MW00873351

THE PRIDE OF BABYLON

THE PRIDE OF BABYLON

The Story of Nebuchadnezzar

Warren Way

To order additional copies of this book, contact:
Xlibris Corporation
1-888-795-4274
www.Xlibris.com
Orders@Xlibris.com

13-WAY1

This first novel is dedicated to:

My wife Nancy, Bob Hostetler, Wilma Porter, Joy Parsley,
And all you who love to study of the Book of Daniel.

013-WAY1

CHAPTER 1

A large caravan plodded its way through the sand, rocks and wadis of the Sumarian desert. It was well fortified and well staffed as befitted the queen of the Chaldean Empire. The final day of their journey began eagerly. Shortly after lunch, the caravan was still far from the gates of Shushan when Queen Yada moaned. "Oh no, not yet."

"What is it, Your Majesty?" her closest attendant asked frantically.

Pain did not allow the queen to answer. Finally, "Tell Jeleu to send a messenger to the palace," she groaned, her words sharp and breathless. The royal midwife must be ready." She inhaled sharply, pain contorting her normally sunny face. "And tell him to hurry!"

Jeleu, the king's chief caravan driver, when he heard of the queen's pains, was visibly shaken. *We never should have made this trip so close to the date of the baby's birth,* he thought. But action was more important than recriminations. He whirled his horse around and came up alongside the queen's camel.

"Your Majesty, shouldn't we give you an opportunity to rest? You're in no condition to travel." Concern marked his weathered face.

"I will not have my child born out here in the desert."

"But, Your Majesty . . ."

"No, just get this caravan moving. I'll be all right. This isn't my first child, you know. Let's move."

Jeleu touched his forehead in salute and spurred his horse to the lead driver of the caravan.

The entire caravan responded, the pace of travel picking up rapidly in spite of the people's weariness. Tension strung the length of the caravan like a tight rope pulling them along to top speed. Everyone thought, but no one spoke, the awful truth: The baby was not due for another four or five weeks.

With the caravan moving as fast as it could, Jeleu returned to the queen and spoke tentatively. "Your Majesty, please tell me if you feel the need to stop and rest."

Queen Yada answered calmly. "Because of me, this trip has already taken far longer than normal. I want to get to Susa. The Shushan palace will be better for the birth than out here, and hopefully it will be much cooler."

The searing heat, certainly a difficulty, had not detracted from Queen Yada's beauty. Her dainty features, dark eyes and hair, fair skin, ready smile, and even her cheery disposition remained intact.

Jeleu remained pensively at her side, his thoughts ranging back three days earlier—back to the Chaldean capital of Ur. *Why did they ever begin this trip anyway?* He knew why, but the tension of the present situation made it all seem foolish.

He had watched the queen, almost eight months pregnant with her third child, mount her camel for the journey to Susa and the palace known as Shushan. It would not have been as difficult if the queen had been able to ride in a carriage, but the rough terrain demanded the four-footed mode of transportation.

The first two days of the trip passed uneventfully. At the rest stops, the noon meal stops and at the overnight camps, Jeleu worriedly watched Queen Yada as she was helped to dismount from her camel, feeling her discomfort.

Two major reasons dictated the necessity of the trip. The court physicians thought Shushan would be much more comfortable than the royal residence at Ur when the birth occurred. The High Priest of Innana, the principal god of Ur, said there was a much greater chance of having a boy if the queen was at the Shushan palace, the king's ancestral home. And, as everyone knew, the child must be a male this time.

By law, it was essential for Queen Yada to produce a male offspring or she would no longer be the queen. The Chaldean

Empire had to have a king to continue the great work that Nabopolassar had begun.

By the third day, the queen seemed to tire more easily, which necessitated an extra night's stay before getting to Susa. The queen had dismounted carefully, grateful for the chance to stretch and move. Jeleu quickly called for Nelo, his first assistant, finding him busy already directing the other servants in erecting the tents for the night's shelter.

Jeleu approached the queen, calling out, "Oh, Queen Yada, live forever."

"Come forward, Jeleu, and please, we are not at the palace; you needn't be so formal. You have known my family since I was a baby. What is it you want?"

Jeleu, flushed and cast a self-conscious glance at the other servants and attendants. He bowed. "Your Majesty, I want to apologize for the inconvenience of not having had servants go before and prepare the resting place in advance."

"Nonsense," the queen responded, "you've made this trip hundreds of times; the problem is your oversized queen whom you have been hovering over like a mother hen. It's no wonder that Polassar sent me in your care." She nodded at the scurrying servants. "See, the resting tent is almost up."

Jeleu smiled at Queen Yada. *Gods that be, give this gracious lady the son that will save her rule*, he prayed silently. "My queen, I think the ladies in attendance are ready for you to go to your tent to rest and be refreshed. I must get this camp organized, or I will no longer be His Majesty's chief caravaner, but will be his stable boy."

Queen Yada laughed. "Never! At least, not while I am queen." Her words were barely out of her mouth when she drew a sharp breath and a shadow passed over her face. She quickly recovered herself, however, and shook her head. "You'd better get to work or I might have to report you to someone—if I only knew who."

Jeleu smiled broadly, bowed, and escorted the queen to the tent and her waiting attendants. As he turned away, he imagined the pain the impending birth might bring to his queen. It was a pain beyond the merely physical, the pain of losing her queenly status, of being relegated to the position of being the mother of the king's daughters, of being rejected as a lover by the king.

There was no doubt that King Nabopolassar loved her deeply. He had been keenly disappointed that their first child, Belyada, a beautiful little girl much like her mother, was not a boy. He could have immediately issued a decree that he was choosing a new queen to replace Yada for failing to produce a son. Instead, he had issued a decree stating that his daughter was to be regarded with royal favor, making her eligible to reign under some circumstances. When Yada's second child was also a girl, the king and his advisors— indeed, the whole nation—grew yet more concerned. The king, bowing to the pressure of his advisors, finally issued a decree that Queen Yada would be replaced if she did not produce a male offspring within a two-year period.

The entire empire was hoping that this pregnancy would result in the essential male child. Not only did the king love Queen Yada, but because of her kind disposition and consideration for the poor the people loved her as well. Much of King Nabopolassar's popularity was owed to the gracious Yada, and he was aware of that debt.

As Jeleu busied himself with getting the camp settled, he couldn't shake off the concern he had for the queen. He had indeed known her since her birth; the lives of their families had been intertwined for many years. *This new baby has to be a boy*, Jeleu vowed.

Directing the set-up of the camp was almost no effort for him, because Nelo was the best assistant that he had ever had. Though not much to look at, the young man sensed what needed to be done and was usually a jump ahead of him. Jeleu allowed himself the luxury of his thoughts until Nelo calling him to inspect the camp broke his reverie.

Nelo escorted Jeleu around the small encampment, pointing out the perimeter fortifications that he had set up, demonstrating his concern for the safety of their special charge. "I think the king would be pleased with the care we've taken for the queen's safety," he remarked, waiting for Jeleu's approval.

"As usual, Nelo, you've done an excellent job. I'm sure if King Nabopolassar himself were here, he'd be pleased."

The sun sank quickly toward the horizon, slowly releasing its heated grip on the desert. Just before it finally set in a brilliant blaze of orange, Jeleu saw something that caused his heart to skip a beat. A lone horseman peered down on their encampment from a distance. Jeleu grasped his assistant's arm and whispered, "Look, Nelo—do you see him?"

Nelo responded hesitantly. "What do you suppose he wants?"

"Get me my horse—but quietly, so no one will be alarmed."

Nelo nodded grimly. "I'll go, too." He moved to get the horses. Jeleu studied the figure on the hill until Nelo returned moments later.

They moved cautiously but steadily toward the figure on horseback; Jeleu rested his hand on the handle of his sword. The mysterious rider seemed to await their advance calmly, comfortably. As they approached, the strange rider, a big, imposing man, turned his horse toward them and straightened himself in the saddle; finally his voice rang out over the still desert. "Jeleu, old friend, I've been expecting you. I see you are on the job as usual."

Jeleu released his grip on his sword. Both men recognized the voice as belonging to Abao, the captain of the king's guard, and they spurred their horses to the important man's side.

"Captain Abao, what brings you here?" Nelo asked.

"The king sent me to Susa to the Shushan Palace to make sure of the comfort of the queen's mother and to oversee the fortification for the queen's safety. When you sent no scout to alert us of your arrival, I decided to pay you a surprise visit."

Jeleu's relief was easy to read. Despite the darkness, his white teeth shone out of his weathered face. "You'll find everything in order." He scanned the vista that surrounded them. "You came alone?"

"Fifteen of my men are deployed around your camp. We'd

better inform your sentries and tell them to use the palace password if anyone comes around. I don't want your bloodthirsty guards slicing up my best men."

"Abao, is there a problem," Jeleu asked, "that our taking an extra day has created?"

"No, there's no problem. We were concerned for anything that might have come up."

"The queen is really tired and an extra day of travel is hard on everybody," Jeleu responded.

The three men returned to camp and settled in for their evening meal. When they were comfortably filled, their conversation turned to their major concerns: the future of the kingdom, the future of the queen, and the games that would be held to celebrate the birth of the newest heir to the throne. When all their views had been expressed and the last wine consumed, they separated to their tents and drifted off to sleep.

Soon after the sun rose the next morning, even before breakfast was served, most of the camp was packed for the last day of the trip to Susa. The entourage eagerly anticipated getting out of the hot sun and beginning the gentle climb to the foothills surrounding the city of Susa. It would be a welcome relief from the heat; the cool breezes coming down from the higher mountains made it a pleasant place to be in the sticky Chaldean summers. The caravan awaited the arrival of Queen Yada on her especially gentle and smooth-gaited camel, whose canopied saddle was so constructed and padded as to enable her to sit either astride or sidesaddle.

As Queen Yada was about to mount, she spotted Abao talking with Jeleu and Nelo. "Abao," she called. "What brings you to this part of the world? Do you think I've never made this trip before?"

Abao bowed as he approached Queen Yada. "Your Majesty, live forever—which is precisely why I am here."

Queen Yada laughed and turned to Jeleu. "Did you know this refugee from the palace was coming to meet us?"

"No, Your Majesty. Nelo and I spotted him looking over our campsite just as the sun was setting last night and we apprehended him before he could do any damage. We've had him under our watchful surveillance all evening. It's good to have him and his men making doubly sure of your safety."

"Abao," the queen said in a scolding tone. "You didn't fear for my safety did you? How could you worry when I had these two nursemaids watching over me?"

The queen threw her head back teasingly and accepted the hands of her attendants as she carefully mounted her camel, which protestingly lurched its way up. The dusty caravan route seemed endless, but near lunchtime the countryside began to take on a more pleasant atmosphere. The bushes were greener and larger. The few scrub trees were more full with foliage and stood taller, less bent by the wind. The ground seemed to have been watered more frequently.

Jeleu sat in his saddle surveying the territory with satisfaction. *It will be much easier traveling after the noon meal,* he thought. *The cooler breezes should be reaching us before long.* Jeleu always loved this last part of the trip. It was invigorating to everyone who had traveled the three or four caravan days that the trip normally took to get from Ur to Susa.

Queen Yada sensed the excitement that Jeleu and all the caravaners felt as she ate her last meal on the road. Soon Susa and the summer palace would appear to rise out of the ground among the distant fortress hills that surrounded the ancient royal city.

When the queen and her attendants finished eating, Abao approached her. "Your Majesty, with your permission, I'd like to take you and my men and begin the journey, so that we could get nearer to the cool area sooner. Jeleu and his men can finish their work and catch up with us later."

"An excellent idea, Abao; let's get going as soon as possible. A cool breeze would please me immensely."

With Jeleu's approval, a group of the queen's attendants and guards began the final leg of their journey. With the sun on their backs rather than in their faces, and their backs shielded with the loose fitting garments that desert life dictated, it seemed as though they were cooler already.

Abao rode beside the queen and commented on the changes in the atmosphere and the topography, and the sharpening focus of the foothills. Trees of good height could be seen more distinctly. The greenery and blades of grass forcing their way up through the sand seemed more lush and vibrant. A cloud appeared on the eastern horizon, wispy and white, but nevertheless a cloud.

By the time Jeleu and the rest of the caravan caught up to the queen's entourage, the first of the trees had been reached. The shade brought relief to the group like a sigh of contentment. Everyone began talking at once, and the animals began to nibble on the inviting blades of grass.

"We are making much better time," Nelo commented to Jeleu. "Both the queen and her camel are in a much bigger hurry to get to Shushan than they were to start this trip."

"I think they are both ready to put this trip behind them. We should be there before the sun sets. I'll send the scouts out to alert the palace of our approach." Jeleu wheeled his horse around and looked for the two scouts that were his fastest horsemen. "Tell them we'll be there for the evening meal—and be sure they make it a good one."

The scouts spurred their horses into a gallop and left everyone eating their dust. No one complained, for Shushan was just ahead.

Jeleu could not help but go over all these events in his mind. It had gone so well until the queen began to experience the pains.

"Your Majesty, are you sure you don't want to stop and rest?"

"No, we can't stop. The pains are getting closer and more intense. Just keep going." The queen grimaced as another pain racked her body.

Jeleu turned his face away. "Your Majesty, we still have almost an hour to go, will you be alright?"

"Of course. We've got to get to Shushan before the baby comes."

The caravan did not stop to drink in the view from the ridge of hills surrounding the city. The weary travelers traversed the fertile valley of fruit trees and farms without a moment's awareness of the beauty, or of the gentle breeze that swept down over the fortress hills.

There was Susa and just ahead the walls of the Shushan palace.

Jeleu and the caravan arrived at the fortifications, the guards saluted and hurried the queen and her attendants through the gates. The members of the entourage caught their breath as the camel seesawed down into its reclining position. Palace servants scrambled to help the queen down and place her in a carriage chair. Four muscular servants lifted the chair and carried the groaning queen, clutching her belly as if afraid it would burst, into the palace.

CHAPTER 2

"We should not have traveled so fast," Jeleu told Nelo as they sat outside the queen's apartment, anxiously awaiting news.

"She might have given birth in the desert if you hadn't driven us. That would have been worse."

"I suppose you're right, Nelo," Jeleu said, but his face wore a doubtful expression. "If anything should happen—"

"Don't borrow trouble," Nelo said, interrupting his friend. "You did what you could. The queen and everyone in the caravan knows that. This may turn out to be no problem at all."

Jeleu nodded without smiling. "We must pray to the gods to be with our queen."

"Yes," Nelo sighed. "We'd better get something to eat. It's been a long day. I'm hungry."

"It could be a long night, too," Jeleu responded. The two men wearily got up and headed to the servants' dining room.

The activity in the queen's quarters imitated the busiest beehive. As the evening continued, comments coming from the apartment were more and more worried. The increasingly anxious midwives going in and out felt that the birth was a very difficult one indeed.

"It's such a pity the queen was so tired before this began," a short stocky midwife commented.

Her partner responded, "If only her strength weren't giving out so quickly each time she needs to push."

"I'm afraid if she doesn't give birth soon, she is in serious trouble." Both of the women agreed. Carrying fresh supplies, they reentered the queen's apartment.

Finally, well past the midnight hour, a faint cry echoed through the stone halls of the palace; the tiny voice alerted all those outside the apartment. The waiting, which had seemed so long, had, in reality, been only six hours after the caravan's arrival, and now there was a birth. The air in the halls felt suspended, as everyone seemed to hold his breath in anticipation: is it a boy?

Word began to spread through the palace, and everyone, including the lowest servants, strained to hear. Jeleu, Nelo, and Abao, the captain of the king's guard, were on their way to the queen's chambers when the cry came singing down the hall. "It's a boy, a boy; it's a boy!"

Abao was the first to find his voice. "I must see her and the child. I must make a full report to the king."

As the trio of men rounded the corner of the hall, they were confronted with the queen's mother. "Oh, Jeleu," she cried. "My Yada—I'm afraid. She may die. She's not good. Not good." Her words tumbled into incoherence as she began to weep. The frail woman collapsed into Jeleu's arms.

Jeleu struggled to control his own emotions; born not only of his sense of responsibility, but also by the love he had for the queen and her family. "There, there, Aia, we're here to help. We will do all we can. The midwives and the practitioners will do their jobs. She'll be all right." He spoke with far more conviction than he felt, but the words and the strength of his arms brought a quietness and peace to the queen's mother.

"She was just so tired, and the birth was very hard on her. She seemed to lose all her strength. They were pulling the baby from her."

Abao took charge. "Let's go find out more so I can send another messenger to the king." The little group, with Aia leaning heavily on Jeleu's arm, moved toward the door of the queen's chambers. The guards saluted smartly and opened the door to the quarters.

The hushed comments of the midwives as they moved about their work helped restore the sense of confidence they all needed.

"Have you heard the good news?" one of the women asked. "It's a boy—not a very big boy, but a boy, and that is good news.

The Chaldean Empire will have an heir to the throne. We've told the queen, I think she heard us; she smiled at least." She faced Abao. "Has the king been notified?"

"That's precisely why I'm here," Abao responded. "I want to send my fastest messengers with the news."

He pivoted on his heels and strode to the guards at the door; he dispatched the older of the two to convey a message to the couriers, who were to ride for the palace in Ur. With good luck, they could make the trip in slightly over one day.

The queen's condition changed little with the coming of the new day. By mid-afternoon she was extremely worn-out from trying to nurse the baby. Her mother and the royal midwife decided to utilize a wet nurse and spare the queen the added strain.

Yada seemed most peaceful when the baby was presented to her to examine and hold. "A boy," she said. She whispered it over and over, much to the delight of the entire palace.

The queen was disappointed she could not nurse her son, but was gracious as she gave her son to a young woman who had given birth to a son two weeks earlier and had plenty of milk for both babies. The young prince responded slowly at first, but was soon eating eagerly.

Three days after the birth of his son, Nabopolassar arrived with his royal entourage. He had gotten the message that the birth had started to take place and left immediately. A few hours into the trip, he met the second group of messengers and upon hearing that the queen was not doing well, ordered his men to ride even faster.

Tossing the reigns to a stable groomsman at the entrance of the palace, swinging his left leg over his saddle, the king was halfway to the door when he landed. Brushing past all the protocol officers, he headed, full stride, for the family quarters.

"I want to see my wife," he said, as he covered the distance to the apartment. "Then I will see my son."

The king was met at the door by the head-midwife, who bowed solicitously. "Your Majesty," she said. "Please see your son first, so that we may ready the queen to see you. You can tell her what a fine son she has given you."

The king's eyes flashed for a moment; then the fire left them, and he smiled. "You are a wise woman." He paused. His brow furrowed, and he asked, "She is better, isn't she?"

"She still is not well, and her improvement is very slow. She will be better for your coming, though."

The midwife raised her hand and the prince's nursemaid bowed to the king. "Right this way, Your Majesty, Your son is just down the hall so his crying will not disturb the queen's rest."

Looking at his long desired son, the king was surprised to see how small and frail he appeared. Gently taking him from the nursemaid and looking intently at him, he wondered if this little boy would have the strength to rule the expanding empire and survive in the very hostile world that was Chaldea. "Nebuchadnezzar II," he whispered, "Prince of Chaldea, Regent of the Gods, Guardian of the Wisdom of the stars." He smiled at the thought that the fate of the world might rest in the tiny hands of that little boy.

The king returned his son to the nursemaid, thanked her, and headed straight for the queen's room. The midwife at the door of the queen's apartment stopped him as he prepared to enter and whispered, "Long live your Majesty, but please do not stay too long on this first visit. She is very excited to see you and will be easily exhausted by too lengthy a stay."

The king nodded grimly as he opened the door to the queen's room. Nabopolassar was visibly startled at the frail paleness of his wife. He took her hand and gently brushed her lips with a kiss. She smiled, a response that seemed to require great effort. "I love you, Yada," he murmured. "Thank you. He is beautiful—like his mother. I am so pleased." Yada smiled again, the biggest smile she had managed since her arrival at Shushan.

The midwives that circled the bed smiled at each other to see the effect the king's holding her hand had on the queen.

The king, exhausted and hungry, kissed Yada again with

whispers of his love. "I'll be back soon." He quickly left the chamber, concern vying with fatigue for control of his face.

The queen's condition did improve for a little while; the king visited her room several times each morning and afternoon. He took his evening meal in her room to be with her and encouraged her to eat and gain strength. However, in spite of all his efforts and those of the staff, her condition continued to deteriorate. Twenty-one days after giving birth to the long awaited son, Queen Yada died.

The king was with her at the time. He stood up from her bedside, set his jaw, and cursed the gods to whom he had prayed. He stormed from the queen's apartment and refused to speak to anyone, refused to be comforted and, as far as anyone knew, refused to cry.

The whole palace, devastated by the death of the queen, reacted: Her mother, inconsolable; Jeleu and all his people, who had accompanied the queen to Susa, overwhelmed with guilt; her servants, quietly weeping. "If only . . ." was heard everywhere.

Customarily, in that part of the world, funerals and burials are performed the next day. In a quiet corner of the west garden, weeping servants dug a solitary grave and the queen's body, in a simple wooden casket, was lowered into the ground. Contrary to custom, however, which called for the husband to fill in the grave as he mourned, the king refused to participate at all. The hardness of his heart reflected in his face as he prepared to leave Susa to return to his palace at Ur.

When asked about the young prince, the king answered with such bitterness that people began to fear for the baby. "Keep him here and when he is old enough to be taught by me, I will send for him. He is not to be coddled. He has cost the life of his mother; see that he causes me no more grief."

The king turned and walked briskly away, leaving the palace guards and the servants with their mouths open wide in astonishment. That night the king and his personal servants left Susa, and Nabopolassar was never seen again in the Shushan Palace.

The entire empire mourned the death of their beloved Queen Yada. It was a bereavement that lasted years, for the king became a different man. Where there had been moderation in the official workings of the empire, there was harshness, the same harshness that enveloped the king himself.

Young Prince Nebuchadnezzar was cared for in the best possible way by his loving grandmother Aia, who in spite of her daughter's death remained in favor with the king. She did her best to raise the boy as befitted the future ruler of the vast and expanding empire. Each year on the anniversary of his birth, Nebuchadnezzar would be taken to his father in Ur, the Chaldean capital. He would remain for several days and his father would check on his progress. He was never allowed to remain at Ur for the anniversary of his mother's death, a day his father marked with bitterness and anger directed mainly toward his son and heir.

In the years Nebuchadnezzar visited the king, he tried to get to know his father and find a means of pleasing him. He was brought before the king, trying hard not to remember the previous year's visit. "Your Majesty, my father," the trembling child would begin. "I hope you are well. It's nice to see you."

"Well," the King responded, "I see you have grown some, your speech is better, but your appearance still leaves much to be desired, if you want to be the king. He still looks weak and scrawny," the king said, as if addressing the others in the room. "It's a shame Belana wasn't the boy. She looks more like a man than he ever will."

In spite of the remarks, many of which he didn't understand, Nebuchadnezzar would smile at the king and ask, "My father, may I sit on your lap on the throne?"

Totally ignoring the request, the king responded, "take him back to Shushan; hopefully he'll be better next year."

In the year Nebuchadnezzar turned twelve, his father remarried and all the realm rejoiced, hoping that the dark time of Nabopolassar was past. But hope soon turned to disappointment. No sooner had the marriage been consummated than the king declared her unfit, and he returned to his abuse of the temple prostitutes. During that year the king married three women, adding them to his harem. Since he, as sovereign, had the right to have as many wives and concubines as he chose, and any woman in the realm was lawfully his; he could take whomever he desired, married or not.

On Nebuchadnezzar's thirteenth birthday trip to the Palace at Ur, he was told, by his father that he would not return to the Shushan Palace but would be trained at Ur to become the next regent. The boy was thrilled to think that finally he would be able to be with his father. He hoped to find some way of pleasing him at last.

The transition from the care of his doting grandmother to his unfeeling father severely shocked Nebuchadnezzar. His sisters, whom he hardly knew, had much better relationships with the king, and they were fearful that their brother would take away from them what little affection their father showed them. They ignored the prince, treating him badly, especially Belana who called him names and made him ill at ease.

There was one compensation: Jeleu. He had been a frequent visitor at Shushan; he had always been the one to conduct the prince and his grandmother to Ur for his birthday reviews. Now Jeleu, because of his age and the expansion of trade, no longer traveled, but was permanently stationed at Ur to coordinate all the caravans.

Jeleu's close relationship with Nebuchadnezzar's mother and grandmother had caused him to grow closer to the young prince each time he was at Susa. Now with both of them at Ur, Jeleu was able to befriend the young prince and become his mentor. It was Jeleu who shortened Nebuchadnezzar's name to Nebuk, a name the king refused to allow to be used in his presence. It was probably Jeleu's relationship with the prince that prompted the king to send Jeleu from the capital on fictitious errands.

Jeleu wasn't the only one whose relationship with the prince caused him personal problems. Nebuk was constantly under surveillance by the king's guard, of whom Abao was still the captain.

Big, blunt, softhearted, Abao had often allowed the boy considerable personal freedom. When jealously inspired reports were made to the King, Abao was retired to his country home.

Almost every pleasurable relationship or activity was denied the prince. He became more and more angry and frustrated in his attempts to please his father.

"You are my son," his father often told him. "You will become my successor." But as often as Nebuk heard those words, he still did not understand what he was expected to do.

The continued friction began to wear on the boy's usually sunny disposition. He seldom smiled, and was often sharp and critical in his answers. He was especially distressed by his sisters who mistrusted him and wanted little to do with him. Even when he tried to talk to them of his mother, wanting to know her better through them, they were unfriendly and angry that his birth had killed their mother.

Finally, on his fourteenth birthday, Nabopolassar summoned Nebuk to appear before him. When Nebuk arrived before the king in the throne room, he found himself in front of a group of boys whom he was told were also fourteen years of age. As he looked at them, he realized that they were all bigger and stronger looking, but that none of them was even remotely as good looking as he was.

"I have summoned you here today to let you know how far short you have fallen in your physical development. You have always been a runt from the day you were born. It is time that you see what real boys and men are really like." With these words the king ordered the boys, who were dressed in toga-like garments, to disrobe and stand at attention. It was very apparent that these young men had been selected for their advanced physical and sexual development.

Nebuchadnezzar, already ill at ease, was ordered by the king to take off his clothes and stand naked before the throne. Nebuk tried to protest, but his father met the prince's appeal with stony silence.

Nebuk stared at his father; hatred growing as he slowly began to remove his clothes. The boys broke into gales of laughter at Nebuk's embarrassment. Soon he stood before everyone; painfully aware his physical development was definitely behind that of all the other boys. He tried to cover the offending organs with his hand and the chorus of derision only grew louder. He became completely unnerved, the room began to spin, and he collapsed.

When Nebuk awoke, he was in his own room and Jeleu was there with him. Jeleu answered the question in the boy's expression. "Your father had the servants bring you back here; I heard what happened."

"I have disappointed my father," Nebuk said. "Again."

"Nebuk, you just haven't developed as quickly as the other boys.

You will catch up in time. You must understand that those boys were selected especially to embarrass you; your father will stop at nothing in his effort to prepare you to rule."

"Why does he make me out to be a fool if he wants me to be something great? Doesn't he know that I will try to do whatever he wants? All he has to do is tell me."

Jeleu sat quietly for a few minutes before speaking, "I think your father was telling you in his own, ah, awkward way." Jeleu cleared his throat. "Perhaps you should get your servants to help you exercise in order to become strong and show your father that you are, indeed, a credit to him."

"Do you really think that will work?" Nebuk brightened at the prospect. "I hope so. I'll do it. Thanks, Jeleu."

As Jeleu left the prince's room, concern for the young man creased his face, and tears filled his eyes. *What is the matter with the king, anyway? If only I could tell him the damage he is doing to his son.*

As the days stretched into months, the results in Nebuk's physical growth began to show. His chest and shoulders seemed to expand. He gained twenty pounds and his thighs grew strong and thick. As he grew, an attitude of greater confidence and self-assuredness also sprouted in him. The results made both Nebuk and his servants smile as they encouraged him in his progress.

In the year between his fourteenth and fifteenth birthdays, Nebuk had changed. When summoned, the prince nervously prepared to appear before his father; choosing to dress in one of the toga-like garments that the boys had worn the year before. He was right in hoping that the gesture would not be lost on the king. His father's comment increased the nervousness that Nebuk felt.

"I see by your dress," Nabopolassar said, "that you remember last year. It is very appropriate for what I have in mind for you today."

The king asked Nebuchadnezzar a few questions about his education and physical training and then clapped his hands three times. Upon this cue, the doors to the king's chamber opened, a small band of musicians began to play exotic music and twelve scantily—clad young dancing girls pranced into the room. They began to dance in front of the young prince, circling around him, moving closer and closer, waving perfumed scarves seeking to entice him.

Nebuk flushed red with embarrassment. His state of excitement increased as the young women began to kiss and fondle him. The prince was just about to run from the room when his father clapped his hands and the music stopped.

"At least this birthday you will enjoy." Smiling, self-satisfied, the King addressed the girls. "Take him to your rooms and teach him the ways of the world."

Nebuk immediately bolted from the room and hid himself in the servants' quarters. It gave him time to evaluate: anger at his father, fear of the unknown with girls, fear that he might not perform right, fear that these girls might be like his sisters, fear he would make a fool of himself, again.

It was late at night when he crept back into his chamber. Just as he was breathing a sigh of relief at being safely in his room, the door opened. The king's chief steward, a man not given to kindness, ordered him, "You are to attend to your princely duties. The king will not tolerate any disobedience."

Hatred for his father was boundless. He pounded his fist into his pillow. He obeyed his father's orders, but the frustration and resentment in his heart welled up to form a vow—a vow to become more cruel than his father.

"By the gods, I will one day make him sorry."

CHAPTER 3

Soon Nebuk's obedience to his father's wishes became more pleasurable. This was especially so, when the partners dared not decline regardless of how amateurish or cruel the prince's efforts or mood. Nebuchadnezzar was no fool; he learned early the ways of a rogue lover and how to use sexuality to his own advantage.

However, knowing his actions were not displeasing to his father, robbed him of the satisfaction that rebellion brings to most teenagers. He only felt he was doing what his father had ordered him to do. He knew his obedience still would not negate his father's rejection of him; he also knew none of his partners felt any love for him.

Nebuk, as he still liked to call himself, was maturing in every way. His interests turned to the politics of the realm. He developed the capacity to listen carefully to all the court conversation, thereby learning the secrets of real effectiveness and power. He developed a fascination with the architecture of the royal palaces and spent much time studying the construction that was taking place in Ur. He began to formulate a plan to build a great city that would one day become his capital.

Nebuk seemed to have inherited his mother's sunny disposition. Though he still battled with despondency, due to his father's rejection, his personality caused people to like and trust him. Coupled with his continued physical development and natural good looks, he was spoken of admiringly in the palace. Rumors of his father's jealousy and fear of his popularity began to circulate among the people.

He was proud of his ability to use his good looks and personality to manipulate and control people for his own wishes. He listened carefully to people and detected hints of dislike or disdain for his father, mentally cataloging them for future use. He endeavored to learn what people really wanted, and discovered he could control people through their weaknesses and fears. Investigating these controlling forces brought him face to face with religion.

The king had forbidden any religious training for his son since he had forsaken the gods after the death of his queen. Nebuk himself nursed a deep resentment for the failure of prayers to save his mother. Nevertheless, he began a careful study of the religions of the empire to see how he could best use them. His conclusions were very simple. Physical appetites (especially sex) and superstition (basically fear) could be blended into a powerful religion and successfully used to control most of the people most of the time.

The idea of control filled Nebuk with eager anticipation; he intended to control their thoughts, their spiritual lives, their emotions, their sex lives, their finances, their jobs, their families, their very existence. As his excitement grew, he realized that he would have to know much more about every area of learning and understand a lot more about human nature in order to fulfill his plans.

Such thoughts consumed him day and night, and he began to neglect eating and his physical exercise. He simply did not have time to waste. He had to know everything and know it now.

The formal education the king had ordered for Nebuchadnezzar was a mere appetizer; the young prince feasted on the Chaldean writings, and knew the code of Hammurabi as well as his own family history. He studied the mathematical calculations of the stars, time, shape, and space. Architecture and military science fascinated him and he devoted long hours to the study of these disciplines, because he knew where he was going.

He was going to rule the world. His would be the greatest empire the world had ever seen. The greatest, strongest, and wisest monarch ever would preside over its inception. "I, Nebuchadnezzar II, will be the greatest ever to sit upon a Sumerian or Chaldean throne. I will rule my kingdom with majesty and power, and its name will endure forever!"

Nabuk's grandiose plans could not long remain a secret. He needed to incorporate others into his plans, and the court gossips were soon wagging their tongues. Eventually the attention of King Nabopolassar was attracted. The king took his son's interest in the realm to be a threat. He called his son into his presence.

"Your Majesty," Nebuk greeted his father. "You sent for me."

Nabopolassar stared at his son for a period of time. "It has come to my attention," he said finally, "you are being divisive to the common good of the Chaldean Empire." Nebuk started to interrupt, but thought better of it as the king continued. "Just what do you think you are doing?"

"I am not sure what you mean, father," Nebuk responded.

"Oh, I think you do," the king bristled. "What is this empire that you and your cronies are going to build?" The fire in Nabopolassar's eyes warned Nebuk to answer very carefully.

"Your Majesty, my father, the empire that I am building is only one in my mind, my imagination. It is only a game I use to sharpen my thinking. Hopefully, one day you will be able to call upon me to assist you in this most noble empire you have built."

The direct answer had its effect on the king and he stroked his well-manicured beard. "Why have you involved others in this project of yours if it is only mental?"

"I have been testing some of my ideas out on other people and they probably were talking with others. I never intended this to be a problem to you or the empire."

Nebuk's ability to charm people was not limited to servants and peasants. Even the king was not exempt. Calming down, he continued, "I don't like anything that causes gossip in the court."

"That certainly wasn't my intention. I shall see that it doesn't happen again," Nebuchadnezzar promised.

"It won't be easy to keep that promise," the king muttered. "I hope you're right." Then as an after thought, "Perhaps some of your ideas might work for the realm we already have, as well as the one that is in your head. Keep on developing your skills; we might be able to use them."

Nebuk controlled the urge to laugh. Only a broad smile of straight white teeth beneath his neatly trimmed, dark moustache brought light to his handsome face. He bowed to his father, resumed his militarily erect posture and walked confidently from the throne room. *Yes, I can win.*

Nebuk's time fairly flew as he devoted more and more of his energies to learning, including his physical development and military studies. People noticed with approval the new resolve, the confidence, and the sense of dedication to the realm that Nebuk exhibited. Not everyone, however, was pleased with the changes in the prince. The many girls who had been his steady playmates were more or less left behind in the search for improvement.

With the approach of Nebuk's twentieth birthday, his father announced that the empire was soon to be expanded. An expedition of conquest was soon to take place, which would add to the Chaldean Empire.

Soldiers trained, officers conferred, and groups of people throughout the city drank tea, and worried. Nebuk approached his father, asking permission to lead a unit of the soldiers.

"Father—Your Majesty—this would be a valuable thing for me to do in terms of knowledge and leadership experience. Check with my military trainers—see if I haven't proven myself able."

His request was refused, but Nebuk did not let his bitter disappointment show as he stood in full military stance on the royal reviewing stand. He saluted the troops as they marched out of the Palace at Ur, some never to return again.

After the parade ended, Nebuk turned to go and noticed his father motioning him to come to him. He stepped quickly to his father, wondering what would prompt him to call him in such a public manner, quite out of keeping with the normal summons to appear in the throne room. Standing face to face with the king was quite different from looking up to him on the throne. Here, they were very nearly the same height, just two men, both military, both handsome, both unsure of the other.

The king spoke with difficulty, "I know," he began, "that you wanted to go with the expedition that just left. However, I could not let you go." Nabopolassar paused, "I have been thinking over many things, things that have caused me much pain. I could not let you go because I promised your mother before you were ever conceived that I would not let any son of ours go into battle until he was fully matured and prepared by me. I have not forgotten that promise. Even though I have despised you, thinking that your birth caused her death, I cannot break that promise. I have been wrong in blaming you."

Nebuk started to speak, but the king continued. "Don't interrupt, for you may never hear these words again. I am sorry I have mistreated you. You deserve better. You are a good man." Raising his finger to stop a further interjection, he continued. "I will, from this time on, take personal charge of your military training, for I know that soon you will lead these men in victorious battle and soon enough you will be ready to lead the empire."

Nebuk was overwhelmed by the importance of his father's words. Finally regaining his composure, he turned to face his father, the Great Nabopolassar, Regent of the mighty Chaldean Empire, only to see him turn and walk away as if he had said nothing. Nebuk's emotions ran the gamut of love, forgiveness, hate, fear, respect, and finally, confusion.

He returned to his quarters somewhat dazed, grateful for the quiet and security that his apartment afforded. There were times when the six rooms only made him feel alone, but more often than not they were his refuge. And now he needed the chance to think and try to deal with all the ragged emotions the last few minutes had dumped on him. He slumped on his bed, clutching the pillow, as his feelings swept him to the verge of tears, "What is happening to me?" A knock on his door brought his straying thoughts under control and his servant, Issima, announced that Master Jeleu wished to see him. "Oh, yes, Issima," he replied. "Make him comfortable in the sitting room. I'll be right there." His countenance brightened by the thought of Jeleu's arrival. "Just the person I need to help me with all this."

Not wanting Jeleu to see a twenty-year-old man crying, he jumped up from his bed, poured water into the basin on the marble wash stand, splashed some on his face, and surveyed the results in the shiny metal mirror.

The sitting room, tastefully decorated for a young man, reflected the prince's interest in architecture, with a large table for clay tablets, for making drawings. Jeleu stood looking at the drawings in the light of a hanging oil lamp.

"Jeleu, I'm so glad you came, I need to talk to you about what my father just said to me." Nebuk crossed the room, gave the man a big hug, led him to a pair of chairs, separated by a small table, and rang for Issima to bring tea.

As Nebuk related the conversation, Jeleu let out a long camel driver's whistle. "Nebuk, I've tried over the years to tell you that your father was not the man you knew him to be. You are just now getting a glimpse of the person your mother knew and loved."

Nebuk felt the tears coming again as he said, "I have hated that man for at least half of my life. The other half, I have spent trying to get him to like me. How can I get to neutral?"

"I don't know," Jeleu responded.

"There is no way to please him. He is suspicious of everything I do. He acts like he's jealous of me. Then he turns. What will it mean? He will probably drive me crazy. I'm so confused. Do you think it will ever get any better?"

Jeleu avoided answering, rubbed his eyes as if trying to clear them to see into the future. "If it's any consolation, your father is probably in just as much confusion over you as you are over him. The only advice I can give you is, take it as it comes. If he's changed, you will know it. If not, you'll know that as well. But don't be surprised if he hardly speaks to you for a while."

Jeleu's advice was borne out very quickly, for the next day the king sent for his son and coldly ordered him to prepare for military tactics instruction, after which he would test him.

Nebuk was grateful that he was being compelled to prepare for the test. His father's orders left him no time to waste. He pushed himself to accomplish the requirements and began a regimen calculated to impress his father. Calling his instructors he asked, "What tactical materials did you emphasize with the troops before they left for battle? I want to go over them in addition to the regular studies you've outlined." He still hoped that he might be allowed to take part in the military campaign.

Many times Jeleu found him humped over the clay tablet desk, now converted to military tactics rather than architecture. He worked as though his life depended on it. In truth it really did, for many a military campaign would be won and his life saved by the brilliance of his tactics. No one, not even Jeleu, bothered him.

The weather began to moderate and since the courtyard of the palace was adjacent to Nebuk's apartment, he often would move his studies outside. He was left alone to study, would-be offenders having learned by the sharpness of his outbursts.

His extreme concentration didn't allow Nebuk to notice the petite, extremely beautiful seventeen-year-old girl, with long black hair braided tightly into one single braid that reached to the middle of her back. Her flawless features were revealed and complimented by the milk-whiteness of her complexion. She looked as if she'd never been in the sun—a near impossibility in that region. She moved with the strong and athletic fluidity of a dancer as she moved into Nebuk's vicinity. Humming and singing parts of a shepherd's song, she danced her way across the courtyard.

By now Nebuk had indeed noticed her and she him. He struggled to try to solve the conflict he felt. Should he be annoyed at the ravishing creature for having disturbed him or should he try to add her to his collection? "Come here, girl," he commanded rather harshly.

"Why should I?" she said. "I have a right to be here."

Her response was so totally unexpected that Nebuk was caught unprepared. "Don't you know who I am?" She did not answer, but stood looking at him, her hands on her hips.

Finally she spoke. "Who you are is really unimportant. Besides, you don't know who I am either."

Nebuk, now completely taken aback by her insolent response, began to laugh. The laughter felt good and reminded him that he needed some recreation, so he decided this would be his playmate. Again he said to her, but this time with the laughter showing through, "Please come here and I will tell you who I am. Then please tell me who you are, fair maiden."

As she approached him, she said, "That's a much better way to speak to a lady, Prince Nebuchadnezzar." With that she turned and started skipping away.

Struggling to control his voice, his anger rising, he called after her, "Come back here! Don't you know that I could have you whipped for your insolence?"

"Of course, Your Highness," she said as she turned back to face him. "You could even order me to be your concubine. You could order me to do many things; but you would never know me, You would never know whether I cared for you or was just being obedient."

The impertinence of her answers startled him, and her words exposed his own feelings about sex. It seemed as if she were reading his mind. Nebuk drew back and started to chuckle. Then roars of laughter overtook him, as the pressures of the long hours of study and the intensity of his desire to please his father melted away.

"You have a very wonderful laugh, your Highness. You should use it all the time; with it, you will rule the world much better than with your sword."

Softly he said, "You need fear nothing from me. Only tell me, fair lady, who you are and where you have been hiding in this great palace?"

She moved quietly to his bench, slid in beside him and looked him straight in the eye. "I would never have dared to be so forward if I hadn't known that you are, at heart, a very gentle man much like your mother, Great Queen Yada." He started to object, but she placed her finger on his lips and he instinctively kissed it. "I came here to see if Prince Nebuchadnezzar is really as great as they say."

Nebuk found himself wanting to put his arms around this girl and hold her out here in the palace courtyard, but her very impertinence made him wary of letting her know his vulnerability. "You certainly have a mysterious way. You haven't told me your name or where you are staying in the palace."

She stood to her feet and pulled her hand away. It was only then that Nebuk realized that he had not let her hand go after he had kissed her finger. "Where I live, you'll have to find, if you wish. Who I am, you will find out in time. For now, my name is Maradebbia. If I may call you Nebuk, you may call me Mara. Good evening, Prince Nebuk." She whirled and raced off into the courtyard. Nebuk was flabbergasted.

As Nebuk walked back to his quarters, she filled his thoughts. His lips framed her name, "Mara".

CHAPTER 4

The name Mara filled Nebuk's mind, as did the questions surrounding her. He inquired as discreetly as he could without revealing too much interest, but failed to learn where the mysterious Mara was hiding. Even Jeleu, who knew everybody, was unable to find her. After several days of fruitless questioning, Nebuk decided the only contact he had with her was in the courtyard. *Perhaps if I did all my work there . . .*

As the weeks passed, his frustration turned to anger and depression that this girl whom he hardly knew could so completely dominate his attention. He couldn't think of anything except Mara.

Nebuk would sit at his table, head down and unmoving for long periods of time. Only Issima, his faithful servant, came near him with food and drink, which he often refused. On one such occasion, Nebuk felt a hand laid gently on his back. Thinking it was Issima; Nebuk promptly pushed the contents of the table onto the floor. But the hand didn't move and a melodic chiding voice spoke. "That's no way for the great Prince Nebuk to act."

Instantly Nebuk swung around, grabbed Mara and kissed her. "You are not going to run away from me this time or ever again. I don't know what kind of a magic spell you weave, but you have completely destroyed my ability to concentrate or behave like a rational being. Everybody thinks I've gone crazy and they are probably right. What evil powers do you have? I am totally under your spell?"

"I don't have any magic powers, but I think your kisses do. Perhaps we should test that again?"

Nebuk didn't have to be told twice to kiss her. They were already locked in a tight embrace. He gently lifted her chin and kissed her lovingly until they both were a little giddy. He relaxed his grip on her and said gently, "Please, don't ever run away from me again."

"I have no intentions of ever running from you again. Now, what do you want to know about me?"

"Everything!"

Mara grinned, and whispered, "That will take a lot of time. What do you want to know first?"

"Well," Nebuk began, "where have you been hiding all these weeks? I've been looking all over for you."

"I know you have," Mara responded, "but I can't tell you exactly where. I have relatives here in the city and I stay with them when I need to."

Nebuk was not totally pleased with her mysterious, half answer, but continued on. "Where have you been that I have not seen you around the palace or in the city? Anyone as beautiful as you couldn't be hidden from my view for long." The air of intrigue about Mara stirred a deep response within him, a response born of need and longing for love. Nebuk looked at her, his eyes sparkling and her eyes answered back.

Tears began to well up in Mara's eyes. "Thank you for considering me beautiful. I have always wanted you to think that about me."

Nebuk looked lovingly down at her luscious brown eyes, took his thumb and wiped an errant tear from the corner of her eye. "How can I feel so comfortable with a girl that I've only just really met and kissed twice?"

Mara interjected, "That's not completely true, you've kissed me two-and-one-half times." Nebuk looked puzzled. "Remember, you kissed my finger," she said, a half-grin playing at the corners of her mouth. "I didn't wash my hand for a week."

Nebuk laughed, and initiated another embrace and kiss. "I do hope you'll keep an accurate record of our kisses." Their voices blending together in laughter filled the courtyard with the music of love.

Suddenly serious, Nebuk said, "How am I going to make sure you will not run away from me again? I don't think I can live without you."

Mara's response set Nebuk's head spinning. "I have no intention of your living without me. That's why I am here." Mara paused waiting for Nebuk to speak. He remained mute.

Finally, his voice vibrating with emotion, Nebuk said, "I have dreamed of you becoming my wife. It's as if this was being thrust upon us by an outside power." He paused, "Will you be my wife? Will you be my queen?"

"Yes, your Highness. I will be your wife. That is precisely why I came here in the first place." She squeezed his hand and continued, "You are right about the outside power; I was told by the astrologers that I would become the queen of the Chaldean Empire. They said it was in the stars."

Nebuk held her close and she rested her head on his shoulder. Mara continued speaking, "I need to tell you more about me. I know much about you, for I have studied you for at least six years. I have wanted to be your wife since I was eleven years old. I first met you when I was thirteen and you were fifteen. I was one of the dancing girls that your father brought in to embarrass you on your birthday." Her revelation brought a startled look to Nebuk. "I have loved you from that day when you ran away and refused to act like a stupid oaf. I have never forgiven your father for betraying you. I've wanted to make up to you for the crudeness of that day."

Nebuk's mind was in a whirl. He wondered if this, his first true love, was possibly one of the many girls that he had used and forgotten. He started but was unable to ask the question. "Did I ever see you again until we met a few weeks back?"

"No, I left the palace and returned to my home in the mountains; it was far too hot for my mother here in Ur and my father's business in the capital was over. No, I was not one of your forgotten playmates, if that's what you're thinking. Nor have I been with any other man, for I have intended to be yours and yours alone.

Nebuk's mouth hung open at the ravishing Mara's ability to read his mind. "I'd better be careful what I think or I'll be in trouble."

"Dearest Nebuk, I can't read minds; I just seem to have the ability to be one jump ahead of everybody. You are not too slow in that department either. That was a pretty fast proposal. What do we do now?"

"I'll request an audience with my father. Then we'll know what to do. Who do I need to ask for permission to marry you?"

"My father," Mara said, "knows of the astrologers' prediction. He will not be surprised when the time comes for you to ask permission."

It took several days for the audience with the king to be granted during which time Nebuk and Mara spent every possible moment getting acquainted. They met each afternoon in the marble colonnaded courtyard. They found a secluded spot, screened by two palm trees, fitted out with what became "their bench."

Mara told Nebuk about her life. "I am an only child; my mother almost died giving birth to me and her health never was good. She died shortly after we left Ur and went back to the north country. My mother and I both loved the mountains; I was born and raised there until I was ten. It was just after your fifteenth birthday that we went back to the mountains. My father recently remarried and he urged me to return to Ur and see what would happen. Which, I guess it has."

King Nabopolassar was not in the best of moods, but when he saw Mara, he became visibly agitated. "Aren't you the daughter of the regent of Ubik that I banished from the court several years ago?"

"Yes, your Majesty, I am the daughter of Ugani of the Province of Ubik. Whether you banished my father, I do not know, for he has never said a word against you in my hearing."

The king muttered, "I certainly would question that."

"If there has been an offense from my house to you, gracious King, I ask that you will forgive it and not hold it against me."

"You claim that you do not know of the offense of your father, for it was over you that your father was banished." Mara drew a sharp breath and squeezed Nebuk's hand. All the girls who danced at Nebuchadnezzar's birthday party were to become a part of my harem. Your father refused. I gave him time to reconsider, but he spirited you and you mother out of the city and I banished him."

Nebuk could stand no more and shouted at his father, "You are a beast! You not only embarrassed me then, now I am ashamed to find you'd take thirteen-year-old girls for your pleasure. Don't you ever care about anyone else's feelings?" Nebuk hung his head and Nabopolassar stared at him. "I came here," he finally resumed, "to ask permission to make Mara my wife."

"That's impossible."

"Your Majesty," Mara interjected, "I have despised what you did to your son at his fifteenth birthday, but I also came to love him because of his embarrassment. If you can forgive me for failing to fulfill your wishes, I will forgive you for what you have done to your son and to my family." Mara's eyes flashed with determination, "I came here with my father's instruction not to be seen by you. Now I understand why. However, that does not change the fact that I came here to meet and marry your fine son."

The king stared at both Mara and Nebuchadnezzar, "I told you that is impossible. My son will not marry a commoner, much less the daughter of a banished former official."

"Again, Your Majesty, allow me to give you some information that may help change your mind." Mara boldly stepped closer to the throne. "You, I am sure, are familiar with the Median Ulai dynasty."

"Of course, that is the line that Nebuchadnezzar's mother came from."

"Precisely, Your Majesty," Mara exclaimed. "Both of my parents were from the Ulai dynasty. My mother was a Median princess and by virtue of my birth, I also am a Median princess. Your objections to my lineage are easily overcome. As far as my father is concerned, he has remained a loyal supporter of your rule. You can believe that or not."

By the time Mara finished speaking, Nabopolassar, king of the Chaldean Empire, was just as much in awe of this beautiful, young, audacious, woman as his son had been. She was obviously in charge of herself and he could not help but think of what an asset she would be to the next king of the realm. *If only my beautiful, intelligent, talented, and sensitive Yada had not been taken from me— how different the world would have been.*

Thinking of Yada made the king slump in his chair. Leaning his head back, he closed his eyes for a long period before he spoke. Nebuk and Mara stood nervously holding onto each other. "I will not prevent the marriage of my son to you. However, there is a requirement; you must produce a male offspring within three years or you will be removed from the lineage as future queen. Do you agree?"

"I accepted your son's speedy proposal and I accept yours as well. I only hope that I can be as good a wife to Nebuchadnezzar II as my cousin Yada was to you."

With that revelation, the king was even more visibly shaken and only nodded his head and waved them out of his presence. When they left, he ordered everyone out of the room; then he held his head and cried. "That girl makes me nervous, and here she is a relative of Yada. Yada, my Yada."

It took time to arrange as grand an affair as a royal wedding. A politically important state wedding demanded the attention of all the court, as well as dignitaries from neighboring countries and all the provinces of the empire. Family and friends from around the country were invited. Fantastic amounts of food had to be ordered and prepared, clothes for the royal participants designed and made. All these preparations were exhausting to Mara and Nebuk. They just wanted to get married.

The wedding took place just before Nebuk's twenty-second birthday. It was a seven-day affair, with the marriage ceremony performed by the High Priest of the moon god, Nannar, the patron

deity of Ur. Parades of the visiting dignitaries wound their way
through the city, swept clean and festooned for the occasion. Each
day Mara and Nebuchadnezzar would be on display at the palace,
greeting all their guests.

The actual ceremony took place in the Nannar temple, which
was quite small, and was attended only by family and top
government officials. Following the ceremony, which was very short
by the king's order, the bride and groom were driven through the
city in an open carriage drawn by four black Persian horses. A
military honor guard rode four abreast in front, four on each side,
and four in the rear. Both dressed in white, both with golden
crowns adorning their black hair, Mara, a radiant bride, and
Nebuchadnezzar, the handsome groom, stirred the people into a
cheering frenzy. There was no doubt they were happy with their
future king and queen.

In the appropriate nine months, a young son, Nabonidus, was
born to the happy couple, one more accomplishment of Princess
Mara.

*   *   *

Marriage agreed with Nebuk. He found great solace and peace in
his family. Nebuk was no longer alone. He had hoped his marriage
would have opened doors of opportunity to serve his father, but
their relationship remained rather distant. He was not the least bit
sure that he was any more pleasing to his father now than he had
been in the earlier days. His life revolved around his military duties
and his family. It was the first time in his entire life he felt some
degree of peace with himself. The drive to succeed took second
place to his concern for those he loved.

The king seemed to enjoy the occasional visits with his happy,
toddler, grandson Prince Nabonidus. He was still somewhat wary
in the presence of his daughter-in-law, Mara. She always seemed
to know what he was thinking and he found that very disconcerting.
He was uncomfortable trying to bring subjects up before she did;

more often than not, he would just remain silent. He hated the feeling that he was not really in command of the situation.

On one of the king's visits to his son's quarters, Mara asked, "How soon do you intend to send Nebuchadnezzar off to oversee the expansion of the empire in the northern front?" Nabopolassar was shaken by her question, for that was his main reason for calling at their home.

"I will talk with my son about this matter; where is he?"

"Nebuchadnezzar is out reviewing the troops that you put under his charge, getting them ready for departure to the front. I told my husband he soon would be going with the troops, because I could sense the confidence you have developed in him. Please tell him of your trust and confidence; he's been waiting to hear it from you for years."

"But as always, you are just a little ahead of everybody," the king answered sharply. "I shall try to convey to him the thoughts I have on the subject." With that he turned and started out of the room and ran into Nebuchadnezzar, who was just coming in.

"Illustrious Father, don't be in such a hurry to get away. To what do we owe the honor of your visit? Where is your beautiful grandson?"

"I did not come to see my grandson." "However, the king added, his anger rising, "He is usually easier for me to deal with than other members of this household who always manage to know things ahead of everybody else." He said it with a sidelong glance at Mara who showed no reaction. "I really came to see you. I want you to lead the contingent of troops I put under your command to the front. I want you to take over the campaign to expand the kingdom into what used to be the Assyrian Empire. You have proven yourself capable, and I want to be sure this campaign is done according to our standards." Nabopolassar cleared his throat and continued softly. "I believe you are ready and I have fulfilled my promise to your mother."

Nebuk couldn't believe his ears and his excitement began to show. "Father, I have waited for this for a long time and I shall do my best to be worthy of your confidence. You do me great honor. Thank you."

"Well, enough of that. Where is my grandson?"

"I will get him from the nursery," Mara responded.

"No, no, I'll go see him there." And with that he was out the door and into the hallway to the child's room. "I've got to see that little one before I go."

Nebuk's face was awash with emotion and as usual, anger took over. "If only he had ever said those words about me when I was little . . . but now it is too late. He can't even stand to be near me even when he is telling me I have his confidence."

"My sweet husband, your father probably never will be able to deal with you as you'd like him to. Just remember the good words he just said about you. 'I want to be sure this campaign is conducted according to our standards.' Coming from him, that means a lot".

"I know you're right, but I need so much more from him. I never know whether to love him or murder him. I can't stand much more of this. It's probably good that I will be away from him for a while."

"But my dear warrior husband, you will also be away from us for a long period of time and I, for one, will miss you. Let's make the most of the time that we have remaining before you march off to war. Besides, I'll still be here and have to put up with your father." Nebuk's laughter filled the room, changing the atmosphere as he embraced his beautiful wife, kissing her passionately.

"That's more what I had in mind than thinking about your father. Go check and see if he has left and we'll get on with our lives." The twinkle in Mara's eye sent Nebuk hurrying down the hall.

As Nebuk entered the nursery he saw his father kiss his one-and-a-half-year old son and tell him to be a good boy. Nabonidus hugged his grandfather. The twin emotions of gratitude for his son's good fortune and the feeling of his own personal lack raced through his heart, side by side.

*   *   *

Three weeks later Mara and her son stood at attention as Nebuchadnezzar II led his troops out of the military compound. He headed them north to further expand the glorious Chaldean Empire that he would soon rule. Mara's eyes were dry. Even though she would miss him very badly, she knew that he would be back and that he was destined for greatness. Her confidence was unshakable.

Nebuk was prepared for the field life, the dry dusty roads, the making and breaking of camp, and the responsibilities of command. But he was not prepared for the loneliness of not having Mara and Nabonidus with him. The days of travel brought Nebuk and his troops to the north country with its rugged terrain and mountains, and they reminded him of Mara again. This was the scenery she dearly loved.

As he thought of Mara and Nabonidus he was reminded of Mara's saying that the flat desert lands lacked the character and the excitement of her hills. "Wouldn't she think it wonderful, when I build my own city, to have trees and gardens just to remind her of her home. I'll do it! I'll make her the finest gardens that the world has ever seen and she will be at home."

The only way Nebuk could break from his depressed thoughts and keep his mind off his family was to dream of his future glory when he established himself as the king on the throne. These thoughts did not keep him happy for long because of external discontent—his men. They gathered in little groups and began to vocalize their unhappiness. When on the move, they grumbled about the slowness of the troops' progress. When camped, they complained about the food. Always they bemoaned the lack of women.

Finally the last days of travel were finished, and scouts were sent out to survey the battle scene. As the excitement mounted, the boasts of the "road warriors" settled into nervousness. Before them lay the great city of Haran and the engagement with the enemy, the Egyptians, who had invaded the former Assyrian city, from which to launch an attack on the Chaldean Empire.

The city of Haran was to be the proving ground for Prince Nebuchadnezzar and show how well his troops would respond to his leadership. Nebuchadnezzar was in no hurry to begin the battle. In fact, his men began to think that he was afraid of the enemy because he delayed the attack that he alone could order. But Nebuk had learned many tricks of military tactics. He knew, perfectly well, the enemy was watching his every move. First he ordered an encampment be made in plain sight of the enemy camp. Then he ordered it dismantled and the camp pulled back in retreat. Equipment was packed and unpacked, giving the illusion of uncertainty.

Nebuk allowed days to go by and he noted with satisfaction that the Egyptian army was becoming agitated by his seeming reticence. Occasionally taunts could be heard. Even Nebuk's own men were edgy about the tactic their leader was using. None were more nervous than Nebuk himself. The strategy was his; *could he pull it off—what if it failed?* All the emotions, attendant to a major test, confronted him. He walked the countryside until he felt confident. It was strange how the earth, the sky, the grass helped him, gave him strength, set his resolve.

Then Nebuk instructed his general to sound retreat and execute a pull back from their major position. As the men grumbled and complained over the decision, the Egyptian army began to charge toward them. It was then the rest of the Chaldean army, which had quietly encircled the city, began a two-prong attack from the opposite direction. The Egyptian army was caught between two advancing armies, and a third, which swiftly turned from their pretended retreat and swept down upon them. They were caught in one of the cleanest of military maneuvers.

Nebuchadnezzar was ecstatic with his victory. His generals applauded him. Their approval was especially satisfying, for many had been his instructors in his earlier training. He longed to get home and receive his father's approval.

When all seemed secure, Nebuk and a small entourage of trusted soldiers began the long trip back to Ur. He was eager to get back to Mara and Nabonidus, whom, he was afraid, might have forgotten him in his absence. He was eager to personally see his father's reaction to his success. He hoped that he had proven to King Nabopolassar that he, Nebuchadnezzar II, was worthy to succeed him on the throne.

These thoughts filled Nebuk's mind as he steadily followed his course homeward. When he neared the strip of land just east of the Euphrates River that held the little city of Babylon, he decided to make the short jog out of his way to visit the city that had once been the earlier capital of the Sumerian/Chaldean Empire. In spite of the prince's unexpected arrival in the city, the people, filling the air with cheers, poured out of their houses and businesses. He was filled with a sense of power and an even greater sense of belonging.

Because of the tumultuous welcome, Nebuk and his men spent two extra days looking over the city and enjoying the hospitality. However, not everyone was pleased with the welcome given the prince and soon a messenger was dispatched to the king, detailing the response of the people and Nebuchadnezzar's basking in the applause.

The night before Nebuk and his men were to leave, the High Priest of Bel Marduk, the chief deity of Babylon, came to see Nebuk. He was a short, round-faced, pleasant man, about fifty, fastidiously groomed, and decidedly used to good food. "Greetings, Prince Nebuchadnezzar. I have come with a very simple message. I believe that your future and that of Babylon are woven together and great power will be yours when you become the next king."

Nebuk thanked the priest and filed these comments in his mind, remembering his conclusions that religion must be harnessed to political power to create a great empire. *This man will be of great service to me in the future. Perhaps he is right; perhaps my future does lie in Babylon. It certainly could be expanded and developed into a great city. It is situated very well and wouldn't need a lot of tearing down to allow my building plans to take place. In fact,*

I could build my city right outside the present town and not disturb the citizens in any way. "Yes, I like it. The New Babylonian Empire' will arise here."

Nebuk's enthusiasm, for the rest of the trip home, was marvelous. The future seemed clearer to him than ever and he was excited to begin the great work that was ahead. He couldn't rest until he could share his dream with Mara.

CHAPTER 5

The trumpets signaled the beginning of the parade. The people standing and waiting for Prince Nebuchadnezzar II to appear were restless. They wanted to see their hero and future king, the one who had defended their honor against the Egyptian army and acquitted himself so valiantly.

First in the procession were trumpeters, followed by dancing girls. Then came the clowns, teasing the children and inciting the people to cheer. Next came the king's gold-trimmed, black carriage drawn by four perfectly matched black horses, which were overlaid with magnificent banners. The king sat stiffly at attention, making no acknowledgment of the crowd.

Behind the king's carriage came the marching soldiers surrounding a shoulder-borne throne chair. All eyes were on the young man in the seat. Nebuk was the object of all the attention as he smilingly waved to the cheering crowd.

The cheerfulness of his appearance masked the hurt the king had imposed on this day, which should have been one of the happiest times of his life. Nebuk had proven himself a valiant and skillful general in battle; he had proven himself able to gain the respect of his men, and indeed, of all the people—all, that is, except his father. He was the only person whose acceptance Nebuk had failed to gain.

As he waved to the crowd, he said, half to himself, "At least you people recognize who I am. I will be great in the eyes of all the world, if not in the eyes of Nabopolassar."

The King, instead of greeting him upon his return, made him wait two days while he jealously brooded over his son's success. "I wish I had not sent him into the battle fields so young. Now he comes parading home, the conquering hero and expects me to fall all over him. Well," the enraged king shouted, "He can just wait. He's going to have to wait to be king." The king justified his behavior by saying his son needed the time with his wife and family.

The reunion with Mara and Nabonidus had been wonderful. The months away from them had made him ravenous for affection and acceptance. Nebuk's family, along with his obsession for greatness, were the only stabilizing factors in his life. He was grateful for both of them. His family gave him unqualified affection and he intended to make himself great.

Mara had declined to ride in the parade. She was adamant that the day belonged to her husband and nothing should be allowed to detract from Nebuchadnezzar. As the king's carriage approached the royal reviewing stand, she stood to her feet and bowed herself before the king, who in spite of his pride, acknowledged her obeisance with the raising of the royal scepter.

It was painful to King Nabopolassar to realize that Mara knew how to react and even control him in the most trying of circumstance. "I hate this," the king muttered to himself, "That woman is a step ahead of me at every turn. She deliberately wanted to be in the reviewing stand to make me know that she is in charge. She made it look like she and my son are in loyal support of me. How does she do it and still make it look so right? The people are just eating out of their hands. I'll straighten it out one day." The king held his head high.

When Nebuchadnezzar's army and his carriage chair drew near, Mara jumped to her feet and saluted him with both arms raised in victory. Then she picked up a bouquet of flowers and tossed them to Nebuk, who acknowledged her by ordering his bearers to the side of the elevated reviewing stand where he stood to his feet and tenderly kissed his wife amid the cheers of all the people.

The public acclamation given his son did not warm the heart of Nabopolassar. Instead, something more like ice water coursed through his veins, further hardening his heart toward both Nebuk and Mara.

When the festivities were over, and it became necessary for Nebuk to face his father, the hostility between them was impenetrable. Mara joined them, insisting that they needed to talk. "This hostility between us has to be resolved; it has already ruined us as a family. If not settled, it will eventually destroy the entire empire. It you can't talk and make peace, you will find, all will be lost." With that she turned and marched out of their presence, leaving them both looking and feeling uncomfortable.

Hesitantly, Nebuk spoke first. "I guess I've got to speak first since I have to live with her." His attempt at lightness was a total failure. "Father, what is it that you want from me? I tried to do my best on the battlefield, not just for me, but for the empire and for you. Then why does everything I do seem only to drive us apart? I feel like you are angry, as if this military campaign was a contest of popularity between us. That isn't the case at all. I only wanted to win the battle so that you would be proud of me and perhaps give me your genuine approval."

Nabopolassar responded very slowly, his face contorted in pain. "That's not what I've heard. I have heard reports from the field, from Babylon, and now here in the palace that you are preparing to take over the throne from me. Now that you have the approval of the people and they all love you, they would perhaps be willing to follow you, even in rebellion against me."

Nebuk's mouth dropped open in amazement. "Your Majesty, that is not true and never will be. Of course, I was excited and thrilled by my first military victory—surely you understand that. All I am asking is for you to say that I did a good job in the field and that you appreciate what we, the men and I, did out there."

"We shall see what the future will tell us about your true attitude. Remember this," the pitch of his voice rising, "There are others who would also like to occupy my throne and the order of succession could easily be changed. You'd better watch your every move. I consider this audience over. Good day, Prince Nebuk."

Nebuk was devastated. He returned to his apartment, rage filling his mind and boiling over into the inner recesses of his soul.

He couldn't even speak to Mara. All the loneliness and rejection that had marked his life swept over him in waves. Finally, when he could speak, he told her, "Nothing was settled. I think my father is crazy. Either he is or I am. I'll talk to you when I can think straight again."

Mara could hear Nebuk pacing the floor, occasionally pounding one fist into the other, and muffled, angry words coming from their bedroom. She longed to go and comfort him but knew that he had to deal with this ongoing problem with his father himself. She wished that she could intervene in some way with Nabopolassar. Gradually a plan began to form in her mind. Nabonidus was the only link to the King that was in any way comfortable. "Perhaps the child could be the means to creating better feelings."

When Nebuk was able to tell her of his father's reaction to him, Mara announced her plan to not allow Nabonidus to visit the king until the strain in the relationship was corrected. They both were so emotionally drained from the day's pressure; they fell into each other's arms and wept. The tears were healing and soon they were able to talk of other things.

Issima, Nebuk's manservant, knocked at their door announcing, "Master Jeleu is here to see you, your Highness."

Mara questioned, "Jeleu is back? Show him in, Issima."

The strain on Nebuk's face was replaced by a smile. The reciprocated bear-hug-welcome for his closest friend brought a sense of peace and hope to his heart. "When did you get back, old friend?"

"I got back just in time for the parade," Jeleu responded. "You looked pretty good sitting in that throne chair. I came to congratulate you on your great victory and to let you know that I believe the whole realm is grateful that you have acted as a valiant Prince of the Empire. I bow in acknowledgment of your achievements." Jeleu's arm swept the floor in a grand gesture of obeisance.

Mara and Nebuk could not help but laugh at the old man's sincerity and they grabbed him and hugged him again before letting him in on the day's bitter news concerning the king. As he heard what the king had said, Jeleu's eyes clouded over and he began to weep.

Nebuk put his arm around the old man, who was now nearing eighty. The years of being the king's chief caravaner had weathered his skin, but had not taken his strength from him. It had been nearly fifteen years since the king had replaced him for befriending and guiding the prince.

Nebuk broke the silence with a question. "Jeleu, what should I do? You've always been here for me and at almost every crossroads I have ever faced, you seem to show up at just the right moment. This is one of those times and I feel the gods, if there be any, must have sent you to me."

Jeleu sighed deeply, turned without speaking and sat down wearily on the edge of a recliner lounge; he wiped his eyes with his sleeve. "My dears, you are facing one of the toughest tests of your lives. As you know, the king is not a man to change his mind easily; no one knows what strange thoughts are troubling him. Nebuk, my son, I believe that since your mother died your father has changed—he is not the sane, rational man he once was."

"I have thought the same thing, Jeleu," Mara interjected, "I was afraid I was only being mean and spiteful concerning him. But since you've said it, I think some of my fears are right." Mara's eyes traveled over the sitting room she had so recently redecorated. Bold colors in geometric patterns dominated the wall hangings and the colorful oil lamps gave off a soft glow. Even the room looked better to her with the knowledge that the problem of dealing with the king may not be their responsibility.

"But, Jeleu," Nebuk said, "What should we do? I am afraid anything that I have thought of would be considered as disloyalty or insurrection. Believe me, I have really entertained some rather radical thoughts. I would probably end up dead; for all he cares for me."

"You may be right, my young friend. You might be thrown away just to satisfy his rage and jealousy. You must be very careful not to incur his wrath. You must not risk his displeasure. I beg you, your Majesty, for the Empire's sake and for your future and your great plans for it, do not cross the king."

Jeleu calling him your Majesty startled both Nebuk and Mara. Nebuk gently said, "I am not the king, Jeleu. If I were, I wouldn't be facing this dilemma."

"Yes, your Highness, I wish you were the king."

Nebuk ignored the remark. "Jeleu, you have always been right in the past when you have advised me to honor my father even when he did not deserve it. I will take your advice again even though my inner feelings are otherwise. You have been a father to me when I had none—now is certainly one of those times. I honor you and bow to your wisdom. How fortunate was my mother's family to have you as friend, but to me you are more, you are my father. Any greatness that may come to the Empire through me is due to you. May you live to see my coronation."

Jeleu responded by rising stiffly from the lounge and bowing to Nebuk and Mara. "May it be so. May it be so."

Very shortly after retiring for the night, Issima knocked at their door, "Your Highness, master Jeleu has been attacked by some palace guards. He was beaten and left for dead. Some people who found him are caring for him nearby." Nebuk was dressing as Issima continued to tell him of what had transpired. "He was asking for you and one of them is waiting to take you to him. May I go with you?"

"Of course," Nebuk said, as he cinched his belt around his robe.

Nebuk was able to get there in time to cradle the old man's head and hear his dying words. "Don't let this stop you. Do what you have to do to become king. Never forget, I love you."

Nebuk's brokenhearted tears mingled with those of the small crowd that had gathered as the old man died. Amidst his tears, Nebuk thanked the people for helping Jeleu. After asking a few questions, he instructed Issima to care for Jeleu and he went home.

When Nebuk returned to Mara, she comforted him and reminded him of Jeleu's love. "You know, Nebuk, I think he must have known that he would not live to call you Majesty, but he did it any way."

"Mara, I think you're right. I think he knew." Nebuk's face reflected the process that he was going through. The love, the grief, the pain, and finally the stress of anger, all were traced on his features.

As usual, anger was the final emotion, the one that always seemed to return. "How am I going to deal with my father after something like this?"

"I have an idea," Mara suggested. "Go to your father and tell him of the tragedy of Jeleu's death. Ask for permission to head the burial delegation since Jeleu had been the king's chief caravaner and deserves some form of special recognition."

Nebuk's request for an audience with the king was granted much faster than usual. Nabopolassar expected this would be a good opportunity to have a fight with his son for he expected him to be in a rage. Instead, a very sad-faced prince told his father of the death of Jeleu and asked the king's permission to do the royal honors for the king's servant who had served him so faithfully for many years. No word of anger escaped his lips. No telltale facial expression told the courtiers in attendance that the prince knew anything of the king's role in Jeleu's death.

The aggrieved approach of his son was so unexpected that the king was unusually sparing with his words. He asked the prince to bear the body of Jeleu to an honorable burial in his home just north of Babylon.

Nebuk returned to Mara and all the pain and anger in his heart over Jeleu's death erupted. "Jeleu was right; I will have to become the model child. We will work until that illegitimate excuse for a man no longer sits on the throne, and that day can't come too soon."

From that very hour, the bitterness and hatred that had been building in his heart was set in concrete. The painful years of seeking for approval and reaping rejection were over. The king, Nabopolassar, was on his way out.

Nebuk bore the body of Jeleu to its burial with great love and grief. In addition to burying his spiritual father, Jeleu, he was just as surely burying his father, the king. So much pain was released through the funeral that Nebuk was emotionally drained and stayed several days longer in Babylon. Here he again felt the renewing power of knowing the destiny of the empire was to be identified with Babylon.

He began to dream again of the great city he would build and of the empire he would lead. "It will be a New Babylonian Empire with Babylon as my city. I must make the plans."

The ideas flooding his mind brought joy and relief to his hurting heart and he returned to Ur with renewed strength and resolve to survive.

Nebuk did not realize how difficult the next several years were to be. When military battles were planned to extend the empire, his advice was unsought. He was not allowed to lead the men in battle as he had at Haran. He had to stand at attention as his father heaped praise on lesser men for doing far less than he had.

Hardest of all was to see the political maneuvering to advance the careers of his sisters' husbands into positions that could allow them to be candidates for the throne if Nebuchadnezzar were out of the picture. Since he had never had any real relationship with his sisters, he became wary of every move they made. He became fearful for his life. "Who are my friends? Whom can I trust?"

Living under the strain of constantly looking over his shoulder became almost unbearable. Had it not been for the deep love of his wife and son, his plans for the future and a growing need to avenge the death of the one man who had really befriended and loved him, Nebuk might have gone completely crazy. As it was, he spent increasingly longer periods of time by himself walking through the fields surrounding Ur in the cool of the evening. Brooding over the events of his life became his daily recreation. Mara worried over his deepening depression.

The king rarely summoned him to the royal throne room and seldom spoke to him when he was called. Most of Nebuk's activities there were purely ceremonial. It was obvious even to the casual observer that the king was displeased with his son. The real reason was kept carefully hidden and, true to his word, Nebuchadnezzar never spoke of it publicly. To the majority of the Chaldean people, Nebuchadnezzar was their hero and someday king.

During these trying times, the isolated family of Nebuchadnezzar continued to grow. Mara gave birth to a beautiful little girl whom they named Aia after Nebuk's maternal grandmother who had died just a few weeks before the baby was born. They wanted to name her after Nebuk's mother, Queen Yada, but knowing the trouble that would cause with the King, they chose the grandmother's name.

Even the birth of a granddaughter did not change their relationship with the king. He had other granddaughters from his daughters' marriages and they were more acceptable than Nebuk's offspring. He paid only "official" attention to the baby, and continued to avoid the family. Even his attention to Nabonidus was perfunctory.

During the years of "Nebuk's exile," as he liked to call it, the Egyptian Pharaoh, Neccoh, continued his campaign against the Chaldean Empire. He continued to press his forces back into position to retake the city of Haran. He conquered the bulk of the seacoast nations, forcing them into servitude. Through political intrigue he created an alliance with the land of Judah, and was poised to strike the forces holding the northern ramparts Nebuchadnezzar had taken from him.

Nabopolassar periodically sent his troops to the front lines and the occasional skirmishes served to remind everyone a bigger battle was coming, and coming soon.

When it did come, the forces of the Chaldean army were repulsed. Reports from the front, detailing massive casualties, caused major panic. Many of the ablest soldiers and generals were killed or captured. People huddled in little groups worrying about the way the war was going; fear dominated their thinking. *What is going to happen to the empire? What's the king going to do? Why doesn't Nebuchadnezzar head up the army again?*

The king was nearly beside himself; he shouted at all the courtiers. Every bad report was always blamed on some incompetent. His usually immaculate appearance became disheveled, giving rise to speculation that he was losing control of himself as well as the war. The King paced the halls of the palace; the plans of his life to expand the Empire were in jeopardy.

Nebuchadnezzar offered his services to his father, hoping he might help rally the troops and perhaps save a defeat from becoming a disaster. The king spoke with bitterness edging his voice. "You'd love another chance to unseat me, wouldn't you? I will not serve you the kingdom on a silver platter." Instead, the king mounted a massive campaign to get more men and materials to the battle areas.

The continuing battles brought no resolution to the ongoing grudge between the Egyptian and Chaldean nations. The only advantage the Chaldeans had, which probably saved them, was the shorter distance of their supply lines. Egypt was certainly holding them at bay.

As difficult as it was, Nebuchadnezzar did nothing to incite any discontent or make any attempt to try and gather forces to himself. He practiced Jeleu's advice. The lack of leadership his father was giving to the empire caused his heart to become increasingly bitter. Knowing the king's failures were working destruction on the empire; he took that as a personal affront to himself. "I will have to rebuild all my father is losing through his stupidity. All I gained at the battle of Haran will have to be redone."

Again Mara gave good council to her husband. "You will be seen as the savior of this empire. Soon the demand will be for you to take charge of the realm and you will be the people's choice. You will become the king."

In less than two months the words of Mara began to come true. The generals in charge of the battle were becoming increasingly concerned about the stagnation of the military and the lack of success on the battlefield. Using a general who held Nabopolassar's confidence, they hinted that he should send Nebuchadnezzar to the battle to lead the men. "Your Majesty, as you know, the people have been upset that you haven't sent Nebuchadnezzar to lead the troops. Any further military failure would have to be borne by him and not you alone. If he were to be captured or, the gods forbid, killed, you couldn't be blamed. However, if you don't use him, you will be. Perhaps it would solve both of your problems, with the people and with your son. We know how eager he is to serve."

Thus an idea was placed in the king's thinking. *If the battle did indeed go badly, perhaps my son would not be such a problem to me, especially if he did not survive.* He never suspected his own generals might have a plan of their own as to who should be the next king of the empire. A hideous idea began to grow in his mind.

Nebuk was surprised by the summons to audience with the king. This hadn't happened for a long time. He stood waiting not with any real anticipation until he was announced to the king. "Your Majesty, how may I be of service to you?"

The king smilingly acknowledged him and said, "My son, I have changed my mind about sending you to lead the army. Are you still willing to do so?"

Nebuk controlled the emotion that threatened to explode. Very calmly he said, "I shall do whatever I can to help in the war effort. Are there any special orders you wish me to follow?"

"No, I am placing you in charge. All the military is at your discretion and disposal."

Nebuchadnezzar's first duty was to call all the generals and strategists together and begin a complete evaluation of all the military. He was furious this survey had not been done previously. It revealed several areas of weakness and lack of support for the field troops. With Nebuk taking charge, the generals' confidence soared. Within six months of the time his father asked him to head up the army, the prince was firmly in charge of a military operation that could beat the Egyptians at Carchemish.

CHAPTER 6

Mara stood with her two children and watched her husband lead the army of the empire out through the city gate. She thought of their last conversation just the night before. "Mara, I will be back triumphant: I will not fail. You shall be proud of me."

"There is no doubt of that, my dear. I am already proud of you. What I really want you to know is that I feel that our struggles with this realm will be over when you return from sending Pharaoh Neccoh back to Egypt where he belongs. I will be watching closely the affair of things here. I shall be your eyes and ears in the palace; much is wrong here and it will not escape me."

The question as to what Mara knew or felt was never asked, for Nebuk knew that he could depend on his wife to be his loyal support. She had known from early teen years that she would be the queen of the empire, having known this before Nebuk knew she existed. *Yes, Mara is the one constant in my life. She is dependable.*

Nebuk's thinking of the consistency of his wife was followed by thoughts of his father's inconsistency, the maddening way that the king conducted himself as the army prepared to march. He called Nebuk to the reviewing stand in front of everyone, raised his scepter in salute and then rested the scepter on first the right shoulder of Nebuk and then on the left, as he would do when conferring great honor on the recipient. No words were spoken between the two but the crowd took the gesture to mean far more than the king did; they burst forth into cheers. The prince was being put to work.

The wordless confrontation left Nebuk with a strong feeling; he better watch his back. The emotion of leaving his family and the question of what his father might mean by his action was more than he could deal with at the time. Raising his sword, he led the men in a triumphant victory shout and paraded out of the city gate past the cheering crowds.

A vague uneasiness settled over Nebuk as he led his men north to their first stop near the city of Babylon. "What was it? The fear of not seeing the family again? Death itself? The battle? The possibility of losing the war? Or was it having to face the king if he won and winning was what he expected. Yes, that was it, there was no way to please the king, so why try? I'll just win the war and then send for Mara and the children and we'll stay up in the north nearer to her home." The decision, even if unrealistic, shook off the uneasiness and he looked forward to the stay in his city, Babylon.

Early twilight found the army at the edge of Babylon where the advance men had begun to set up tents for the stay. As Nebuk dismounted from his horse, a servant of the high priest greeted him and asked if his master could have a word with him. Nebuk was flattered that the most influential religious leader in the whole realm wanted to talk to him. Nebuk was very surprised to be told that Belardos, the High Priest of Bel, was here at the campsite awaiting his arrival. He had hoped to spend some time talking with the priest, but to have him waiting for him was exciting. He went immediately to the tent where the priest was resting. He was greeted with high praise . . . so much so that Nebuk became nervous lest anyone overhear and report the flattery to his father.

"Prince Nebuchadnezzar, I wanted to meet you here and share my feelings concerning your upcoming war against the Egyptians. You will win, but you must take lots of time to do it. The Pharaoh of Egypt is expecting to make quick work of the army of Nebuchadnezzar. He was delighted when it became known you were leading the forces personally. In fact, he has been preparing for this battle since you defeated his forces at Haran several years ago. He has studied your military tactics at that battle and is also personally taking charge of his forces at Carchemish. For him, this is personal revenge. Your victory, therefore, is all the more important.

"You know some things already from your intelligence scouts. However, what you may not know is that a trap has been laid for you as you approach the battlefield just below the city. My spirit emissaries have just brought me this information this morning as I was sacrificing to Bel Marduk."

"Excuse me, your Eminence," Nebuk interrupted. "What is this about spirit emissaries? I am not sure what you mean?"

"Oh, Your Highness, I have much to tell you about spiritual things. Suffice it for now to say, I often know things that are going to happen when the spirits of Marduk send me messages. I listen carefully to hear these things, because they are always right." He paused to let the prince take in his words and then continued. "Bel Marduk, our greatest god, has assured me that if you will make Babylon great again and promote him to be the chief god in your kingdom, you will be able to overcome and rule the realm. Your reign will start very soon."

"Oh, Your Eminence, Great High Priest of Bel, it would be my extreme pleasure to make the fair city of Babylon great again as well as restore the worship of the great god Bel Marduk as the chief god in all the realm. You must, however, realize one thing. I do not believe in the gods people make. I use religion to cause the people to work for me and for my realm. I have prayed for many years for the gods to favor me in a great area of my life and to this day they have not answered."

"I know the reason you pray and your father will never be around long enough for that prayer to be answered. I have no great problem with your failure to believe; however, if you will promote the worship of Bel you will have my approval."

Nebuk's face registered his surprise at both the words and the speed of the acceptance of his terms; but more so, that the priest seemed to know of his prayers. "Tell me, Great Priest of Bel, what do you know of other men's private prayers?"

"Please, call me Belardos." A kindly expression tinged with sorrow lighted the priest's round face. "As I told you, my spirit emissaries give me much information. More important is the warning I have been given for you. You must be very careful on the battlefield. I am sorry to have to tell you this, but the king's men are there to cause you to fail. Use only the men you personally know and can trust, for the king plans for you to be killed in this battle so that he can continue to rule without your competition."

If Nebuk was surprised before, he was now completely devastated by the priest's words. His tanned olive skin seemed to drain of all its color and he struggled to maintain his composure. Finally he said, "Forgive me, your Grace, I am aware that somehow there must be power from your god to give you this kind of information. I must spend some time with you and learn more of these things before I proceed further into battle."

"That is why I came out to meet you here and to invite you to spend time with me. There is no need for you to hurry to battle. Take time to prepare. Please be my guest, come to my home and make it your personal headquarters. Tonight we will discuss the battle of Carchemish the right way, as directed by the gods.

Nebuk was embarrassed by his reaction to the news of his father's duplicity, and so emotionally drained and confused by the rapidity of the events, that he had forgotten he needed to settle his troops. Before any personal activities, duty called. Leaving the priest's tent, he thankfully accepted the priest's offered hospitality and quickly called his chief of staff.

Nebuzaradan was the most completely loyal member of his staff; so strong was his affection for the prince that he added the Nebu prefix to his name. Addressing the handsome thirty-one-year-old career officer, Nebuk said, "I am leaving you in complete charge of settling the troops for an indefinite stay here in Babylon. I will be at the High Priest's home adjoining the temple should you need me. I realize there are some things I have to know from this man before we can begin our campaign against the Pharaoh of Egypt. I shall contact you tomorrow. I trust you completely to do as I would."

Nebuzaradan bowed before the Prince. "Your Highness is most gracious. I will do as I feel you would do. If you are sacrificing to the God Bel, mention me in your devotion as well. Good evening, your Highness."

Nebuzaradan was pleased with the prince's expression of confidence. It had been a long way for a boy, raised by his mother after his father had committed suicide, to become one of the youngest generals in the Chaldean Empire's history. Zaradan, as the prince often called him—they'd been friends for years, had worked hard to gain his position. Shorter than average, he compensated by demanding perfection from himself and his subordinates. He was a tough administrator, a strict leader, a performer, and a valuable asset to the prince.

Nebuk gathered his personal bags, giving orders to his aids to deliver the other things to the High Priest's house. He was eager to sample more of the priest's thoughts and learn the sources of his knowledge. *This promises to be an exciting evening.*

Belardos's servants had prepared a sumptuous meal for the Prince. Dinner over, the two settled down to serious conversation. The evening was spent in opening Nebuk's eyes to the world of the spirits. Bel, Ishtar, Innanna were all-important gods connected to the spirit world. As such they could provide information and help to the persons they favored, just as Belardos's spirit guides did for him.

Nebuk had always known of the obligatory nature of the worship of these gods and goddesses, but had never really believed in any supernatural powers other than the hold superstition had on the masses. He was fully aware of the sexual nature of the worship of the gods, but had no other understanding of the spirit realm.

After talking for nearly four hours, the Priest suggested an early rise for morning sacrifice at the ziggurat; the pyramid shaped tower at the center of the city dedicated to the worship of Bel. Nebuk was exhausted but readily agreed to learn all he could from this fascinating man who had become his friend.

Nebuk's sleep was fitful and frequently disturbed by sounds that seemed to swirl in his room. The most disturbing sound was a voice that sounded much like his father, the king, attacking him and telling him that he would fail. He tried to shut these sounds out of his mind by sitting up and straining his eyes to see what or who was in his room.

Finally, he fell back on his bed, slipped into a deep sleep and began to dream. Not only was the dream disturbing but it replayed over and over. Try as hard as he could, he could not stop the dream. He tried to scream, but no sound would come forth. Cold sweat drenched him as he watched the repeated sequence of his father gleefully ordering him to be made a eunuch. Knowing his father's attitude toward him made the dream more real. He felt the humiliation and the pain that the procedure involved.

As suddenly as the dream came, it left, and he slept peacefully. He was awakened by one of the servants who had readied his bath and was prepared to give him a morning massage. Nebuk was so fearful after the dream, which he remembered vividly, that he would not let anybody touch him. The servant sensing the Prince's fear, tried to reassure him that he meant him no evil. "I am, after all, just a harmless eunuch, and would not hurt such an honored guest."

Hearing the word eunuch, he began to tremble, shaking visibly he ordered the servant, "Please leave me."

Finally calm, Nebuk was able to recall the servant and ask him how and why he became a eunuch. The servant, much relieved that the Prince was not angry with him, told him how he had been taken captive in a battle King Nabopolassar had conducted 20 years earlier. He had been made a eunuch to keep him from being dangerous to the realm. Later he had been taken to the High Priest's house because of his devotion to the god, Bel. Here he served the High Priest because as a eunuch he was not eligible to be a temple prostitute.

The view from the top of the ziggurat was breathtaking and so was the climb up the steep steps which took the worshipper to the pinnacle of the seven tiered, pyramid-like structure. It was old and the steps well-worn by the faithful who had practiced their faith with physical exertion. It was obvious that Belardos, in spite of his weight was in good shape, having made the climb many times in his career.

All morning, even the exhilarating climb and the impressive view could not keep Nebuk's thoughts off his dream. *What if that happens to me?* It was not so much a question as a declaration of fear. He was depressed. The priest, noting his preoccupation, asked him to share his feelings. At first Nebuk tried to pass off the problem as not worthy of wasting the priest's time, but with further prompting, he shared the dream and the fear created by the servant. The priest immediately called his advisors and magicians to interpret the dream.

The interpretation revealed a simple matter that his father did not accept him as a man or a fit heir to his throne. In the king's thinking, emasculation would rob the prince of his strength and power to rule. As the simplicity and truth of this settled into his mind, Nebuk began to relax and ask the questions the priest was eager to answer.

The rest of the day was spent in discussion of the work of spirit emissaries, dreams, and their interpretation. Nebuk was fascinated to learn that much of what Mara did and knew was similar to the things Belardos understood. "You and Mara must be kindred spirits. I am impressed with the control you seem to have over your own emotions and even over the spirits that give you answers."

It was a stimulating and exciting day, and when it was time to retire, Nebuk was exhausted and ready to sleep. However, all the stimulating ideas caused him to toss and turn.

When finally he slept, he dreamed again, this time, a pleasant dream of Mara, Aia and a new baby, another boy. This boy seemed to grow very fast. In his middle age, he was seated on a throne in what looked to Nebuk like a beautiful and expanded city of Babylon. There was no picture of Nabonidus in the dream but that did not seem to be of any importance to Nebuk. He slept peacefully the rest of the night and when he awakened, he was refreshed and excited about what was happening.

After morning exercise, climbing the Ziggurat and sacrificing to Bel Marduk, Nebuk carefully told Belardos his dream and asked for an interpretation. The magicians, seers and prognosticators were quickly called and they listened carefully to the dream and asked detailed questions about parts of it.

"Mara is even now with child and his birth will occur just after the battle of Carchemish, just after . . . just after." They drew a blank. "The child will be the one who will succeed you on the throne but he will be more than forty years old when he begins to reign. Your older son will, by his own choices, disqualify himself from reigning."

Nebuk was amazed at the ease with which the interpretation of the dream came to the magicians. He wanted to go to his room to sleep and dream so that he could hear more of these mystical bits of information. When he said as much to the high priest, Belardos laughingly said, "You don't have to be asleep to hear things. You can have visions as well as dreams." And with that began a long series of descriptions of visions he had experienced.

"I remember one particular vision that has to do with you. I was standing outside the city wall here at Babylon. I saw a very handsome young man dressed as a king standing on the wall and surveying the city. Something bothered me at the time. The city was the same as it is today, and even though Nabopolassar was King, as he is today, yet the man was not he. It was you. As I watched, the city grew and became very beautiful and powerful. You became older and I watched until you were old and feeble."

"What excites me so much is seeing the beginning of the vision come to pass. I believe that you will be the king who will bring great glory to the nation and particularly to the city of Babylon. See what the spirits can do to help you?"

Nebuk's responsive excitement was infectious to the priest and to the temple officials. They found much enjoyment in the prince's discoveries. In the middle of all this stimulation, Nebuk's sense of duty kicked in and he realized that he had not checked back with Nebuzaradan. Elation gave way to guilt; as commander and chief of the troops he had not prepared them adequately for their extended stay.

When Nebuk reached the encampment, he was happy to see everything that he would have done, had been done. When Nebuzaradan saluted the Prince, it was obvious that Nebuk was pleased with his chief of staff. "Zaradan, you've done it again. There will never be another like you. When we finally get into battle, you must take good care of yourself. I can't do without you. Thank you, my friend."

The well-deserved praise was answered with a smart salute, "As you ordered, your Highness. It is my pleasure to serve you." It was obvious that the prince's approval meant a great deal to the officer. Zaradan, being younger and shorter than the other officers, needed the prince's approval. Nebuk's affirmation made him stand taller and straighter, adding inches to his mental image.

"Enough formality, Zaradan, let's get to your tent so I can bring you up-to-date on some of the things I am learning." Nebuk spent the next hour apprising his chief-of-staff of the dreams, the interpretations and the suggestions the high priest had laid out for him to consider in making his battle plans. When he told Nebuzaradan about the disloyal troops they were going to have to find and neutralize, Zaradan interrupted.

"Your Highness, I've already identified some of the ones who we will have to watch. Some of the men, and I won't tell you who yet, are already trying to cause discontent. They are unhappy because we have set up a semi-permanent camp so close to home and not nearer the battlefield. Some of them are saying you are not courageous enough to carry out the war and you are just stalling for time."

"Good job, my friend. Just keep your eyes open and mark them for future reference. We will know where to put them in the line-up when the battle gets hot. Now, I must get back to the city and continue learning all I can about the upcoming campaign."

Nebuk and the high priest spent the evening working over the plans for the Carchemish battle. The maps of the area substantiated the things that Belardos' spirits had told him. It was easy to see how Pharaoh Neccoh could try to ambush him in the approach to a battlefield below the city. They needed a plan that enabled them to skirt the area and make camp far enough away to cause the enemy to doubt the imminence of attack. They would build what would give the appearance of a permanent campsite and in the middle of the building, stop and attack the Egyptians. The plan consisted of running away from every encounter with the enemy, making it appear the Chaldean forces were fearful and still awaiting reinforcements.

Belardos continued his advice, "I think you should stay completely out of sight, as if you had not arrived and the troops were really waiting for your coming with more soldiers. Making the permanent camp larger than necessary will also imply more troops are expected. Also, don't forget to put all of your traitors in the front ranks of your forces when you finally do attack."

Prince Nebuchadnezzar thanked the priest for his advice and said, "I certainly will consider your suggestions." As Nebuk retired for the night, his mind was a whirlwind of military planning. He was excited about the future, he liked the idea he could know in advance what things were coming and that nothing seemed to be denied him.

When he finally settled down for the night, a tremendous fear gripped him. *What if I lose the battle? What if I'm killed and leave Mara and the children all alone to fend for themselves against my father?* The "what ifs" drove him into a deep state of agitation. After rolling and tossing for several hours, unable to sleep, he rang the bell for the eunuch servant.

In a few moments the servant, a tall slender balding man, came rushing into the room tying his toga-like robe about him. "Your Highness, what can I do for you?"

"Please prepare a bath and massage for me, I don't seem to be able to sleep. Too much is on my mind."

The servant hurried from the room to make the arrangements. Soon other servants, carrying buckets of water and a cradle of hot rocks to heat the water, completed their work. It was several minutes before Nebuk could slip into the water to soak the confusion and depression of the night away. The servant stood ready to do the prince's bidding. "What is your name, my good man? The least I can do is call you by your name, for I certainly gave you a difficult time when I first came and now I roust you out of your sleep."

"My name before I was captured was Akkakah, but when I entered the temple service my name was changed to Belakah. Please call me Belakah as I delight to be in the service of Bel Marduk."

"Well, Belakah it shall be. Tell me about yourself. It will help to get my mind on other things."

"I don't know what to tell you."

"Well, how old are you? Do you have a family? Do you always want to be a servant in the house of the high priest? How's that for starters?"

"Your Highness, I am fifty two years old. All of my family was killed in the battle in which I was captured. Bel Marduk and the high priest are my family. I am happy to serve here. I only wish I was whole so I could be one of the temple prostitutes. I would gladly have served the men and the women who came for their fertility cleansing. But right now, I am who I am. And I am glad to serve you, the future king of the empire, in any way that you might wish."

Nebuk stepped out of the bath water and wrapped himself in a towel. Nebuk lay on the massage table and Belakah anointed him with oil. The servant's soothing hands began to work the tightness out of his muscles; soon he found himself relaxing and enjoying the massage. In spite of his earlier fear of the servant, he felt the stress begin to leave. He felt renewed, comfortable. In the dim glow of the candles, as Belakah worked, he felt the servant's strong hands gently restore him, and he felt as if he were a small child ready to be tucked into bed. The sense of comfort was overwhelming to him. "Belakah, you are wonderful."

"Thank you, Your Highness. I could feel the tension leaving your back and arms and shoulders. As I touch you, I can feel you relaxing into me. That is a great compliment you are giving me, especially after how much I frightened you when we first met. Now, let's turn you over and I will finish the rest of this massage."

As Belakah was completing his work, he spoke to the prince. "You have a very muscular, well-built, strong body. Your emotions are also very strong, but not so well built. You are very sensitive, very feeling. The hurts that you have sustained will plague you, but must be controlled. You must learn to relax. While you are here, let me give you massages each day and that should help you."

Nebuk hurriedly dressed, thanked Belakah for the massage and then dropped wearily into his bed. "What is this, even the servants here are prophets. What was it I was feeling as he massaged me?" Weariness and relaxation overtook him and soon he was resting peacefully.

He slept peacefully until he began to dream again. This time the dream was very real and the feelings were equally powerful. He dreamt that Jeleu, his old friend and the only man who had ever really loved him, was holding him in his arms and comforting him, just as he had when Nebuk was a small child. The scene was very soothing until suddenly it was a rerun of him holding Jeleu as he was dying. Still sleeping, Nebuk began crying louder and louder until finally he was shouting out his hatred for his father who had ordered Jeleu's beating and death. Strong arms were wrapped around the sobbing prince's shoulders and as he became calm, he opened his eyes and realized that Belakah had his arms around him just as Jeleu would have done.

"Belakah? What is happening? Where did you come from?"

"Your Highness, I heard you call out; I sleep just down the hall when I have a guest to care for. What can I do for you?"

"I have bad dreams which upset me greatly. Promise me you will never tell anyone about this. No one must know about my weakness. Promise me you will be silent."

"Your Highness, your secrets are as safe with me as they were with your friend whom you saw in your dream."

Nebuk jerked his head in amazement at the servant's ability to know what was going on in his dream and he pulled away from Belakah's embrace. He stared at the eunuch, the dim candlelight casting eerie shadows on Belakah's face. "Who and what are you? How do you know what's going on in my dreams?"

"Your Highness, I am merely a lowly eunuch in the service of Bel. I only know what is given to me. Since it is my privilege to be your personal servant while you are here in the house of the high priest, the spirits are giving me information that I need to help you, to comfort you, however I can. Right now, you needed someone to hold you. I am sure that you will be able to relax and sleep now."

When Nebuk awoke, he was surprised to find Belakah sleeping soundly on the floor beside his bed. It had not been just a dream, but a dream with a real human encounter. As Nebuk stirred, Belakah awoke with a start and jumped to his feet. "Your Highness, what can I do for you?"

"Two things, first remember your promise of confidentiality. Second, I want you to find a place where you can rest today, for I seem to need you in the night times. You have become very important to me. Perhaps you'd consider going with me when I leave?"

"I will do whatever you wish, Highness. My life is to serve you. You need not fear, for I will keep your confidence. I will also rest so I can serve you when you need me. If you ask the high priest for me, I'm sure he will agree to your request."

CHAPTER 7

Mara and the children had just returned home from seeing Nebuchadnezzar march off to the war when the house steward startled her by telling her that the king was there. She was puzzled and fearful for it had been several years since the king had come to their home. *Why now, when Nebuchadnezzar isn't home?* "Your Majesty," she said as she greeted him in the vestibule. "Please come in." She hoped the fear and suspicion wasn't noticeable to the king as she spoke. "We have just now gotten back from the military send-off. What can I get you, some tea perhaps?"

"Tea would be fine. I have really come to see Nabonidus, but I have a somewhat delicate matter to discuss with you, first. His father and I do not seem to be able to communicate."

"Your Majesty, that situation is completely in your control. Your son desires more than anything to please and serve you in whatever way he can. He certainly would like to do all in his power to comply with your wishes. I shall try to do the same. First, let me have Sala bring the tea. Excuse me for a moment."

Mara needed the time away from the king to gather her composure. She smoothed her hair, straightened her dress, took several deep breaths to settle her nerves and then returned. She spoke graciously to the king. "The tea will be here in a few minutes; now, let's not sit out here, let's go into the sitting room. We'll be more comfortable while we talk." The king followed her into the adjoining room. "Now, please proceed, Your Majesty."

Nabopolassar hesitated before his wily daughter-in-law. He stroked his well-manicured beard. Age had not changed his still regal bearing, but then age had not modified the bitterness that seemed to flow from his very presence either.

Softly and slowly, he began to speak. "You know, Mara, that I respect you very much and I would never want to be the bearer of bad news, but there are some realities that we must face." The ominous tone of the king's voice, calculated to cause fear, succeeded. "It is possible we could lose this battle with Pharaoh Neccoh and we could lose many men in the process. Your husband is a very brave man to lead the army against such a worthy opponent."

Sala interrupted with the tea, placing it on the table between them. "That will be all, Sala, thank you." Mara, grateful for the interruption, seized the opportunity to gain the control of the conversation. She asked the king, "How do you want your tea? You use lemon, if I remember correctly." When he answered, she poured his tea and asked in a totally non-belligerent tone, "What is it you are trying to say, Your Majesty"?

The king was flushed by her direct approach and stirred his tea before answering. "You, dear Mara, are the most direct woman I know. I have grave fears of what would happen to the empire if your husband should be killed on the battlefield. As you know, he is very popular and the people have great hopes for his succeeding me. Without him, great demoralization would set in and we would become a broken people."

"What does that have to do with Nabonidus?" This time there was more than a hint of an edge in her voice and the king, detecting it, reacted by taking a deep breath before answering.

"I want to reassure the people of the empire that my grandson is being prepared to succeed me in the event that his father would be unable to do so. I want to personally see to his training, just as I did for his father, so he will be ready in case . . . " His voice drifted off and his eyes searched Mara's face for her reaction. Finding none, he continued. "There is another reason." He paused as if groping for words. "You see, I am not well and I don't know how much longer I will live. I must see to the well-being of the empire in whatever way I can."

"I am sorry you are not well." Normally Mara was aware of many things, but this caught her by surprise. Alarm was in her reaction. "Have you been to the physicians? What do they say? Surely they can help?" The tone of her voice, no longer edged, but filled with genuine compassion, registered with the king and he felt further discomforted by her caring. That was not his reason for coming to see her.

"I want to talk to Nabonidus and tell him to delay his studies for a while and allow me to direct him in the role that might be thrust upon him. I trust you can understand my reasoning?"

"Certainly, and whatever is best for the realm would be what I and his father would want. If you feel this is the right course, I'll call him to speak to you right now. However, there is one thing I must interject. I am confident Nebuchadnezzar will be successful and I certainly hope it will be a long time before you relinquish your throne to him."

"As usual, you are most gracious and I hope you are right. Please call Nabonidus, for I want to begin his training as soon as possible."

Nabonidus was not hard to find, for he had heard his grandfather's voice in the sitting room and was curious. After so many years of absence, now he was here. He waited a few moments before entering the sitting room then he burst out. "Grandfather!" Then remembering the formalities, he corrected himself and bowed. "Your Majesty, how good to see you here."

The king could not help but smile, for he realized that at least someone in this household held some affection for him. He fixed his eyes on the handsome young man before him and noticed with satisfaction that he was taller and larger of build than his father. The king stood to greet him "Do you realize that you are as tall as I am? How old are you, seventeen? You are certainly developing very well. "Come, my son, sit down, it's been too long since we've been able to have a talk." Nabonidus only grinned happily and the king continued. "What I'm about to say has already been discussed with your mother and now I need to talk it over with you."

Nabopolassar quickly briefed the young prince concerning his

role in the future of the realm. The king expressed concern for the
well-being of the people in the event his father was killed in the
battle with Pharaoh Neccoh. Nabonidus sat quietly while his
grandfather unfolded the role he might have to play in the future.
He was respectful and attentive as the king spoke.

The king finished speaking, he looked first at Mara and then
at Nabonidus who also was looking at his mother for some form of
guidance. Finding none, Nabonidus swallowed hard and began to
speak very slowly. "Your Majesty, I hardly know what to say. We
have not even considered the possibility that my father would not
be successful. He and my mother are very confident that it is the
will of the gods that my father sit on your throne . . . ah, that is,
in the distant future. You and my father have not been close in the
years I have been growing up. For me now to be suddenly
confronted with being my father's replacement is very hard for me
to accept. I will do whatever you wish. However, I will do nothing
to replace my father in the affections of the people." Pausing to
take a deep breath, he continued with greater strength in his voice.
"I will receive whatever training you deem necessary, but I will not
parade or be on display until my father, for whatever reason, is not
able to be the legal heir to the throne. I will not be a party to the
political intrigues that do not have my father's interests at heart."

Mara straightened herself in her chair, reflecting her pride in
her son's answer. The king also looked at his grandson with a new
perspective. "Mara, I see that you and Nebuchadnezzar have done
an excellent job in raising your son to be such a fine young man. It
will be a joy to spend time with him and watch his progress. I
shall expect you at the palace tomorrow, Nabonidus. We shall begin
immediately." With that the king stood and strode to the door
where the servant let him out.

No sooner was the king out of the door than Mara's arms were
enfolding her son. "I am so proud of you. You were superb in the
way you answered your grandfather. He has always loved you far
more than the rest of us, but you let him know that you are your

own man. If your father were here, he would be thrilled with your ability to handle yourself."

"Mother, I don't like this whole thing. Oh, I'll do my best, but you know grandfather. He always has some ulterior motive behind what he does. You know how I hate the intrigues that rule the palace. If I had my way, I'd really like to not be in line for the throne."

"Well, there isn't much you can do about that, being the firstborn in a royal line, and up until now, only having one sister." Nabonidus turned to look at his mother and see her blush. "It's really too early to say for sure, but you may be having a little brother or sister in a few more months. Even your father doesn't know it yet. I shall send a messenger to him with all this news very soon."

It was now Nabonidus's turn to put his arms around Mara. "We shall have to be very careful of you, little mother. With father away, winning the war, I shall see to your welfare. After all, I am seventeen and even the king thinks I'm the heir apparent to my father!"

"That you are, my dear, that you are."

It was several days later that Mara decided she would send a messenger to her husband. A carefully worded message was prepared and the servant, a trusted, loyal one, was dispatched with the message, which was carefully concealed in the lining of his cloak. It contained word about Nabonidus's training at the king's hand, about the king's supposed illness and about the soon arrival of another child in the Nebuchadnezzar household. It also contained encouragement to be careful and instructions to be very wary of any who might be disloyal in the forces. It was sealed with love and kisses from all the family.

To keep suspicions from being aroused, the servant left Ur looking very much like anyone just going out for the day into the countryside. He was found three days later, throat slit and his cloak missing.

*   *   *

When a message arrived back at Ur from Nebuchadnezzar, it contained nothing in reference to the message that Mara had sent. She was surprised that the news in her message did not warrant a more direct response. Nebuk's excited message told only of what had happened the first few days in Babylon and the events of staying at the high priest's home. That information, interesting enough under other circumstances, only caused her concern. She felt better when she assumed the messengers had probably crossed paths. Soon a letter would contain the proper responses, she was sure.

Later that day, a courtier who was known as a gossip surprised her by coming to the house and asking coyly about the possibility of a new arrival in the family. Somehow the very private knowledge had gotten out and Mara was furious to think her physician or her personal attendants were leaking information to the palace gossips.

When Nabonidus returned that evening from the palace, she questioned him sharply. "Did you say anything to the king or anyone else at the palace about the possibility I may be having another baby?"

"Absolutely not, mother, I never tell anyone, not even the king, any of our personal family business—even though I'm sure he'd like to know of anything that takes place here in our house. He is always asking if everything is well with you and Aia, or have we heard anything from father."

Nabonidus' remarks only deepened the concern Mara felt. "Your father's message to us didn't contain any of the expected responses and the messenger I sent to him has not returned. I'm worried about what is going on. I'm sorry to have to say this to you, Nabonidus, but I don't trust your grandfather. He has always been a difficult man for your father and me to deal with, and now . . . I just don't know what to think. I don't want to believe he would do anything to harm your father and the security of the realm, but I just don't know."

"Well, mother, I really don't know what to think, either, but I do know that Aunt Belana and Uncle Youini have become very frequent visitors at the palace and grandfather seems to be in confidential conversation with them whenever they come. We both know there is no love between them and father."

"That certainly is an understatement. Please be very careful around them. I don't trust them at all."

They have treated me well, but they certainly know how to get in the king's good graces. If Aunt Belana had only been a boy, she surely would have ruled the realm. I think that she is angry with father for being born. I believe if Aunt Belyada hadn't died a few years ago, she would have cheerfully put her to death. I wouldn't put it past her to plot to have father killed so she could reign."

"Nabonidus, do you realize what you are saying? Do you realize that if that were true, you, the next in line for the throne are in danger of being eliminated, too."

"Yes, mother, I am aware that I need to keep my eyes and ears open to all that is going on. I just hate this business, the gossip, the palace intrigue, the politics. I don't want to be king. I just would like to be somebody else and forget all this.

"I am sorry, son, but you are who you are and it is necessary for you to be very careful to watch out for the future of the realm. Perhaps later you will be ready and eager to succeed your father."

"Perhaps, but I shall be glad when this war is over and father is home and finally on the throne. Perhaps then everything will settle down and we can be a family and I can get on with my studies. I want to study people, not politics, and learn all I can about their languages and customs and their history. I'll find out what makes them do the things they do."

Mara's laughter interrupted his words and he gave her a startled look, "Son, you are right now in the best place in the world to learn about people. Your grandfather, a great king, is one of the world's most difficult, mixed-up individuals you could ever want to study. If you can figure him out, you'll do the world a great service. If you can figure out what has made him such a difficult ruler to be under, you will be well prepared to rule the realm in a much better way. There's your assignment. But be careful."

*   *   *

Mara was awakened by Sala, her maidservant. "There's a crazy woman at the door. She refuses to go away or be quiet until she sees you."

"Take her to the sitting room and fix her some tea. Tell the guards to watch, but that it is all right. I shall dress and be there shortly."

When Mara entered the room she recognized the woman as the mother of the messenger that she had sent to Nebuchadnezzar. The woman appeared to be quite distraught. She spoke to the woman, "Mozel, what's the matter? What I can do for you?" The woman stood up and lunged at Mara. As she did, she pulled a dagger from her shawl. In her haste, she stepped on her dress and tripped over the tea table in front of her, sending cups and tea flying. She pounded her fists on the floor and began to cry. The household servants quickly surrounded her, taking the knife. Once subdued, Mara realized the woman was not really dangerous, only upset. When her sobbing finally subsided, Mara asked again, "What is the matter, my dear, and what do you want?"

Struggling to control her voice, she asked, "Why did you send my son out to be killed? They just brought his body to me." She began sobbing again. "His throat was slit and he was left for dead in the fields." Mara gasped. "The animals started to eat at him. His cloak was missing but his money was still on him. Why did you sent him out to be killed?"

"Oh, my poor, poor dear. I didn't send him out to be killed. This is the first that I knew of his death. I did not know that he didn't deliver my message to my husband. I am so sorry for your loss. I did everything I knew to do to keep him safe. The message was sewn into his cloak so that no one would see him carrying a message pouch and identify him as a courier. We hoped that would keep him safe from robbers as well. Please believe me, I am so sorry for what has happened."

Mara paused, searching the tear-stained face of the brokenhearted woman. She was a mother; she could feel her pain and grief. She continued, "I selected him to carry the message for a very special reason; you know, he was very loyal to the prince. Because of his injuries early in life, he could not serve in the army. He told me he would welcome the chance to be with the soldiers for a short time. I had no idea I was sending him to his death. Again, I am so very sorry for you. What can I do to help you?"

"I am a widow and he was my only child. I can't afford to bury him as I should. What can I do?"

Mara embraced the devastated woman. "Mozel, I shall take care of his burial expenses, and you shall come and work with my household staff. Your son shall be considered a hero of the army and shall have honor from this household. And when we find who killed him, they shall be treated to the same fate." The woman's sense of relief conditioned another round of crying, and Mara hugged her again.

"Princess, you are a good woman. Forgive me for accusing you and trying to hurt you."

Mara could not go back to sleep. She knew that her entire household was in danger from whoever intercepted the message to her husband. *Is that how they found out I was expecting a baby? Is the king behind all this? I must do whatever is necessary to defend my household.*

CHAPTER 8

It was midday when soldiers bearing a message from Mara got through to Nebuchadnezzar in Babylon. When he read the news of Mara's pregnancy, he knew the words of Belardos, the high priest, were true and he became more excited. His excitement was short-lived as he read further of his father's plan to subvert his son. His anger rose to a fever pitch when he heard of the death of the first messenger and the events surrounding his murder. His first thought was to take his troops home, drive the king off the throne and establish himself as king. However, he soon realized to do that would leave the empire vulnerable to the Pharaoh of Egypt and bring possible defeat to his future plans.

What should he do? Hesitating only slightly, he went to see Belardos and told him the news in Mara's message and the events in Ur. Nebuk began to list what he felt were his options. Belardos listened patiently to the prince's ideas and finally spoke. "It is time to send the pharaoh back to Egypt. Go and get the battle over. You will win if you do not allow yourself to be distracted by the things back at the palace."

"Yes, but what if they kill my wife and children while I am not there to defend them?"

"They would have done it by now if that were their plan. Your father will try to force your son into the role you should play. But remember, that son will not succeed you on the throne, for he does not want any part of ruling the empire. He will eventually succeed his brother, but that will only be for a very short time. Go finish your job. You will return and be the king. You are the man of destiny."

"You are right, as you have been about most things. I have no doubt of your truthfulness, for Mara is, indeed, expecting a new baby and it shall be the boy who will follow me on the throne. Thank you, my friend. I shall do my best to bring glory to Bel Marduk, to Babylon and to you. Thank you for your help and hospitality. I shall prepare to leave for battle in two days."

"Aren't you forgetting something else?" Nebuk's surprised and questioning look made Belardos laugh. "This is not as serious as your winning the war or taking your place on the throne, but could be very necessary to your personal comfort and sense of security." He chuckled again and said, "I am referring to Belakah; you do want him to go with you, don't you? He will be my presence with you as you go."

Nebuk was embarrassed that he had not asked the priest, but obviously Belakah had, and he felt glad he wanted to go with him. When he mentioned this to Belardos, the priest told him Belakah had not said one word to him. Nebuk just shook his head, but he thought *this certainly is a different world. I wonder what else he knows about me?*

The preparations for the departure filled the two days. The excitement gripping the camp was contagious. Even the people of Babylon were affected by all the excitement. The soldiers, flexing their muscles and boasting of their ability to drive the enemy out of the land, created the sense of invincibility that the people needed.

Nebuk huddled with Nebuzaradan, who had already made detailed plans for him to examine. They were excellent, and Nebuk's comments only fine-tuned details that were based on Belardos's original ones. Both men were confident of victory. While their major goal was to send Neccoh back to Egypt either on horseback or in a box, they were eager to put into action the trap that would neutralize the conspirators in their own forces.

The trap was carefully laid out and called for the traitorous leaders to plan a campaign that would cause Nebuchadnezzar to be killed. At the last moment, pretending great illness, Nebuchadnezzar would not go and the traitors would be forced to go in his stead. Should they refuse, they were to be killed by other loyal officers in some fashion that would keep from demoralizing the rest of the men. Nebuzaradan had planned thoroughly; his men would be there to carry out the plan if it became necessary.

Earlier, Nebuzaradan had asked the generals under him to submit specific plans of attack to use in his battle preparations. As these plans began to come in, the identity of the traitors became clear. Their plans, all very risky, all very similar, appeared to have been well thought out by several people.

Nebuzaradan had reviewed closely each plan as it was submitted. Each was critically proclaimed as definitely worthy of consideration. He congratulated each general on his original thinking and promised full accreditation for his skill in planning. More often than not, the traitors feigned modesty and proclaimed service to the prince as reward enough.

"Again, superior work." Nebuk's praise for Nebuzaradan caused his chief of staff to flush with pride. His undivided loyalty to Nebuk was an encouragement to the prince. As they both realized, soon the battle would be theirs. The world would know that Nebuchadnezzar was indeed a power in the empire, perhaps the world.

"You, my general, are not only an efficient chief of staff, you are a good friend and I appreciate all that you have done for me over the years. Now as we advance this campaign, we shall be more dependent on each other. I am glad that our relationship is more than just professional." In a totally unexpected move, Nebuk hugged the officer and quickly left the tent.

As Nebuk walked back to where his horse was tied, he felt himself questioning his propriety in hugging a subordinate. Nonetheless, it felt good to have done it and he began to realize that being kind to another human being really helped to solidify relationships. It made good sense to share feelings and not just words. Had Nebuk known what was going through the mind of Nebuzaradan, he would have been aware of how right he was. His chief of staff was wiping tears from his eyes and promising "until death loyalty" to the man who had just given him the greatest compliment of his life. Not only was it complimentary, but it was the first hug from another man that the general had ever experienced. He and the prince had much in common in missing the affection of a caring father.

As Nebuk thought of the reasons why hugging was not out of order, he began to realize how different his life might be if his father had only been able to show acceptance and affection to him. Dark impressions of hatred for his father arose dominating his thoughts. Realizing that he could not risk feeling depressed at this critical time, he shook off the thoughts by thinking positively about the upcoming battle. Also, he must be sure his own children were aware of his feelings for them.

Thoughts of his family always brightened his disposition and he began to concentrate on Mara, Nabonidus, Aia, and of course, the new baby—the boy who would succeed him on the throne. "That one must never know the pain of a distant father," he said out loud.

When Nebuk arrived back at Belardos's house, he found Belakah had already packed his things and all was in readiness for the early morning departure. Belakah was saying his farewells to the other servants and making sure that all his responsibilities were in capable hands. He greeted Nebuchadnezzar cheerfully and assured him that he was ready to go to the battle scene.

After another sumptuous meal with the High Priest, Nebuk asked him, "Do you have any last minute thoughts concerning the battle or the future?"

Belardos stroked his flowing beard and began to speak very slowly, measuring every word for its import. "Your plans to trap the traitors will work; however, one of the conspirators will escape and get the word back to your father that you were not killed in the entrapment. This information will have a great effect on your future. Don't look for him, for he will succeed and get back to Ur. When you return to the palace, you will know how the news affects you. When you have defeated Neccoh, chase him beyond the land of Israel and you will be able to bring Israel and Judah under your control with little or no effort."

"I had not thought of expanding the empire in that direction until I was on the throne. Is it necessary for me to do it at this time?"

"Much in your future will have to do with the lands of Israel-Judah and your domination of them. They are pagans—they do not worship the great Bel Marduk. They need to have their eyes opened to the greatness of our god. Remember your goal is to bring greatness to Bel and you must do it in the way the spirits direct. This is the direction my spirit guides tell me you must go. You will be guided in these ventures, for I have given spirit charms to Belakah and he will help you. Do not be afraid to allow him in your closest confidence as you have already done. He will do more than give you a massage and comfort you when you can't sleep. He will give you my direction, for my spirit guides have a direct connection with him."

Nebuk's face flushed with the awareness that Belardos knew that the servant had indeed held him. He also knew that it was not Belakah who told the priest.

When the evening conversations were over, Nebuk gratefully submitted to Belakah's suggestion of a massage and bath to help him sleep and be ready to travel. The prince was very thankful Belakah was to be with him and let him know he appreciated him and his caring. "Your Highness, I love to serve and now to be able to serve you gives great meaning to my life. I am ready to do whatever you should need."

"Belakah, since you know me more intimately than any other man on the face of the earth, please call me by the name my good friends know me. Call me Nebuk."

"Your Highness, I couldn't do that, it would not be right for a servant to call his master in such a familiar way, especially the future king."

"Did you not say that you would do whatever I needed at anytime and way? Well, I am ordering you to call me Nebuk when no one else is around and you may call me by whatever title you choose when in public . . . that is an order."

"Yes, Sir, . . . Nebuk."

"I'm glad that's settled. Now let's get this massage over and get ready for tomorrow."

It was still dark when the Chaldean force abandoned their camp near Babylon. Nevertheless, a large number of the residents of the city made their way to the encampment to watch the soldiers, under the command of their Prince Nebuchadnezzar, march out to the battle. Their waving and cheering stirred the men to step out vigorously. Nebuk mounted his horse, raised his sword, and the flag bearers raised the colors. The grand procession in ranks of authority paraded past the High Priest Belardos, who held his serpent staff aloft for the troops to pass under. The future glory of the empire and that of Babylon rested with these men.

It was a six-day journey to the area where the main encampment would be made to the northeast of Carchemish. The level sandy terrain of the Shinar plain quickly gave way to the rough hill country and finally to the mountainous north. The going got tougher and the men had to work harder to maintain the speed necessary to make the trip in the appointed number of days. The nearer to the battle scene, the more the excitement mounted. The more the excitement mounted, the more the braggadocio gave way to quiet fear and in some cases outright panic. Some of these men would not come back alive. They were facing the most formidable enemy in the world. The prolonged wait for the confrontation, both through the several years since the victorious battle for Haran and the almost six weeks spent in Babylon, had put the soldiers in a mind-set that entertained doubt.

They weren't alone, all the officers responsible for carrying out the orders of the prince were wondering if the plans that Nebuzaradan had outlined to them would, indeed, do the job of routing the Pharaoh of Egypt. There were seven other officers who had additional concerns. How would their other plans work? How would they get away with them? How would they escape the

Egyptian army when their plans were carried out? Would the king
leave them alive to tell the story? Being the king's confidant was
one thing. Being a traitor to the king's son was especially difficult
when the king tells you to come back successful or your families
will suffer.

When camp was made, the troops settled in. The officers had
to wait for the reconnaissance to be completed and the plans
readjusted for the terrain. Only then did they allow themselves to
relax a little.

As soon as Nebuzaradan had assured himself of the viability of
the plans in the territory, he began to call in each of his trusted
generals and their staff officers to develop assignments to their
theaters of operation. He carefully listened to each and then called
in some of the potential co-conspirators, under the guise of acting
as a final advisory board. These men were older and had more
experience than some of the younger officers. Nebuzaradan was
impressed with the work the seven had done to coordinate their
individual plans into the general plan. These plans looked as if
they had been developed as a strategic part of the work of
Nebuchadnezzar himself.

When Nebuzaradan was able to be alone with Nebuk, he
shared with him the final details that the conspirators had given.
They began to see how the traitors would play into their hands.
"You must arrange to be sick on this particular day of the operation,"
Nebuzaradan commented. "They will certainly expect you to be
in charge when this attack is started."

Nebuk grinned in agreement. "Who have you selected to be
my replacement? All seven of them can't be Officer of the Day in
my absence, even though that is precisely what it should be."

"I have selected General Al Bufassah. He seems to be the main
leader. The other men seem to listen to him more than any other.
He is the natural one to do the job.

Nebuk winced at the name of Al Bufassah. Here was the father
of one of his school friends and a man that he thought would be
one of the least likely to betray him. "Well, so be it. You've done a

good job, my friend. Now if the weather stays good and the next two days pass smoothly, we shall be in the thick of the battle, without the threat of rebellion in the ranks. Thanks to you, my chief, we shall be ready. You'd better get all the rest that you can tonight, for you won't have much other time to enjoy sleep. Good night and call me if you need anything."

"Good night, Your Highness. I trust you, too, will rest comfortably."

It was not rest that Nebuk was concerned about; it was pain. The pain of his own father, sending him off into the battle, to be killed by a trick of some of his "trusted" officers. "For once in my life, couldn't the joy of victory not be pulled out from under me? I feel like I'm on some magic carpet that will not hold still. But, Al Bufassah...I can hardly believe he is the main conspirator. What am I saying? He's not the main conspirator. It's that man who sits on my throne. That's it! It really is my throne! He has no right to set on it any longer. Anyone who would sacrifice the security of the empire to get rid of his own son ought to be . . . ," his voice trailed off. "I wish I'd taken troops back to Ur and deposed him myself. Listen, Nebuk, you've got to get hold of yourself or you will be as dead as that bastard wants you to be."

It was almost impossible to defeat these thoughts and they certainly were not conducive to a good night's rest. Nebuk was extremely grateful that Belakah had prepared a massage and hot bath even out in the field. The heat and rub down relaxed him and he wearily dropped into his cot and was asleep almost instantly. If only it had continued.

In less than two hours the dreams began. It was the old dream of being made a eunuch by his father. The original dream, coupled with the knowledge of the king's plot to have him killed, had blended into one; and the pain was more than he could bear. The fear and dread of his father's actions flooded his heart, and before he was aware enough to know what was happening, he shrieked.

The soldiers on guard could be heard drawing their swords

and trying to find the source of the sound. Belakah was at Nebuk's side in a second. "Your Highness, what is it?" he whispered.

"The dream, my father is trying to do to me what he had done to you. It's the same dream over and over again."

"Let me tell the guards that it was just a bad dream, so they can quit stirring around out there."

"Yes, yes, Belakah, please take care of it for me, and then come back here."

Belakah quickly stepped to the door of the tent and motioned to the captain of the prince's guards. "I just had a bad dream and woke myself up. Sorry for the problem; I hope I haven't disturbed the prince."

The captain of the guard thanked Belakah for telling him and went away muttering something about non-Chaldeans; especially those in the priestly service bring a strange lot.

Nebuk heard the exchange and when Belakah returned, he put out his hand to the man who was friend enough to keep him from looking bad in the eyes of his men. "Belakah, you are a true friend. You shall not be forgotten when I sit on the throne."

"Your Highness . . . ah, Nebuk, I want only to be of help to you. Now tell me of the dream again so we can send it away."

As Nebuk recounted the dream to Belakah, he began to weep, as if he were a child. He cupped his head in his hands until he felt Belakah's arm around him. Belakah listened quietly and held the prince firmly. "We need to assure that the dream will not happen to you, either physically or emotionally. Let me send the evil thoughts away by using the charms that the high priest gave me to use on your behalf. Nebuk, you will have to let me do to you whatever is necessary."

"Please, please do whatever you want, only get rid of the dream. It is bad enough to know that my father is trying to kill me, let alone dream he's trying to castrate me."

Nebuk's submission to Belakah and the charms of the high priest were more involved than he expected. He was perplexed and distressed by the servant as he administered the intimate ritual, but he was desperate.

After Belakah completed the spirit cleansing, Nebuk dropped peacefully off to sleep in the knowledge that Belakah was even more his friend, confidant and mainstay. As soon as Nebuk was sleeping peacefully, Belakah slipped quietly into his own cot and thought happily to himself, *now, for sure, this young man will bring glory to the great god Bel, for he is willing to allow the powers of our god to work in him.* The next morning Nebuk was cheerful and said to Belakah, "I think I had a couple of dreams last night, but they didn't seem to disturb me."

It was several hours later that the captain of the guard came to Nebuchadnezzar and asked to have a word with him. "I don't want to be a trouble maker, Your Highness, but last night your personal servant let out an awful shriek and if that were to continue, we'd be in danger of the enemy discovering your whereabouts. I just felt you should know."

As Nebuk dismissed him, he became aware of the events of the previous night. They were not a dream; they were real. A reality of need was bringing him into a greater dependence on his servant. How could he face the servant and face himself?

"Nebuk, I did what I knew was best for you. I hope these things will not disturb you, for you are a great man and your needs will remain secret. The good night's rest you experienced is proof you need relief from the tension of not only this battle, but the battle that has been raging in your heart for the greater part of your life. I am here to help you anyway I can."

"We shall never speak of this again." Nebuk wheeled and left the tent and walked out over the field. "How can my life be so complicated and filled with contradiction? Perhaps, I should just put a knife to my throat and let them have the rest of the world. I don't know what to do. I wish I were a dog or a horse or some wild animal. I feel like I'm going crazy. Now what little respect I had for myself is gone. Mara, where are you? I need you."

Nebuk felt helpless in the grip of the negative feelings. It seemed that there was no place to turn.

But turning was required. There was a battle to be waged, a war to be won, and a king to replace. There was no time for personal feelings, only the need to drive away the intruding thoughts. "All in proper order. I must go see Nebuzaradan."

His chief-of-staff had all in readiness for the next day's attack. Nebuk was supposed to be killed by a contingent of Neccoh's forces that had purposefully been provoked. Sickness was to save the prince from actual involvement. He had no problem in feeling sick, for he was sick at heart. The whole of life seemed enough to make him sick.

The attack as planned was moving on schedule. The soldiers and their officers were all ready for the prince to lead them. They waited past the appointed hour and were getting unsettled by the delay. As Nebuk rode up to the men, he was slumped in his saddle. He started to dismount and collapsed into the arms of one of his guards, who laid him gently on the ground. "I'm sick," and his eyelids fluttered shut.

"Get His Highness back to his tent. Get the company physicians and his servants to care for him." Nebuzaradan commanded. "And, don't forget to post guards around his tent. All right men, we can carry out this campaign for the prince. General Al Bufassah, you will lead the charge as the prince's replacement."

Al Bufassah tried to object, but Nebuzaradan insisted, "The plan is yours and you will execute it the best." The general's face was white, but bowed graciously to the Chief of the Army.

The plan worked flawlessly, Al Bufassah and five of the other generals were killed along with several enlisted men. One of the seven 'special' officers was missing in action and Nebuzaradan had to do some very fast explaining to the other officers that had not been alerted to the conspiracy. When told, they were furious, wanting to get the last officer, too.

Nebuk was elated with the results. The good news conditioned a complete recovery from his "sickness." He congratulated the men and further explained the strategy of the battle. "We will wear down the patience of the enemy by using minor skirmishes like the one today to cause the enemy to betray their weaknesses. Our plan is to keep the enemy from knowing I am actually here and to act like we are waiting for further reinforcements. As they become more careless, and they will, we will attack and put an end to them.

"Thank you all, and special thanks to my brilliant chief, Nebuzaradan." As he was leaving, he turned and said, "If you find the other traitor, bring me his head properly dressed for the occasion." The men knew what he meant and several cheered.

Nebuk slept very well that evening, for the pressure of the traitors was over. He felt badly about the men killed in the combat, but that was war. War is not pretty; war is breaking and killing.

A messenger from Ur interrupted breakfast. The message was from Mara. "Your father is dying. He is trying to install your sister on the throne. They are holding Nabonidus in the king's palace and we are being watched. Come quickly, or there will be no kingdom for you to rule. I love you. Mara".

CHAPTER 9

Between angry outbursts Nebuchadnezzar read and reread the message that had come from Mara. The thought of his family being harmed was driving him into a maniacal frenzy. He slammed his fist on the table and sent the dishes rattling to the floor. Jumping to his feet, he paced around the dining tent. He cursed. He spat. He cried, not because of his father; he cared little for the impending death of his father . . . "Good enough for him," but for the years of struggle with him that were coming to a conclusion. He was so far away. "I can't stand this, aren't we ready to go?"

In short order a contingent of men to guard the prince was equipped with the fastest horses and provisions for the several days journey. Swinging into the saddle, Nebuk spoke to Nebuzaradan, "Pursue the war as we planned. Remember, slow and steady! I have confidence in you to do the job just as I would and perhaps even better. I trust your judgement. I hope to be back in time for the kill when it comes to the Egyptian leader."

"Take care of what you need to do in Ur, for without the throne, there is no way to carry out your plan. May the gods be with you! Belakah, you take good care of him. He is very important to us, you know. Safe trip, Your Majesty."

With Nebuzaradan's "Your Majesty" ringing in his ears, Nebuk signaled for the trip to begin. It would be three very hard days of travel to Babylon and one more to Ur. Four days and yet it would really be eight days since Mara sent her messenger. A lot could happen in those eight days. I wonder if he is still alive?

Making camp at a military outpost afforded protection while the exhausted travelers rested. But Nebuk was so pent-up with emotion, the only relief was to walk in the fields and let the fresh night breezes wash away some of the anxiety. Still uneasy over the events of his dream a few nights earlier, he stayed clear of too close contact with Belakah, who did his best to make things comfortable for him.

The second night's camp brought rain just before settling down to sleep. Lightning, thunder and rain added to the other elements of misery. They fueled Nebuk's morbid imagination further. His sleep was fitful and his dreams full of dreadful omens. Twice Nebuk awoke to the awareness of Belakah standing near his cot. When it happened the third time, Belakah was at his side and this time without hesitation the servant massaged his neck and shoulders and held him. Nebuk felt the anxiety and tension flow out of his body. *If only I could maintain these relaxed feelings my world certainly would be different,* he thought as he went back to sleep.

The balance of the trip to Babylon was wet and dismal, the unrelenting rain slowing their progress. When the walls of the city came into view there was a general expression of relief. Nebuk was thinking of how to get his entourage settled for the night when Belakah noticed a servant of Belardos, the High Priest of Bel, riding toward them. The servant rode directly to Prince Nebuchadnezzar. "Greetings, Your Majesty. His Excellency, Belardos, has been expecting you and has provisions for all your men. Please follow me."

Again, Nebuk was awed by what the priest knew and he hardly realized that the servant had called him Majesty and not Highness.

Belardos was waiting for Nebuk when he arrived at the house. His servants took care of the other men and he brought Nebuchadnezzar and Belakah into the house himself. A fine meal, much better than travel rations, was awaiting them both and Belakah quickly excused himself to greet the other servants.

"Belardos, did you know this was coming when you sent me off to Carchemish and the battle?"

"No, I did not. I only became aware of what was happening after you had been gone a week or two."

"Is my father dead?"

"Yes."

"What is happening to my son and family?"

"I know only they will be safe, but the throne is not really yours. Your sister and her husband have plotted to take it from you and your father was a willing participant. He planned, after your death, to train Nabonidus to succeed him. Your father has become so callous to his own children that he would have disposed of your sister if she had any real potential to take the throne from him. However, she has been plotting to take the throne from you since you first came to Ur from Shushan. She got eager. With you out of the country, fighting Neccoh, she began a slow and steady physical poisoning of your father, in addition to the mental poisoning she has done for years."

Nebuk, in spite of his bitterness toward his father, appeared grieved at the words of his sister's duplicity. Then he spoke slowly and bitterly. "Isn't it ironic! It seems I owe my sister a debt of gratitude. She spared me having to get rid of the king myself. But, of course, now I shall have to deal with her."

"That is true, Your Majesty . . . and I use the word correctly. However, remember the country expects you to show great sorrow at the death of your father. They do not know the bitterness and hatred attendant to your relationship. Spare the country more pain, for the war has already taken a heavy toll on them over the years. Deal with the nation kindly and with your sister firmly. The people are already yours and you shall succeed."

"I'm sure you are right. But when will all this end?"

"Never, my boy, never. The older I get and the more I learn, the more I serve the great god Bel Marduk, the more I see trouble and struggle. You will be great, but your way will not be easy."

Nebuk stood to his feet and turned away from the priest. "I must sleep for I have to travel early in the morning. I really don't want to hear any more. I've already heard more than I can bear. Good night, my friend, and thank you."

"No need for thanks, Your Majesty, it is my duty as well as my great pleasure. You will bring glory to Babylon and Bel."

Nebuk retired to the suite of rooms that he had occupied earlier and was not surprised to find Belakah ready with a hot bath and massage oil. Belakah's strong hands worked out the tension that he had felt building up on the trip. Belakah was careful not to cause any embarrassment to the prince as he completed the massage. "Belakah, you are a true friend. You must be just as tired as I and yet you care for my needs. You truly are my good friend. Sleep well."

"And you also, Your Majesty."

Morning came all too quickly for the weary travelers, but the urgency of their mission spurred them on. In record time the walls of Ur were sighted. Nebuk was rejuvenated at the sight of the capital. He was greeted with great respect and reverence as he passed through the city gate. The cheers were more subdued because of the period of mourning, but soon word of the prince's arrival was wafted by voice to the entire city.

Mara was waiting in the courtyard of their home when Nebuk arrived. He swiftly dismounted and swept her into his arms, kissed her tenderly and looked approvingly at her enlarged shape. How are you, my darling? Where is Aia? What about Nabonidus?

Mara placed her finger against his lips, which he instinctively kissed. She kissed him again and whispered to him, "I will tell you all in a moment, but not out here. I'm so glad you got here so fast. I have missed you so much."

Nebuk realized that Mara had never met Belakah and introduced his faithful personal servant. After the introductions, they quickly moved into the house. Nebuk's first question, "Are the guards here loyal and trustworthy, especially now that I am home?"

"Oh, yes. I would not have had a moment's peace if they hadn't been. You can let your personal guards go to their homes. We're safe. You take care of your men and I'll have Sala prepare a room for Belakah. Belakah, you look tired. I hope you'll be comfortable here."

No sooner had Mara left the room with Belakah than in swept the joy of Nebuk's life, his daughter Aia. "Oh, Daddy, you're home."

She flung herself into her father's arms and they mutually began to smother each other with kisses. How good it felt to be home and loved.

Mara returned and brought further strengthening of the sense of wellbeing. Her soft nearness and the sweet smell of her perfumed hair took much of the travel weariness away from him. "Tell me, what is really happening?"

"My darling, I know you already know that your father is dead. He died two days ago just before sundown. He died of the strangest illness. To look at him you would say that there was nothing wrong, but internally, he felt and acted like death before he died. The medicine doctors do not know what was wrong with him. It is just as if he died of meanness."

"Ultimately, that is probably true; however, Belardos believes that he was poisoned . . . by my dear sister and brother-in-law. That probably would account for the strangeness of his death. Belardos also said Belana and my father plotted to keep the throne from me, and father really intended for the throne to later be given to Nabonidus. Where is my son?"

"He is safe. We were able to rescue him from the palace during the excitement following the king's death. We have him in safekeeping. He's in the little apartment that I lived in those long ago days when you were trying so desperately to find me. Remember just after we met?" Mara's laughter over the memory of how she taunted the young prince by hiding from him caused Nebuk to smile. The relief of knowing that Nabonidus was safe caused an even bigger smile to wrinkle his weary face and laughter escaped from deep within.

"I told you all those years ago, my handsome husband, that you would rule the world better with laughter. It sounds wonderful to hear you laugh and see you smile. Nabonidus is fine and he has plenty to tell you. He should be your first action. What do you intend to do?"

"I'd like to let my dear sister and her husband sweat for a little while. When will my father's funeral be held?"

"The state funeral has not been set as yet, because you were not back. If you hadn't returned when you did, they were going to bury him tomorrow. I am sure, your sister has heard you are back, but why not send a messenger, letting them know you have arrived and that you want the funeral to proceed. Don't let them know that you are aware of their plot to usurp the throne or how they killed your father. Possibly you could expose them and have them arrested in the middle of the funeral exercises."

"Mara, you are very devious, but I love your deviousness. I will send the messenger right now. That should give them a somewhat sleepless night. I will also notify the court of my arrival and that I will be prepared to assume the responsibility of governing. First thing in the morning, I must recruit loyal forces. Then I want to see Nabonidus."

"So you shall. However, my darling, I have taken upon myself the responsibility of recruiting the forces we will need to protect ourselves and also deliver the throne to you. I have over two thousand men who are Nebuchadnezzar loyalists. They are poised and ready for your orders. I hope you won't think me presumptuous for seeing to this detail while you were away 'playing war games' with the traitors, but we needed security, especially since you were gone."

"I am certainly glad that you are on my side. The kingdom would have crumbled away from me if you had been on their side. Thank you my dear, dear wife."

In spite of the day awaiting them, the night's rest was very sweet for both of them. For Nebuk, holding and being held in his wife's arms was certainly the tonic he needed. He desperately needed to hold her close and be to her what she needed. Yes, life would continue as it should; the future king was already with them.

Early morning found the prince/king pacing the floor and talking to himself. "After I see Nabonidus, I will proceed to the royal embalmer's and see my father. Then I shall go pay my respects to the Princess Belana and Youini. Why she ever married that rat, I shall never know. He must have been the most visible favorite of father's whom she knew she could control." As he thought further about his schedule, he heard voices in the entry vestibule and heard the voice of Sala, the housemaid, taking a message that she promised to bring directly to him.

"What is it, Sala?"

"A messenger from the Palace, Your Highness . . . oh, forgive me, Your Majesty."

"That's ok, Sala. I'm not sure who I am right now either. Thanks for the message.

Taking the message from her hand, the prince broke the seal. Unfolding the papyrus parchment, he read: "Your Highness, we are profoundly grateful that you have arrived before the interment of our beloved Sovereign, Nabopolassar. The service has been planned for high noon today, if that is satisfactory with you. We shall await your wishes. We are ready to proceed with the funeral, as all the arrangements have been made at His Majesty's direction and the advice of Princess Belana."

The message was signed: The Royal Council of Physicians and Embalmers.

Mara came into the room as Nebuk finished reading the message. He quickly explained the message and his plan of action. "Do you wish to come with me?"

"Of course. You would never find Nabonidus if I didn't take you there. And I am ready to see all that is going to make this day a day to be remembered."

Mara led Nebuk and the guards to one of the oldest sections of Ur. She slipped between buildings as if she were taking a shortcut home. "I see why I never knew where you were all those years ago when you were hiding from me. How did you know of this place?"

"This was the apartment that my parents lived in before they were banished to the north-country." She rapped a secret code on the door; a rather nervous looking old man opened it.

"Ah, Mara and Your Majesty. I am so glad to see you. Nabonidus, your parents are here. Come quickly." He led them into a rather darkly lit room, furnished sparingly but comfortably. Soon Nabonidus was hugging his father and mother.

"I am so glad to see you, son. Are you all right?"

"Oh, yes, Father, Mother and Uncle Baris have taken good care of me after their spies spirited me away."

Nebuk looked carefully at his son to see if he showed any pain resulting from the death of his grandfather. They had been so much closer than he had ever been with his father. His fears were swiftly put to rest as he listened to Nabonidus tell of the things that he had learned being under the king's tutelage.

"Father, I am so grateful that grandfather wanted me to be trained by him. I learned so much of the politics and the hatred that makes the palace work. I hope this doesn't offend you, but I know more than ever that I do not want to be the king. Father, you can have the job. However, it certainly wasn't grandfather's wishes for you to succeed him. In fact, he made an agreement with Aunt Belana to allow her to be his successor until I reached the age of thirty and then I was to be crowned as king. I doubt that they'd have allowed me to even reach age twenty. I am sure that you know that Aunt Belana and Uncle Youini have been plotting against you for years. When you went to fight the war, they decided it would be a good time to take over the throne while you were gone."

"How do you know all this, son?"

"Mother told me to keep my eyes and ears open and learn all I could. I have made friends with people in places where they would discover things. Things that if they were generally known would cause our not so dear relatives to be hung as traitors."

"Do you mean such things as that they were steadily poisoning your grandfather?"

The relieved look on Nabonidus's face spoke volumes, "Whew, I am so glad that you already know. I was afraid to have to tell you." Nabonidus hesitated, "Do you also know that you were supposed to be killed—by grandfather's order?"

"Yes, son, I did."

"I knew that you were still alive, because one of the traitors came back and reported to grandfather, just before he died, that you were sick and did not fall into their trap. Is that right?"

"You are right again. What else do you know?"

"Well, I know that just before grandfather died, he issued several orders. The traitor who came back was to be killed as a deserter from the army. He ordered that no one was to be king until after his funeral. He called for me and told me that Belana and Youini were plotting to take the throne from me, if you were killed. He told me to get away from them and get mother and Aia out of the city as fast as I could. I almost believed that he really cared for our family. Now I think that was just another scheme to make it easier for them to take the throne."

Nebuk resisted the angry words he felt, seeing the pain on his son's face. Squeezing his hands firmly together, letting them take the pressure of his anger, he wearily rested his chin on his thumbs. "Maybe because of the mental problems which he has had all his life and the fact he was dying caused his actions? He might have meant to be helpful." Nebuk drew a deep sigh and continued, "How did you know about the poisoning?"

"Well, one of the physicians who attended grandfather was an instructor of mine in school. We developed a friendship and he would tell me of grandfather's condition. He began to investigate the cause of the problem. One day he was there when Youini brought him his special health water from the spring outside of town. Grandfather drank only a little bit of it and set the goblet down. My doctor friend busied himself attending grandfather and deliberately picked up the drink. He took it with him. He let his cat drink it and the cat was dead within the day. There is other proof, too. Another court friend, supposedly loyal to Aunt Belana, overheard her saying that one more dose of the health water should take care of the king's problems."

"Nabonidus, I am very sorry that you have had to deal with all of this. It is now over. I shall take charge after the funeral."

"Father, with all due respect, you had better have all of the loyal soldiers there. They are going to arrest you for planning and hiring people to kill your father. They have people who are willing to swear that you ordered the king killed."

"Thank you, son. I shall follow your advice and your mother's. She suggested that I take charge in the middle of the funeral. We shall have fun. Now, we must go to the embalmers to see my late father, the king. Let's get on with today's duties. Are you ready to go with us, Nabonidus?"

"Yes, father, Your Majesty."

"Son, I am first and foremost your father. Save the Majesty for the court performance." With that, Nebuk moved to Nabonidus, putting his arms around his son's shoulders, he hugged and kissed him. Both men hung on as if their lives depended upon it. Mara smiled.

Nebuk's pride in his son helped to mitigate the pain and disappointment that he felt toward his father. But he must, for the country's sake, carry out the responsibility that was his by virtue of his royal birth.

"I am now the King."

CHAPTER 10

As Nebuk, Mara and Nabonidus emerged from the royal embalmers, Nebuk whispered to Mara, "Take me to the officer in charge of the your troops. I have an order to give them."

"That's no problem. Just stop for a moment right here." She raised her hand and a group of beggars following them hurried to her side.

"Your Majesties, how may we help," one particularly disreputable looking beggar said as he stepped to Mara's side and bowed as if in great pain.

"What a motley bunch of loyalists," Nebuk chuckled. He was impressed with the disguises; especially when he saw the scimitars and swords carefully enfolded in their beggar rags. As he was thinking of their cleverness, his own bodyguards drew swords, preparing to send the beggars away. "Its all right, Zelaph, believe it or not, they are my wife's bodyguards." His eyes twinkled with a new idea to 'enliven' the funeral.

Nebuk called the leader of the beggars to him as if to give him money, and spoke softly. "Gather several hundred men. Dress them all as beggars and be at the funeral. Push your way in, asking to pay homage to my father, the king. The guards will try to stop you, but I shall call for you to come forward. Wait until I'm speaking to everyone before you try to come in. Have your swords and daggers sharp. I shall order you to arrest my sister and brother-in-law as soon as you have your troops in place.

"Yes, Your Majesty. We shall be there with swords, awaiting your orders. We pledge our loyalty to you, your family and the future of the realm only under your leadership."

"Thank you, my friends. In the future you will wear the garb of royal guards, not beggars. Until then, thank you."

Nebuk grinned at Mara, and the mischievous light in his eyes brought her beautiful smile to surface on what had been a rather serious face the last several years.

"Now to call on my sister and her worthless husband." The entourage moved toward the west wing of the palace where Belana and Youini had set up their dwelling during the king's illness, just to be near in case of emergency.

A group of people had gathered near Nebuk and his family as they had spoken to the beggars. They parted to let the royal party pass through and the cheers for the prince buoyed his heart even further. "We're with you, King Nebuchadnezzar. Oh, king live forever. May the gods guide you."

Their approach was stopped at the gate of the princess's compound by the palace guards who asked them to wait until they had notified Her Highness of their arrival. Nebuk agreed and very simply said, "Please tell my sister that we are here to talk before the funeral."

It was only brief minutes until they were escorted into the entry hall and were greeted by a tall muscular-looking woman in her late-forties dressed in mourning garb. She was daubing her eyes as if she had been crying. She opened her hands to her brother in greeting. "Oh, Nebuchadnezzar, I'm so glad you made it back in time. I'm so sorry you didn't get here before father died. Mara, my dear,—Nabonidus." At her side a short, pudgy man in his late-fifties held out a greeting hand which Nebuk shook perfunctorily.

"Belana, I'm sorry you had to bear the illness and death of our father without my being here. However, I know you were closer to him than I, so I'm glad you could care for him."

Mara could hardly control herself and coughed several times to regain her composure. "Are you all right, mother?" Nabonidus asked trying to control his rising laughter by diverting his attention away from his father's superb acting.

"Oh, yes, I'm all right, just a slight cold. Thank you, son."

Youini spoke up, "Let me have some tea brought in—we can sit down and talk. That will help soothe that cough."

"Excellent idea, come in and sit down," Belana said, regaining control of the conversation. "Let me explain what I've planned for the funeral." She launched into the details as she escorted them to the sitting parlor. Before the tea was served, the plans had been discussed and Nebuk was agreeable to all she had planned, especially the part allowing him to speak to the assembled dignitaries. Belana smiled appreciatively.

Following the tea, an awkward silence fell upon the group. This was not unusual, considering the huge barriers that had existed for so many years between these two branches of the family. Finally Youini broke the strained silence by asking, "How was the war progressing when you left?"

It was now Belana's turn to cough and her husband looked embarrassed, but Nebuk answered. "Well, we were just beginning the campaign when I received word of father's illness. At the same time, we learned of a plot by several generals to try to kill me and take the throne for one of them. Can you believe that? They probably would have tried to kill you and father as well. Fortunately we discovered it before it was too late."

Now Belana's already-pale complexion was about the same pasty white as her father's corpse and Youini mumbled something about how glad they were he'd escaped without injury.

"Well, that's all past now and we don't need to worry about any threats to our empire which father worked so hard to expand." There was nodded agreement as Nebuk continued, "I need a little time to prepare my remarks for the funeral. Thank you for your hospitality and all your preparations for the service. We shall join you shortly before noon."

Nabonidus waited as long as he could after leaving the palace before he exploded into laughter. He pounded his father on the back and exclaimed, "I can hardly wait for the funeral."

"Now listen, you two. We've got to remember this is supposed to be a serious occasion." Mara chided them.

The ensuing silence turned all their thoughts to their own feelings, feelings running the whole gamut from pain to relief. His personal loss had yet to be dealt with. Nebuk finally broke the silence, "You are right, Mara, and I have much work to do before this funeral."

During the next hour, Nebuk sent out messages to several people who promptly answered his summons. A brief consultation with each, and then it was time to go.

When the whole family emerged for the trip to the palace for the funeral, a royal coach drawn by four black Arabian horses was waiting to convey them. Accompanied by a military honor guard as well as their own personal guards, they ceremoniously paraded to the palace throne room where the traditional funeral for a king was held.

The body of King Nabopolassar, still handsome and regal, dressed in his royal robes, rested on a magnificent marble slab supported on the backs of four bronze lions. Even in death, he was the focus of attention as he had been all his life. Thanks to their enemies, the Egyptians, the Chaldeans had learned the art of embalming their royalty.

The king's family was seated immediately in front of the deceased and immediately behind was the empty throne draped in black. Slightly to the right and rear of the body, held in an upright position in plain sight was the Scepter of the Realm, signifying the authority of the Empire had departed the king's hand. The brilliantly colored, hand-stitched wall hangings were also over-draped with black, heightening the somber mood.

As the priests, government officials and courtiers took their places, the paid mourners paraded before the assembly. Their weeping and wailing as expected increased the sense of loss even as they secretly rejoiced over the death. Without the death, they would not be working.

Such an emotional swing was extremely difficult for Nebuk as

he thought back over his relationship with the king. In spite of the
hatred he had for his father and the relief he felt over his death, he
was distressed that his sister, his father's favorite, had poisoned
him. A sense of pity for his dead father swept over him and that
particular emotion was certainly unwelcome. Thoughts of what he
must do and what would be happening very shortly crowded out
the grief and a sense of excitement replaced the pity.

The ceremonial service began and soon the High Priest of
Innanna was extolling the exploits and beginning the genealogy of
Nabopolassar, tracing his ancestry back to the glory days of
Nebuchadnezzar the 1st. At the mention of the name of
Nebuchadnezzar 1st, Nebuk's thoughts shifted toward his plans
for the future. *I'm going to make what my father, and his fathers
before him, did as of nothing. I will make the name of Nebuchadnezzar
II a household word throughout the world and I will make a new
Babylonian empire out of the foundation of the old Chaldean. I will be
the greatest ruler the world has ever known. I will be* . . . Just then he
heard the name of his sister, Princess Belana being called.

Belana arose amid the quiet applause of the gathering. She
slowly made her way to the side of her father's body and began to
speak. "I am devastated by the death of my illustrious father. I
have tried to be the child that he wanted. It is my desire to be of
service to the realm and to the people of this great empire. I pledge
myself and my family to the greatest good of this dynasty." She
paused and motioned for her family to come forward. Youini, her
two sons and her daughter joined her at the front of the gathering.
Her oldest son, Belo-Phane, strikingly tall and handsome stepped
behind his mother and rested his hand on the arm of the throne.

Suddenly it was all clear to Nebuk. *My father had really planned
on Belana's son carrying out the lineage. Nabonidus was only a cover
up in his plan to rid himself of the hated son and his family. It was now
clear. They all must go.* The hatred won out over the sympathy and
the ice was again in his veins.

Belana finished her eulogy to her father with a dramatic
statement of her love for the king and her intense grief. She daubed

her eyes with a white handkerchief that stood out in marked contrast to her black mourning clothes.

Then Nebuk heard, "The king's third child—a son and heir apparent, Nebuchadnezzar the II." Nebuk stood, resplendent in his military uniform, and hearty applause broke out in the assemblage. He was pleased, and the response continued as he made his way to the position behind his father's body and directly in front of the throne, a position that did not go unnoticed by the crowd.

He did not begin to speak immediately, but looked down directly in front of him at his father's form, then at his sister and finally at his family, who sat tensely waiting what he was going to say and do. "My dear countrymen, it was with sorrow I learned that my father, the king, had departed the throne in such an untimely manner. I am sorry to have to be here; I would rather be pursuing the battle against the Pharaoh of Egypt. However, I have just received word this morning—the war is going in our favor."

Thunderous applause greeted the news and people smiled approvingly at the prince. Nebuk again paused awaiting the attention to come back to him.

"We've been through great strife on the battlefield, and now the emotion of the death of our king. It is my desire to secure the kingdom in peace and prosperity for all of our people." As Nebuk spoke, he could see the anger and hostility on Belana's face. She deeply resented his extreme popularity. "My first official act will be to make the continuity of the governing of this realm as sure as possible. Therefore, I now ascend to the throne." Nebuchadnezzar reached over, picked up the scepter and stepped back and sat down on his throne.

Belana was on her feet screaming, "You can't do that. You can't do that. Father changed the order of succession." But her words were lost in the thunder of approval that Nebuk's bold move had unleashed. Belana's face was so red that Youini tried to calm her, fearing she'd have a seizure.

As calm began to be restored, a commotion at the doors of the

throne room diverted the crowds' attention. Zelaph, captain of
Nebuk's body guards rushed to the front to tell Nebuk that a
group of beggars demanded to pay respects to the king. Nebuk
raised his voice; "A group of our poorer citizens has arrived to pay
respects to our former king. Send a delegation of twenty of their
people to come forward."

A murmur arose in the assembled dignitaries and there were
nods of approval of the way the new king graciously handled the
situation. Belana was outraged at the interruption. A small
contingent of beggar men made their way forward. First they bowed
to the king's body and then to Nebuchadnezzar. Arising, their
spokesman said to the new king. "We are here to pledge our
allegiance to you, Majesty, for we are not beggars, but Queen Mara's
personal forces." At that signal, all the "beggars" threw off their
rags and revealed themselves as trained and well-equipped soldiers.
They positioned themselves around the king. The amazed
government and religious leaders began to clap, slowly at first and
finally in an enthusiastic cadence.

Nebuk motioned to Mara and his children to join him at the
throne. Their movement elicited an even greater outburst of
applause. Belana and her family made moves to leave the room
and the queen's guards drew their swords and blocked the way.
Youini whispered to his wife, "sit back down." She did, looking
like a woman stricken with death pangs.

The other "beggars" now filed into the throne room and
surrounded the entire assemblage. People began to be fearful and
looked nervously at the soldiers. Quickly a hush descended over
the room. Nebuk continued, "There is no need for anyone to be
afraid unless they have been involved in the plot to keep the throne
from me." He paused and looked directly at Belana and Youini.

Again a ripple of excitement passed through the crowd. The
king continued. "There was a plot to ensure my death on the
battlefield. All but one of the conspirators died in my place. I am
sure many of you know who he is and he has, by my father's order,

already joined the others in their reward." He paused to let the facts sink in.

"The Captain of Her Majesty's Guard is now prepared to take into custody other members of the conspiracy. We know some of these conspirators, and others will be discovered. The queen, my beloved and beautiful Mara, and my son and heir, Nabonidus, have worked, and will continue to work to bring justice to this kingdom.

By this time Belana could stand no more, jumped to her feet and turned to the crowd and shouted, "My father didn't want Nebuchadnezzar to rule this realm and he left new instructions for the succession. He made out these orders just five days before he died." With that she told her son to deliver the order of succession to Nebuchadnezzar. "See the signature and the seal of the king," she screamed.

By this time the entire room was in an uproar and began to be polarized into two camps. Some were shocked at Belana's actions. Others called for the matter to be settled immediately. Perhaps King Nabopolassar had changed his mind on the succession. He was the king.

"As king of this empire," Nebuk continued in a calm reassuring manner. "I am prepared to deal with all of these questions. I shall do so now as I have no time to waste until I can get back to the battle front." His control, in the face of the dissention, gained him respect, even among those who had a more normal affinity with Belana.

Nebuk examined the document Belo-Phane handed him. He called Nabonidus to his side. They conferred quietly and then Nabonidus moved to one of the guards who nodded as he received the orders from the prince. He quickly left the room. The action conditioned speculation and fear.

"I have examined the document and it looks to be official and to all appearances the king's wishes are different from mine. However, there are some questions yet to be settled." A satisfied look settled over Belana's face. She squared her shoulders and settled back comfortably in her chair.

The guard returned with two men who followed him to the throne. As Belana saw who they were her smug confidence turned to terror. It was the keeper of the king's seal and one of the king's physicians.

"Gentlemen, what can you tell us about this document?" Nebuk gestured to the physician.

"The king almost died on the day this document was issued. Princess Belana and Prince Youini insisted he sign it and swore at him when he hesitated. I overheard the conversation. He was almost unintelligible when he finally agreed. Afterwards he wept and I stayed with him all night. The next day he had no recollection of what had transpired but he was much stronger."

"Thank you. I have other questions for you. Please remain here. Now, I ask the Document Keeper for his memory of the events. Please tell us what you know."

"Your Majesty, I . . . I know that the king did not place the official seal on the documents." A murmur swept the crowd.

"He didn't? Why not? There is a seal on the parchment."

"Well, Your Majesty, the king was too weak to lift his hand and the seal is of a very heavy stone that requires more strength than the king had."

"Did the king ask you to put the seal on for him?"

"No, Majesty."

"If he didn't put the seal on, then, who did?"

"Majesty, I don't know for sure." He looked nervously at Princess Belana who was glaring a warning to "say no more." Taking a deep breath and gathering all his strength, knowing his life was in the balance, he continued. "All I know is, two days later after the documents were signed but not sealed, the princess and her husband came to see the document in my vault. The princess asked to read the document again and I left her in the room to do so. When she called me back to put the document away, it was neatly

THE PRIDE OF BABYLON 115

folded and had been sealed. I wondered at the time how the seal got there, but I am but a servant. I do not question royalty, Majesty."

"That's fine, my good man, that's perfectly all right, except for one thing which you told my son. What else do you know?"

"Well, Majesty, when I examined the seal again, I got out the king's seal which I pressed on another parchment. The seal on the document is not the official king's seal." Gasps could be heard all over the room. "See—there is no curl under the lower mark. King Nabopolassar had that small curl mark made to look like an accident of craftsmanship. Only he and I knew about it. Someone forged the seal to make this document look more official."

"Thank you. So now we have a document signed under duress and forgery. Physician, come here again." The crowded room was buzzing with the controversy, but quickly quieted as the physician stepped forward again. "What can you tell us concerning the king's death?"

"Your Majesty, I have, along with other court physicians, treated your father for several years. We all know he was ill for some time, but it was not a life-threatening illness. He should have lived much longer. Suddenly he began to get weaker and sicker. There was no good explanation. One day I took some spring water he had been drinking and tried to see if it was causing him to have trouble. It smelled and looked ok, but when I fed some to a cat, the cat died the next day. I believe the king was poisoned."

The crowd could no longer contain itself and pandemonium broke out in the throne room. Princess Belana tried to act shocked and dismayed, but fear was squeezing her in its ever-tightening grip.

King Nebuchadnezzar raised the scepter, calling for attention. It took some time for order to return to the room. Addressing the physician, Nebuk asked, "Who do you think poisoned my father?"

"Your Majesty, it was the spring water that was brought to him by Princess Belana and Prince Youini." This time the gasp was more like the audience being choked on the very thought that the princess would do such a thing or even be accused of it, especially since she was so close to her father.

"You are a liar," cried the trembling, ashen-faced princess. "That's all lies."

"No, Princess, the very poison you obtained from the apothecary has been found in the same cupboard where you stored the water jars. You started bringing the spring water to your father at the very time his illness changed to being life threatening. You poisoned your own father. You caused His Majesty's death."

A stunned silence fell on the room. Princess Belana struggled to her feet and pointed at her husband. "It was not my idea. My husband made me do it so our son could be the king." The princess's eyes rolled back in her head and she collapsed in a heap on the floor. Youini made no move to help her.

"Now that you know the truth, you know why I shall be the king. My very own sister, the daughter of my mother and father, is not fit to live, much less reign. I shall issue orders for her and her husband's execution after this terrible ceremony is over." A subdued whisper of approval swept the room. Nebuchadnezzar had begun his reign in tragic triumph, as the queen's guards escorted Princess Belana and her family to the prison.

"Before this day is forgotten we shall build an even greater empire and the glory of Bel Marduk will be established. I shall now issue several edicts. First, my father will be buried in Shushan beside my mother. The time before my mother died giving me birth was the only time my father was a truly happy man. Second, I shall not have a coronation until the Pharaoh of Egypt has been buried in the dust of battle or has ridden his horse at top speed back to his palace. Third, my queen and my son, Prince Nabonidus, and my daughter, Princess Aia, shall have the power of the throne until I return from battle victoriously. Should I not return, the power of succession is in the power of the queen to determine. Fourth, I shall build a new capitol in the city of Babylon to serve the greatly expanding empire and we shall again be the great Babylonian Empire, combining all the greatness of the Chaldean and Sumerian and Babylonian empires into one. These are my words. This is my will. This we will do. These edicts I will sign and seal immediately. May the gods be with us. Go to your homes in peace."

The people were stunned by the turn of events. No one was sure the funeral was finished until the Chief Mourner cried out, "The king is dead, Oh, King Nebuchadnezzar live forever." The cry of "Oh, king live forever," echoed through the palace and throughout the entire city.

The next few days were extremely busy for the royal family. Plans were made for the burial of the king's body in Shushan with Prince Nabonidus carrying out the official duty. The arrangements for the executions of Princess Belana and Youini needed to be made. The palace was to be prepared for the family to live in. Preparations were made for the king to resume control on the battlefield.

Nebuk and Mara plunged in to get many things accomplished. Nebuk stepped into the role of king as easily as he directed his troops in the field. A confident and festive air filled the palace. The excitement of the future with a vibrant and considerate king, a beautiful and kindly queen, coupled with a soon victorious army ending the war, quickened everyone's spirits. The nation was at war, but peace and contentment were theirs.

Nebuk left the palace arrangements to Mara to complete. He commissioned the captain of the Queen's Guard to oversee the family's safety. Everything was falling rapidly into place and he felt good about returning to the battlefield.

He and Mara had only one area of disagreement. That was the deaths of Belana and Youini. Mara reminded him, "Don't you remember how grateful you were you did not have to depose your father since Belana had done it for you. I think there must be a better way of dealing with them."

"You may be right, but I don't know what!"

It was Princess Aia who suggested, "Daddy, why don't you banish them for life. Give them fifty days supply of food and send them out into the Arabian Desert to live or die by their wits."

When Nebuk heard her suggestion, it ignited his imagination. "How just it would be, especially if they had to struggle to get their water? It would probably be a more severe lesson than death." And so the sentence was changed to "life in the desert." Their children were not allowed to go with them and were punished less severely since they had no actual part in the death of the king.

When Belana heard of the sentence change, she again passed out and later was able to meekly thank Nebuchadnezzar, King of the Chaldean/Babylonian Empire, for sparing her life. She many times later wished she had been killed rather than have to live the life of being sentenced to live with a husband who now hated her.

With the duties of transfer of power completed in record time, the departure for the battlefield of Carchemish was upon the king. He hated to leave Mara and the children with all the work there at Ur, and especially with Mara's time to have the next king coming so soon. But since they both believed the prophecies of their new son's destiny, they agreed everything would be all right.

CHAPTER 11

Nebuk left Ur with mixed emotions. He hated leaving his family, but his sense of destiny and desire for greatness led him on. The future was his to make. Now as king he thrilled to the challenges that were possible before him. Each step toward the battle spurred his inner excitement.

Reaching Babylon, the first leg of his journey, he headed directly for the home of the high priest Belardos. Again, he and his men were made welcome. Belardos was thrilled with the words he'd heard about Babylon becoming the capital of the revived Babylonian Empire. He was so excited he grabbed Nebuk's arm and swung him around and did some fancy footwork. Suddenly he stopped and looked embarrassed. "Oh, I am sorry, your Majesty."

It was the king's turn to laugh and he grabbed the priest's arm and demonstrated some of his own footwork. They fell into each other's arms and embraced. "That's what we both want and that is what we both shall have." It felt good to have a friend like Belardos with whom he was so comfortable. If only his father had been that kind of a man, but he wasn't. He knew those thoughts were dangerous.

Nebuk slept very well that night. With Belardos's acceptance and Belakah's massage and care, he was well rested and ready to continue the rest of the journey early in the morning. This part of the trip was aggravating to the king. It was too long, and he wanted to know how the battle was going. How was Nebuzaradan managing the battle? Would Pharaoh Neccoh know that he was now the king? Would such knowledge intensify the battle and Neccoh's resolve, or would his own position be strengthened and his enemy weakened? Would his own men be happy over his coming to the throne?

He had only to wait until his arrival at the main camp. Handmade signs of welcome and the cheering of his men reassured Nebuchadnezzar that he was, indeed, a hero here at the battle site. Nebuzaradan was on hand to welcome the king and brief him on the battle. "Your Majesty, it is with great pleasure I welcome you to the sight of one of your greatest victories as you lead this great empire." He bowed to the king and asked Nebuchadnezzar, "how soon will you be ready for a briefing?"

"I am ready right now. Belakah, see to my things and have meals prepared for us. I shall join you shortly. Come, Zaradan, let me know all that is going on." The two men headed for the command tent a few yards away.

"Your Majesty, Pharaoh's main forces are in the same place they were when you left. Two smaller groupings have moved from place to place and back again in an attempt to divert our attention from the main camp. We have engaged the enemy in six different battles in as many weeks. In each we have held them off and caused them to retreat. We have not had any major battles with the main force. We have succeeded several times in cutting their supply lines from the south, but there is almost no cover for our men to build an encampment to keep their supply lines stopped. We can easily win the battle if we can keep the supplies from reaching them when we attack the main camp."

"Have they utilized the locals in providing for their needs? If they are abusing the people, can we count on them to help us get rid of them? We need to infiltrate the citizenry and see what we can do to sabotage their relationship with the people."

"Your Majesty, we have several men who have come to us from the city and they are willing to help us. We have already used them to scout and give us information. The Egyptians have already done some raping and confiscating of the people's goods. I think the people are rapidly turning against the Egyptians."

"That's good. What else?"

"You know how Belardos told us not to be in too big a hurry to engage them in battle? Well, in this case, he certainly was right. The people at first welcomed Neccoh's forces as deliverance from the Persian influence and fear of us. As time has gone by, the Egyptian forces have become more hostile to the people and they in return have become more helpful to us. It's almost like we could wait them out and they would just disappear."

"That seems too good to be true, and therefore it is. However, we can use their discontent to help us drive the enemy out even faster. I think it is time to engage the enemy head on. How soon can we be ready to mount our main offensive?"

"Our plans have been ready for several weeks. We have only to cut the supply lines south of the city again and at the same time attack the main camp to the north. We can act in as little as two days."

"A thought just hit me. Why don't we attack through the city and let the people see us as liberators and then march on to the main camp. That way we can also hold the area on the south side of the city and effectively cut their supply lines. The city would provide us the shelter we need. The bulk of our forces could then proceed and attack in the original manner we'd planned. Could we still do this in two days?"

"I would think we'd be able to do it. But let's plan three days just to be safe. I want to introduce you to the men from Carchemish and perhaps they can organize some liberators of their own."

"Good, for I want to lead the forces that liberate the city so people can think in terms of 'Good King Nebuchadnezzar' who set them free from Egyptian control. Since we have the future job of administering this territory, I want as good a relationship with them as I possibly can. Alert the troops to maintain respect and good will with these people who are not to be a conquered people, but liberated."

"I will send for the men to meet with you tomorrow. You must be very tired from your journey. Perhaps when you are rested, you can tell me more of the events at Ur. My spies tell me that things got pretty exciting."

"We shall have time for that tomorrow. Now I am famished and very tired. Thank you for all your good work while I was gone. I hold you in the same high esteem I did as prince. Now as king, I need you more than ever."

The praise, as usual, caused Nebuzaradan to feel embarrassed and he blushed in his pride. "Your Majesty, I shall endeavor to serve you faithfully throughout your reign and may it be a long, long reign. Rest well, Your Majesty. We shall continue tomorrow."

Nebuk, returning to his tent, noticed more than the usual number of guards were there. Even the trappings of being king followed to the battlefield. He was grateful his men seemed genuinely pleased that he was their king. Once inside his tent he saw Belakah had everything under control. The table was set for him to eat. The cooks were standing by with hot foods being kept warm, waiting for his arrival. Water was being heated for a hot bath and the massage table was ready. Belakah had seen to everything.

"Belakah, you must be as tired as I am. We can skip the massage tonight."

"No, your Majesty," and seeing the king frown, "Nebuk. I think that we both shall get a good night's sleep if you are most relaxed and rested. It will perhaps be a shorter massage than usual, but we will get it in."

"This is really terrible, here I am the king of the empire and everyone is ordering me around." In spite of his tiredness, there was laughter in his voice. "Don't you dare let it be known how Mara, Aia and you just tell me what to do and I do it."

"Well, somebody has to do it. And since Queen Mara and Princess Aia aren't here, I guess it's my job. You don't want me to get fired for neglect of duty, do you?" Both men realized the effect of the laughter in relaxing them. It was good to laugh.

Dinner was soon over and Nebuk was in the bath and on the massage table in record time. By the time Belakah finished with the massage, Nebuk was sound asleep and hardly awakened as the servant helped him into his bed. He felt good and slept well. Morning brought a day filled with plans for the attack that was coming in two more days. Nebuk was pleased with the men from Carchemish. So pleased, in fact, he determined to make them the administrative council after the war.

The King of Carchemish, Nikomee, was a nervous little man who had not ruled the city/state properly. Spending most of his time currying the favor of Pharaoh Neccoh, he neglected his people. He hoped to become the regional adjutant for Egypt as well as having an expanded kingdom backed by Pharaoh's power. Guessing wrong, he chose to align himself with Egypt. He had no way of knowing the battle over his city would be the turning point in the Babylonian Empire becoming the greatest empire the world had ever seen.

The two days passed agonizingly slow for some and very rapidly for others. The excitement of the preparation for the big battle was wearing on everyone. Nerves were exposed. People snapped at each other causing arguments and fights. Some soldiers became quiet and withdrawn. The officers did their best to prepare the men for battle.

The troop movements began before dawn and the eerie quiet pervading the encampment added to the tension. Men went through their routines as in an automated state. The training of many months and years paid off as they mechanically did what was needed; no unnecessary words were exchanged.

The first group, smaller than the other, and led by King Nebuchadnezzar, moved out first. They marched south by southwest to cut off the supply lines just below the city. They took a sizable enemy encampment completely by surprise and made quick work of taking the south flank of the city. The gates of the city opened to them and they were greeted with quiet welcome. The underground had done its work well.

Since the city fortifications were not all that strong, even Pharaoh Neccoh had decided against using the city as his defense.

Instead, he had chosen to battle outside of the city. This caused King Nikomee to feel quite safe in his palace.

Moving quickly, the Babylonians captured the king and delivered him to Nebuchadnezzar who quizzed him about his relationship to Neccoh. The king, hoping to save his neck, tried his best to insist that he had only befriended Neccoh to gather information, which would be of help to the forces of Nebuchadnezzar. His chin trembling excitedly, he told all he knew under Nebuchadnezzar's prompting. Soon he was bound and in his own prison. Nebuchadnezzar installed the leader of his spies as the temporary city governor.

The information the King of Carchemish provided gave Nebuk further ideas on how to surprise the Pharaoh. He spent a few hours securing the city, making sure it could not be used as a defense for the fleeing Egyptians. Nebuk and his men began the move on the enemy through the northwest city gates. Waiting until he was sure Nebuzaradan had begun his attack on the main camp from the east, he began his assault on the western flank of the encampment. The two-pronged attack, one of which came from the city, an entirely unexpected direction, had the desired effect of making the enemy unsure of where the main forces were. They became ineffective in their deployment of their men.

The battle raged the remainder of the day and into the night. Finally, retreat sounded for the Babylonian forces and they pulled back to the safety of the areas they had conquered. When Nebuk and Nebuzaradan conferred, they were extremely surprised to find that they had lost relatively few men. Most of their units were in good condition. Many men had superficial wounds and the medical people were busy binding up the cuts and slashes of swords and arrow punctures.

With morning light the attack began again. This time the response to their attack was very slow and soon the white flag of surrender appeared. King Nebuchadnezzar was disappointed when he examined the enemy's encampment. It was obvious that the remaining soldiers were hardly able to fight. The pharaoh had taken most of the able-bodied men, skirted the city and headed back to Egypt, leaving primarily the sick and wounded. Calling to Nebuzaradan, "I see Belardos was right again. It looks like I'll have to chase Neccoh to the Land of Judah, just like he said." Conferring briefly, they left their most trusted generals to finish mopping up at the camp and returned to their command center.

It seemed like the wrong thing to do, to follow Neccoh and try to capture him. However, the idea of bringing the whole Egyptian Empire down with the subjugation of its king was very tempting, especially when you've been the king of your empire for only a few weeks.

Finally Nebuzaradan said, "Let's do it. You will be the undisputed ruler of the whole world once the Egyptians are under your control." Nebuk struggled with the idea; it certainly fed his ego; it felt good.

"If we do it, we'll have to dispose of most of the prisoners that we've taken. We would have to leave too many men here to guard and care for them. We'll need a great many of our men to pursue Neccoh. What if he should regroup and try to turn the tables on us further on down the road?"

"You are right, Your Majesty. I was thinking of what you said you did to your sister and her husband. Why don't we do the same thing to these men? Take their weapons away from them and give them a supply of food. Let them find their way back to Egypt or stay here. Some of them ought to become slaves. Castrate the best of them and send the rest away."

Nebuk winced at the mention of castration, but did not dare show his chief-of-staff he was unwilling to carry out such an idea. "Do it and get our men ready to travel to overtake Neccoh."

Nebuzaradan quickly translated the command into action with men ready to do the work. He rapidly selected the units of men that would be traveling with them and briefed them on the need for speed in their preparations. They would be leaving the next morning at dawn.

Nebuk told Belakah of their plans and instructed him to prepare for their moving. "I have already been gathering our things back into the travel packs. The spirits have told me that you will be successful, but you will need to be very careful when we get near Hamath. Neccoh is already there setting up fortifications which he thinks will hold you and send you back home, leaving him in control of this area."

"Belakah, you are amazing. What would I ever do without you?"

"I hope that you never have to find out, Nebuk."

"I must tell you that I ordered some of the captives to be made eunuchs. I hope that doesn't bother you too much?"

"You are the king. You have to do what you have to do. Besides, they are only Egyptians. They aren't Chaldean as you are."

It surprised Nebuk that Belakah would take it so calmly, especially since he knew of the dreams that had troubled Nebuk in the past. Also surprising was his ascribing inferiority to other enslaved peoples. *He is right, of course, we are the Chaldeans,* and that thought satisfied him. A reawakened sense of power stemming from his ability to control the destiny of other men flooded his mind. *I am the greatest king in this part of the world and when I get done with Neccoh, I shall be the undisputed world ruler.*

At dawn the men were ready and eager to depart. Leaving the last orders to the general in charge, Nebuzaradan saluted and led the men out of the camp toward the south. The king, surrounded by his guards and all his entourage, left after the first units were under way. The balance of the force, which was about seventy-five percent of the troop strength that he had brought to Carchemish, followed him.

The main road was known in later years, as the "Way of the Kings," because of such people as Pharaoh Neccoh and Nebuchadnezzar. The road wound around the mountains and sometimes through the valleys. Taking the high elevations whenever possible offered protection from bands of marauders. From the higher outlooks they could see who was coming toward them and who was following them. It was harder travel, but clearly advantageous.

In two days they passed through the city of Aleppo and found no evidence of the Egyptian forces. Local informants told them that Pharaoh and his men seemed very eager to put distance between themselves and the Babylonians, whom they were sure were following them.

When Nebuk and Belakah discussed these reports, Belakah was suspicious of their motives and reminded Nebuk of the spirit guides that had warned of danger at Hamath. "It seems to me that these informants were told to tell you that Neccoh is afraid of you. They want you to think they are on their way to Egypt as fast as they can go, when in reality they are readying an ambush in Hamath."

"I believe you are right, Belakah, and as we get to the Hamath area, we are certainly going to be very watchful."

Several days of hard travel brought them to where they could see the Orontes River and finally the city of Hamath in the distance. They began to notice the Egyptian forces were in the area. In fact, the signs were so obvious you could tell Neccoh wanted them to attack the city of Hamath as if their main forces were there in hiding. Nebuzaradan, much impressed with the king's description of Queen Mara's guards' operation, sent scouts dressed in beggars' rags into the city. They found very little evidence of Egyptian forces in the city. The people were angered at having their food and supplies taken by the Egyptians and being left unprotected to face the force of the Babylonian army.

When all the information was gathered together and the most likely ambush location identified, Nebuk and Nebuzaradan laid out a plan to bypass the location and attack from the rear with a small elite force they would send up the river to divert their attention. They would think they were being attacked from the rear; however, the main force would come straight on from the north.

The Babylonian force made camp just out of sight of the

impending battle, but close enough for the enemy to scout them.
They wanted them to see what they were doing, creating the image
of resting before continuing their journey. Make the Egyptians
wait again for the battle.

The people of Hamath were terrified at the thought of getting
involved and not knowing which side to favor. Suspecting that the
Egyptians were running from Nebuchadnezzar, they refused to
deliver more supplies to them. Angered by the loss of supplies,
Pharaoh Neccoh sent marauding bands of his men into the city to
confiscate what they needed. Knowing the Egyptian supply
condition gave the Babylonians a distinct advantage.
Nebuchadnezzar sent men to intercept and destroy Neccoh's raiders
as fast as he sent them out. The residents of Hamath responded
appreciatively.

After a few days of this interception, the king and Nebuzaradan
sent their men, under the cover of darkness, up the river to the
south side of the mountain where their enemy was hiding. They
were told to wait two more days in hiding and then to begin a
noisy, harassing attack intended only to draw the enemy's attention.
When the main attack began they were to leave the area, giving
the Egyptians a way to escape and run home.

The two days dragged by. With their swords in hand and
ready to fight, the main Babylonian forces awaited the sound of
the horns signaling the start of the battle. When the sounds echoed
through the mountains, they waited an additional hour and then
began their own attack. In the ensuing confusion, many of the
Egyptians began running toward the main force. In a reverse
ambush, they were picked off one by one by expert archers.

The battle didn't last long, as the demoralized and confused
forces felt betrayed by their leaders, whose battle plans had failed
again. The sight of Pharaoh and his best soldiers slipping out from
their safe hiding place and running brought the white flag of
surrender. Again the forces of Egypt were at the mercy of the
Babylonians.

This second victory and the scent of Neccoh's blood, coupled with Belardos's words ringing in his ears, caused Nebuchadnezzar to quickly gather the highest officers of the captives and demand to know the plans of the Pharaoh. At first the men were reluctant to divulge any of the Egyptian plans, but the threat of emasculation and being left on the road to die without food quickly convinced them to save their necks and tell what they knew.

Neccoh was retreating to Jerusalem, to refortify his troop strength and return to attack this new King of Babylon again. The supremacy of Egypt in the area was at stake. Egypt had controlled the region from the Arabian Peninsula to the coastal plain. His men had killed Josiah, the King of Judah, who had fought against him, and he had replaced him with Jehoiakim. He now needed to capitalize on all his threats and power plays that would enable him to turn defeat into victory and reestablish his control and win the war. He was gambling that the Babylonians would not pursue him into the land of Judah.

It was just such thinking that finally put Nebuchadnezzar at the gates of Jerusalem and found Neccoh running for Egypt, abandoning the young King of Judah to fight the battle with the Babylonian forces. Some of the prophets in the land of Judah had encouraged the people to believe they could overcome the strength of Nebuchadnezzar's resolve. It was now a question of Judah's defiance of the new King of Babylon and his right to rule over this entire part of the world.

Nebuchadnezzar found himself thinking, *what am I doing here fighting with this motley bunch of heathens. I will make quick work of this and get home in time for the birth of my second son. I guess Belardos will expect me to subdue these rebellious cousins of ours. He'll want them to get back to the true worship of Bel and all of our other gods.*

It was amazing to Nebuchadnezzar how easily he overcame the resistance of the army of Judah. What further amazed him was the number of the people of the city, carrying white flags, who flocked out to meet him and welcome his control. They kept talking about a prophet of the Lord, a Jeremiah, who had told them it was God's will for them to be under Babylonian rule, and safety for

WAY1

them was only possible under Babylon. "What could they possibly mean?"

"What a strange people with a strange view of God. They say there is only one God and not many gods who are in constant conflict with each other for supremacy. What a shame to be stuck with only one god to choose from."

Of course, the battle for Jerusalem was not long because of the divided opinion of the people. It was soon clear even to King Jehoiakim that surrender was the only way to save the country. Nebuchadnezzar found himself facing the problem of what to do with another country. Here he was, barely on the throne, and a second conquered nation added to his Empire all in just a few short days. This one was so far away from his capitol and these people were so different in their beliefs. "Our cousins certainly have become strange since they left Ur."

CHAPTER 12

Nebuchadnezzar, in his makeshift throne room located off the temple plaza, became impatient waiting for King Jehoiakim to officially surrender. He paced angrily. *Where is he, doesn't he know that I could have his head. Who does he think he is?*

Finally Jehoiakim arrived with his courtiers, and Nebuchadnezzar accepting his apologies, took full note of his appearance. Of average height, lean and strong, regal in his purple coronation robes, he bowed himself humbly before Nebuchadnezzar. For a Judean, he was unusually fair skinned which was made more noticeable by his short dark curly hair. He stood bareheaded signifying he was in the presence of a superior king. Though young and nervous, he said all the right things as he presented appropriate gifts signifying the national and personal surrender.

The Judean king's speech officially recognized the King of Babylon as victor and ruler over the land of Judah. He announced his full cooperation with and allegiance to Nebuchadnezzar. This wasn't the first time Jehoiakim had spoken words of submission, for he owed his throne to the Pharaoh of Egypt, who had chosen him instead of his more belligerent elder brother. Survival to him was being in the right place at the right time with the right attitude. He had every intention of surviving the Babylonians and especially this new king on the Babylonian throne.

Listening to the Judean king, Nebuk was impressed with the ability of Jehoiakim to handle himself. *Perhaps the easiest way to manage the conquest of Judah is to keep this present king on the throne— on a very tight leash. I think I will leave Nebuzaradan here to 'oversee*

His Majesty's loyalty.' I'll have him continue as puppet king. This time he'll know he has a new master pulling the strings.

Nebuk excused himself for a few minutes and kept the Judean king standing anxiously before his empty throne. A brief consultation with Nebuzaradan produced the positive response that he expected and he returned to the throne and addressed the waiting Judean courtiers. "King Jehoiakim, it is my desire for you to retain, first of all, your head . . . and your throne as well." The relief on the face of Jehoiakim was enough to make Nebuk smile. "I see that meets with your approval. This will be under the supervision of my chief of staff, Nebuzaradan."

"Oh, yes, Your Majesty. I shall do everything in my power to work with you and your chief of staff to make a smooth and safe transition from Egyptian to Babylonian rule. You will find that I am a very adaptable administrator. I hope you will be very satisfied with my cooperation."

"I am very certain you will do all you can to save yourself . . . and your country. Now, there are some things that must be taken into account. First, the people who came out to greet me, or as you say, defected to my advance, must not be made to suffer in any way. They may stay here if they wish, or they will be allowed to travel with me to my new capitol of Babylon where they will be put to work in building the world's finest city. They will not be slaves, but paid workers. Those who choose to remain here will be under our protection.

"Second, all male relatives of royal lineage will come for review before me. I shall decide which of them will be able to remain here. The rest of them will be taken to the court in Babylon.

"Third, all males eligible for higher learning by virtue of their giftedness will be examined by my people for use in our great schools of learning. We shall see how much of your Chaldean heritage remains in your heads.

"Fourth, any rebellion brought about by royal insurrection is a signed death sentence. I will tolerate no insubordination. I will be swift in quashing any rebellion against my rule. Your heads will continue to be on your shoulders as long as you use yours and recognize me as your head.

"Fifth, we shall send priests to you to instruct you in the worship of the Great God, Bel Marduk. You have forgotten who your gods are. Are these terms clear to you?"

King Jehoiakim bowed his head to Nebuchadnezzar, and said, "Your terms are perfectly clear and we shall abide by each of them. One request, Your Majesty, as my children are very small, I request a minimum age be established for the transporting of young men to spare mothers undue distress over their young children."

"That seems a reasonable request. No children under the age of 13 will be taken from their families."

"Thank you, Your Majesty, that is very favorable. I am sure our people will consider it as a gesture of goodwill which will enable them to feel more kindly toward you."

"That is all well and good; however, it was not my intention when I left my own country to travel this far in pursuit of the Egyptian Pharaoh. Had he not attacked us at Hamath, and had we not learned that he intended to regroup and attack us again, it is very doubtful we would be having this conversation. You owe your present condition to pharaoh who used you and caused you this defeat. I demand you have no further dealings with him, on penalty of death. Please pass this bit of information on to your people. Their anger must be directed at Pharaoh Neccoh, not at me."

Jehoiakim again bowed his head and the audience was over. Nebuchadnezzar conferred again with Nebuzaradan and soon the administrative procedures were being worked out with the Judean courtiers. Nebuchadnezzar satisfied himself that things were going well and retired to his quarters where Belakah surprisingly began to make suggestions.

"Nebuk, I wonder if it is wise to take so many people back to Babylon when the government hasn't really been shifted there as yet. I am concerned about the infusion of so many heathen thinkers into our midst. We should be very selective in the people we take

back to our country. I think all of the men you take should either
be married, taking their whole families, or they should be made
eunuchs so there will be less possibility of unrest."

"Belakah, I am surprised you would make such a suggestion,
since you, yourself, are a victim of the same action against you by
my father."

"I expected you to question me about that, but my experience
has been very good. Here I am, in the closest employ and
relationship with the greatest king the world has ever known. If I
hadn't been taken and enslaved, I wouldn't have had this
opportunity. Losing some of my body parts has not been too high
a price for this great service. Besides, I know some of the people
you will bring with you will have a great effect on your future and
your ability to rule this great Empire that you've expanded to twice
the size it was just a few weeks ago."

Nebuk stood with his mouth agape as the words of Belakah
poured forth. "I can hardly believe I am hearing you say what I
have just heard. You know of the horror I experienced just dreaming
about the things you have lived through. Here you are acting like
it was nothing, and in fact, your passport to a better life. My
friend, you are either a great, great man, or you're losing your
mind. I prefer to think of you as a great man, but I reserve the
right to change my mind." Nebuk just shook his head and grinned.

"You are probably right about the number of people Babylon
is prepared to receive. We must get the city ready for the government
and perhaps as we build we shall need the work of many more
people. I shall certainly take your suggestions into my final
decisions. Thank you, my friend."

It wasn't two hours before the same basic suggestion Belakah
made, came to him in the form of comments from Nebuzaradan.
"Your Majesty, I'm concerned that taking a lot of people from this
country would demoralize the general population. Perhaps it would
be better if the only ones you take with you would be the nobles
who could cause the greatest problem if they were left here."

Nebuk laughed and told Nebuzaradan, "I think you are trying

to get rid of all the troublemakers from off your back. You, my general, are the one who will be left here to deal with any insurrection."

"That's true and I sincerely hope you will manage to take the worst of the potential trouble with you," Nebuzaradan grinned. "Perhaps making enough of them eunuchs will take the rebellious spirit out of them."

"It seems you and Belakah have come to the same general idea. I shall begin making plans and inspections will follow very shortly. I am eager to get back to Ur before the new baby arrives. If all goes well, I should be able to be there about a month before he is due."

"You seem very sure that it will be a boy. What if it turns out to be a girl?"

"It won't. Belardos and his seers have told me it will be a boy and he will be the one to eventually succeed me on the throne. I have even been told he will not reign too long and that he will be succeeded by his older brother who will only reign until his oldest son is able to control the Empire."

"That is very spooky. I am not too sure I want to know what is going to happen before it does. I am certainly glad you are the king and I am your servant; all I have to do is whatever you tell me. If I should marry, I will wait to find out what sex our children are as they arrive."

"Have you no spirit of adventure? It's fun to see how things you know of will come to pass. I will admit it is strange knowing some things that are coming, but my experiences so far with Belardos's prophecies are all very good. I shall expect the future to be revealed to me. After all, I am the king of the largest empire in the world."

"That you are, Your Majesty, and may your reign be long and fruitful." Nebuzaradan bowed to the king and said, "Your humble servant."

"I am counting on your long and faithful service to make all the dreams and goals I have for the Babylonian Empire come to fulfillment. Don't you let these strange cousins of ours do anything to prevent you from being in the forefront of our great future. Please be careful, my good and faithful servant."

Nebuk didn't have very long to think of how good it was to have servants and officers like Belakah and Nebuzaradan. No sooner had he turned his attention to the work at hand than a messenger from King Jehoiakim was at his door. "The King has assembled all the princes of the country in his palace and the throne room is yours to make your inspection."

"Thank his majesty, but I shall inspect the princes here in my present quarters. The work I have to do must not be associated with his majesty in any way. Please have the princes assembled here in one hour. I will make decisions at that time."

The hour of preparation for the job Nebuchadnezzar had to do was not enough and the princes were kept waiting. The waiting increased their edginess just as it served to calm the King of Babylon. As the inspection was to begin, Nebuk called for Belakah to come and assist him in the job. Nebuzaradan was already there, having brought the princes into the king's chamber.

The first group of seven was the youngest of the princes, ages thirteen through fifteen. They were a pretty average-looking bunch of kids. They were scared and nervous about what the future held for them. They reminded Nebuk of himself when his father so rudely embarrassed him in front of the more developed boys. None of these princes were sons of the king. His children were all too young and according to the orders of the surrender, children under thirteen would not be taken from their families.

"All of these children are to remain here." And that was all there was to it. The relief on the faces carried much thanks to the king.

The next group of twenty-one young men, ages sixteen through twenty, demanded much greater scrutiny. The king ordered them divided into three groups. The first group was to be close enough to the king to be in line for the throne. The second group was to consist of those who were physically more attractive and strong.

The third group was to be those thought to be the most intelligent, so the Chaldean wisdom and language could be imparted to them.

The first group consisted of four young men, cousins of the king. Nebuchadnezzar questioned them as to their relationship to the king and found that one cousin was the son of the sister of King Josiah who was the father of Jehoiakim. The other three were brothers and second cousins of the king. They were sent back to the group of princes waiting to be judged.

The second group consisted of twelve young men who were the best physical specimens. Some were extremely handsome and others were very athletic and strong. They were ordered to stand forward and disrobe. The embarrassment was electric in the room. Nakedness was not a practice of the people of Judah and there was resentment that the King of Babylon would dishonor them in such a manner. The murmuring began to subside and the king spoke. "There will be many discomforting moments for you in the years that lie ahead. This will seem very small. Disrobe."

The removal of their clothing was finished after much hesitation. The embarrassed posturing reminded Nebuk of his experiences and he felt a twinge of guilt over why he felt the need for such a maneuver. However, he wanted to take back only the best specimens as the first evidences of his conquest.

He was impressed with the majority of the young men. He was much surprised by the fact that all of them had undergone the curious rite known as circumcision. He made a note to discuss the reason for the circumcision with them at a more appropriate time. Their bodies were smooth and well proportioned in general and several were obviously very muscular. He noticed the same four young men who had been in the first group were also in this group. He selected eight of the twelve, which included the four cousins of the king.

Group three created the most interest for Nebuk. Ten young men were selected and brought before him. As he asked questions, he was pleased with the ability of several of the young men who had not appeared before him in either of the earlier groups. It excited the king when he realized that four of these princes he had seen twice before. His interest in these young men prompted him to question them very closely. Their answers indicated good education and understanding of science, mathematics and the arts. *Very valuable assets to building up the Babylonian Empire, and dangerous assets to leave to a newly subjugated nation.*

Nebuk asked the four repeaters to remain and asked them several more questions. Still further impressed with their answers, he finally asked, "What are your names?"

"My name is Hananiah, Your Majesty."

"My name is Azariah, Sire."

"My name is Daniel, Your Majesty."

"My name is Mishael, Your Majesty."

"You have high qualifications. I think that I shall use you in the court. If, after your training, you turn out to be what I think you can be, you will have a very useful life in the city of Babylon. Remember your place and you shall prosper."

Nebuchadnezzar announced his choice. "I will take fifteen of the twenty-one young princes to be educated to serve the Babylonian Empire. The other six will remain here under the direct supervision of Nebuzaradan. All twenty-one will be made eunuchs. The six remaining in Jerusalem will be castrated immediately, the others after we arrive in Babylon, so as not to slow down my departure and travel for home." The King also thought the wait would cause them to be more subdued by the time they arrived in Babylon.

The rest of the inspections took several more days to complete. There were families to consider, the age of the older princes and their position in relation to the king and the power structure of the nation. When Nebuk had satisfied himself that the three hundred people who would go back with him were all that he wanted at the time, he announced the departure to begin in two days.

The caravan gathered in front of the temple area when the King and his party were ready to leave for Babylon and finally to go on to Ur. The king, resplendent in his dark uniform and white cape sat astride his black horse in the center of the procession. Gathered around him were his soldiers, caravan drivers and all the people being taken back with him to Babylon.

It was a very difficult time for the families of the people who were being taken to live in a hostile world and live a life of servitude. They had never been prepared for slavery and now their lives would never be as they had imagined. The tears of mothers and the grim faces of fathers betrayed love that was deep and real. The king felt jealousy stirring in his heart. Love of parents . . . love of family . . . love that he had never had. If only he could have ordered love as easily as he ordered this deportation. Steeling his heart against the pain, he waved the procession into its march out the gate on the road to Damascus.

The day was pretty well gone before the first refreshing glimpse of the Sea of Kinneret came into sight. The sea was a beautiful small body of water shaped like a harp, especially when seen from the highlands on the western flank of the sea. Some called it Galilee, but the natives all referred to it as Kinneret, the harp.

Resting for the evening and bathing in the cool refreshing water of the sea helped to wipe away the depression that the captives felt. Since this would probably be the last time they would ever see this body of water, they relished every moment of its pleasure.

The next day, winding their way up the slopes of Mount Canaan they had their last look at the Kinneret and forged ahead toward the city of Damascus and on to Babylon.

Nebuk was eager to get the caravan to Babylon so then he and his men could continue on to Ur. His wife and family and what was happening to his kingdom, were now uppermost in his mind. He was not fearful of what he would find at home, for he knew Mara and Nabonidus would have everything under control.

He was also eager to see whether his plans to move the palace back to Babylon were progressing satisfactorily. He was ready to begin the great building project that had been his pet from the earliest days. The days when he, as a young man, used his building plans to escape pain and fill his dreams with glory. Glory that he had, at one time, hoped would enable his father to respect and honor him. His mind had never been really very far from the plans since he first made the decision to rebuild the city of Babylon and make it the capital again.

Belardos was ecstatic when King Nebuchadnezzar brought him some of the vessels of the temple in Jerusalem. The custom of taking religious artifacts from a people of a different religion signaled the superior power of the conqueror's god. Belardos was very happy with the slaves since he considered them heathen who had turned away from the true god, Bel Marduk. He would show them the error of their ways, even if it took much enforcing.

In spite of being weary of travel, Nebuk allowed his men only one day of rest before they traveled on to Ur. Most of them were as happy as he, to be going home and soon the final long day-of-march was past. They entered the city just before the gates were to be shut for the night. The whole city was there to welcome the conquering heroes. Shouts of joy as well as wails of grief for other fallen loved ones filled the air most of the night.

Nebuk swept what he could of Mara into his arms. She was in the last stage of her pregnancy and obviously was waiting for her man to come home to have this new baby. She greeted the king with warm grateful kisses. Nabonidus and Aia were eager to hug their father and welcome him.

Nebuk noticed as he released Aia and turned to Nabonidus that there was a very stately young woman standing beside his tall handsome son. Black hair reached to the middle of her back complimenting her milk-white skin. Almond eyes of azure dominated her regal looking face. He hugged his son and said, "Who is this beautiful young thing standing next to you, my son?"

Nabonidus blushed and said, "Father, this is my friend, Niyan. She has become very special to me."

"Well, Mara, it seems that my son has inherited some of my better traits. He too, knows how to pick a good-looking woman to be his friend. I am glad to meet you, Niyan. I shall look forward to getting to know you better."

"The pleasure shall be all mine, Your Majesty. If you are anything like your son, my pleasure will be double."

"Homecoming is always pleasant, but you have made this event even more enjoyable. Nabonidus, she is not only beautiful, but also wise. Better look out, those kind of women make the best wives."

Nabonidus again blushed, but said under his breath, "I sure hope so."

Nebuk turned his attention to Mara and asked, "How soon before the next little prince will be born?"

"Now that you are here, he can come at anytime. We were just waiting for his conquering father to be in attendance at the birth of the next king." Mara's laughter filled Nebuk's heart with peace and joy and confidence in the future.

They didn't have long to wait, for their youngest son put in his appearance in less than two weeks after Nebuchadnezzar's return. He was a feisty and strong baby boy, just as predicted by the high priest, Belardos. They decided to name him after the god Bel and called him Awil Merodach, another way of spelling the name Marduk. This additional tribute to the god Bel brought great joy to the high priest. Nebuchadnezzar had, indeed, kept his promise to honor Bel.

Nebuchadnezzar could now command whatever he wished, not just because he was the king, but because he had stirred the hearts of the right people and more especially, most of the people. His popularity and sense of destiny filled the population of the entire realm with expectancy and pride. The Pride of Babylon was their king, king of the entire world, Nebuchadnezzar.

CHAPTER 13

With the wars over, the routine of running an empire settled into predictable patterns, and Nebuk was able to devote a great deal of his time to the building of Babylon. He was excited about his overall plans and began the groundwork necessary to get construction started.

There was a myriad of things to be done before the government could actually be transferred from Ur to Babylon. Buildings had to be readied to receive the officials who operated the government. Then too, walls had to be built to protect the new buildings.

Soon King Nebuchadnezzar was spending almost all of his time involved in the building business. Unfolding his plans to the royal architects thrilled them that their new king had such an interest and understanding of architecture. They were amazed by the detailed plans of the construction flow he had developed.

Plans for the government offices, the palaces, and the temples were surpassed only by the scope of the plans for the walls and the river. The city walls were to be magnificent, higher than any other city, seventy feet wide, enabling chariots to be driven side by side for the entire eleven-mile encirclement. The main entrance to the city was planned through massive bronze doors forming the Ishtar Gate, to celebrate Ishtar, the consort of the city-god Bel Marduk. The gate would be surrounded with blue glazed brick and large sculpted lions. Through it, all the ceremonial parades would be brought down a broad boulevard, called the processional way, past the yet-to-be built palace into the heart of the city with its Temple of Bel and the new future ziggurat.

The plans called for the city to be built over the river on multiple bridges, giving the effect of being one gigantic bridge, providing the riverfront areas for the loading docks and commerce centers of the city. With so many innovations, the architects marveled at the vision of the king. This was to be no ordinary building program; it was to going to be the most magnificent city in the known world. Nebuchadnezzar was eager to establish his personal reign from Babylon. Consequently, the first order of business in the building program was the conversion of some of the existing buildings into temporary quarters for his family and for his court. As the renovations neared completion, Nebuk, Mara, Aia and the new baby, Awil Merodach left for Babylon.

Nabonidus remained in the palace at Ur to be his father's chief liaison with the government there. He was most happy to do so, primarily because of Niyan, and he was not interested in pursuing the throne of his father. His interest continued to be in the culture of the empire, the nobility, the middle class, and even the slaves. Nabonidus, true to his scholarly nature, found more pleasure investigating history and learning why things happened the way they do than in making them happen.

When Nebuk and his family arrived in Babylon, they were greeted with the most elaborate celebration that the city had ever known. The people had always viewed Nebuchadnezzar with great warmth and affection, and this reception proved it.

Belardos and the priests of Bel Marduk were overjoyed; Babylon was becoming the great city that Nebuchadnezzar had promised. Belardos welcomed the royal family and entertained them in his home while finishing touches were completed on the king's temporary palace. For Nebuk it was like his second home. Mara felt somewhat an outsider and rather uncomfortable, but Belardos's obvious affection for her husband saw her through the rough times.

In getting better acquainted with Belardos, Mara found out she had a great deal in common with him, and he freely shared with her his spiritual experiences. His knowledge of spirit-activity helped Mara understand how she often knew things in advance of their happening. The more time they spent together, the greater their affinity for each other; and they became close friends.

Shortly after his arrival in Babylon, the king called for an inspection of the prisoners whom he had brought to Babylon from his wars in Carchemish, Hamath and Judah. Much training had been given many of the slaves to prepare them for their service. The king was especially eager to know about the young Judean princes. He was concerned how they had made the adjustment to Babylonian life and if they were ready to undertake rigorous training in the Chaldean wisdom.

When the Judean prisoners came before the king for review, he saw that many of the young men had suffered physically. Their being made eunuchs, their exile, and probably the strange diet, had taken a toll on them. Several were depressed and were suffering extreme melancholia. If something weren't done to help, his prime specimens would die before they could ever become useful to him. He had to do something dramatic to alter the direction things were going.

His hope had been to train several of his slaves, especially the Judeans into becoming loyal Babylonians, as Belakah had become, and use them in his ambassadorial staff to deal with the countries surrounding the empire. He wanted to prove to the world what a beneficent ruler he was.

Nebuk made a very quick inspection of the men and read the reports that his Master of Eunuchs, Aspenaz, had written on each man. The reports verified the choices the king had made in Jerusalem. The fifteen young princes obviously possessed the high qualifications he had expected.

"Ashpenaz, I want you to give these eunuchs the best of food and wine that the palace can provide. I want them to be given exercise, treated with respect and given every comfort. If we don't, they are going to die and all my efforts wasted."

The king spoke to the captives, "Three years of training will be provided for you, covering all the fields of Chaldean learning. The very best of you will be chosen to serve the empire at my pleasure." The king spelled out to them that their future was entirely in their own hands. "If you do not apply yourselves, Ashpenaz has the right to send you out to the labor gangs where you can choose to die, if you wish. It is of no matter to me. I can get as many slaves from your hometowns as I need. You have been chosen, but it is up to you to succeed."

The building of Babylon progressed at tremendous speed and so did the passing of the years. The people caught the vision of making the city into a magnificent capital. The cheers of excitement that greeted each new project were very pleasurable to the king. The people enjoyed the economic security that the building projects afforded them. Food was plentiful and there was plenty of work for all. The great city of Nebuk's dreams was taking shape in brick and stone.

Most of the slaves Nebuchadnezzar brought to Babylon were integrated into the life of the empire with little problem and they provided valuable help in the building. A number of them had been chosen because they had been involved in the architectural field before their captivity. They gave tremendous help with some of the engineering and stone-cutting feats that the massive buildings required. The king's life revolved around his increasingly obsessive desire for the city to be the fullest expression of his great plans. He was excited as each new project was started and completed.

Nebuk had been searching for new developments in construction and building materials. He conducted contests among the engineers and architects to develop these new methods. The most successful of these contests resulted in stronger bricks with colored glazing that made his projects visually spectacular. The use of bitumen in cementing stones together enabled new design capabilities, further enhancing the beauty of the developing city.

When the three-year training program was completed for the fifteen young Judeans and they were presented before the king he was surprised that some of them still looked like they were not well. The best of food and care had not been enough to keep them flourishing. However, four of the young princes looked like they had just finished training for athletic competition. They were vigorous and healthy looking and very alert. The king paid special attention to these young men as they were questioned, noticing even their attitudes were much better than the others. All of the young men seemed to be intelligent enough, but they were not infused with life as were these four.

Dismissing the princes, Nebuchadnezzar called Ashpenaz to him. "Why are these four men so much better than all the others? They seem to be almost of a different nationality. What's the difference?"

"Your Majesty", Ashpenaz replied nervously, "I have examined these four young men very closely and they refused to eat the food provided for them. They ate only vegetables and the simplest of foods. They believe the fancier food you ordered for them would cause them to sin against their god. I don't understand it, but I gave them a ten-day test concerning the food and they were better and stronger than all the rest and so I allowed them to continue on the diet they preferred."

"You mean, the only difference is in what they ate and that has made them so much better physically than the rest?"

"I think it mainly has to do with their devotion to their god. They pray regularly, quote their scriptures to each other and they don't get angry, curse or complain. It is very strange to me, but I find I like these four young men better than all the rest. They are the best students; they learn quicker. They are the most concerned to excel in whatever I order them to do."

"Thank you, Ashpenaz. Please send in the four young men. I must question them further. By the way, what are their names?"

"Majesty, I have given them Babylonian names that I hope will please you. Their names are Belteshazzar, Shadrach, Meshach and Abed-Nego. Their Judean names were Daniel, Hananiah, Mishael and Azariah."

"Are these the same four men I was so impressed with when I brought them from Jerusalem?"

"Yes, Majesty, the very same."

"Bring them in. I must talk with them immediately."

The four young princes were ushered in to the king again and he began to question them about their appearance, their attitude and their development in the Chaldean wisdom. As Nebuk asked the questions, he was intrigued by the quiet and peaceful way in which they conducted themselves. They had to have been nervous about the audience with him, but they very steadily answered him, remaining calm and controlled.

"Why do you insist upon eating only vegetables?"

Belteshazzar, who, though not the oldest, seemed to be the leader of the group, spoke up. "Your Majesty, it was not our desire to offend you in our choice of food, but we determined that to be faithful to the Lord our God, we would abstain from strong drink and fancy foods. We chose rather the simple diet that seemed best to our bodies. We hope we did not offend you in our refusal."

"No, no. That is of no consequence. It obviously suits you well and my purpose is for you to be of great service to the Babylonian Empire. Being physically fit and healthy is essential. Tell me how you survived being made eunuchs?"

Again, Belteshazzar answered. "That was very difficult for us, Your Majesty. Our God has told us to be fruitful and multiply and to lose that capacity was a great sorrow for us. We could have become very angry and, indeed, some of us did. However, our God has given us peace concerning this loss. Your Majesty, a man is not a man because of the presence or loss of genitals. A man is a man because of what he is on the inside."

"I am impressed with your answer, however, aren't you angry at me for taking you captive and ordering your castration?"

Abed-Nego spoke up. "With all due respect, Your Majesty, it was our God who delivered the nation of Judah into your hand and caused us to become your servants. We accept this as the will of God for our lives. We will endeavor to honor and serve you to the best of our ability." The other men all nodded in agreement with Abed-Nego's words.

"Hmmmmm." The answer caused the king to hesitate in

pursuing the questions. Pausing briefly he continued. "Tell me more about your rite of circumcision. That is evidently a custom among your people."

Shadrach broke his silence and said softly to the king. "It was our father, Abraham, your distant relative, who left Ur of the Chaldees and traveled to the land of Canaan and there received the order from the Lord God to cut off the foreskin of every male born in the family as a sign of covenant with Him. We are all circumcised in accordance with this word of our God. Even some of our people who do not worship and live for the Lord God practice it because most of the laws of God have good healthful reasons behind them, as well as the conforming to God's words."

"You keep talking about your god as if he were alive and he was a personal friend of yours."

"With all due respect, Your Majesty," Meshach spoke up, "You are right on both things you mentioned. He is alive and He has become our best friend. The Lord God of Israel is the true and living God. We are here to honor Him and serve Him because He has placed us in your hand. Whatever you bid us do, in reality, is the service that we have for Him."

"Do you all feel this way?"

"We certainly do, Your Majesty, We are here to serve you because we serve the Lord God. I can't speak for all the others, but the four of us have committed ourselves to serving God while we are here and our service is to do your bidding as long as that does not stop us from following our God."

Shadrach's bold words to the King caused him to lean forward on his throne. "You mean that if I ordered you to serve the god Bel Marduk you would or would not do so?"

The young men did not answer immediately, finally Belteshazzar answered. "We hope that will never become an issue between us. Our desire is to serve you, oh great king. However, we are ordered to worship the Lord our God and Him only. We will serve no other gods. Please, Your Majesty, understand we are not being rebellious; we are here to honor and serve you; our God has ordered us to serve you personally. It is our hope that we will sufficiently prove our loyalty is to you, and to our God."

"You are certainly fortunate that I am a very understanding person. I hope you realize I could have your lives for such bold statements. However, I am sure you meant no offense and I am eager to see the results of our having you in our service. I will be extending your assignments to you very shortly. You will be in the direct service here in the palace. See to it that I do not have cause to be disappointed in you."

The king was pleased with the interviews and set about planning how he could best use the young men. Even more than their usefulness, he was intrigued by their devotion to their God. They served a god that could not be seen, but obviously was felt by them, felt to be very real and very present. "I wonder if their God is able to tell the future, as is Marduk? I wonder if dreams can also be interpreted by these followers of the God with no name and no idol?"

When the assignments were distributed, the four young Judean princes plunged into their work with a vigor and enthusiasm that surprised even Ashpenaz. They were eager for productive work. They seemed to thrive on putting in long hours and their work was judged to be excellent. The king was pleased with each report of the fine job "his men" were doing. He prided himself on having picked out the best for his staff.

CHAPTER 14

Nebuchadnezzar was pleased; things were going his way; the construction in the city was progressing nicely, but of course, he wished it were faster. The pride of the people in the development of the city was encouraging. The economy of the state was good. Every able-bodied person could find work in the construction. The many slaves seemed content with their provisions. Food was plentiful and available to all thanks to the extensive system of irrigation canals that brought water to the fertile fields. The people of Babylon were happy.

His family was growing. Awil Merodach was now six years old. Aia and her husband, Idib, had just produced his first granddaughter and Nabonidus and Niyan, still living in Ur, were happily married and expecting their first child. Mara, under Belardos's teaching was learning much about the spirit side of the worship of Bel Marduk and the many other gods of Babylonia.

Mara and Belardos were returning from an expedition to the ancient ruins of the original Tower of Babel from which the empire derived its name and the name of their god, Bel Marduk. As their carriage was nearing the city, Belardos was explaining to Mara some of the unusual symbolism they had seen at the ruins. He coughed several times, dropped his head on his chest and fell over on Mara's shoulder, and died instantly of a heart seizure. Mara was devastated and his unexpected death disrupted the peace and tranquility of the city of Babylon.

The royal family, because of their close ties with the High Priest, felt his death very deeply. As the word of Belardos's death reached the priests of Babylon, chaos broke out. The political maneuvering and infighting, which had always taken place regarding who would be the next high priest, now became an epidemic.

Mara, upset over losing her friend and mentor so dramatically, reacted bitterly to the attitudes of the priests. When she spoke, anger spilled out. "They can't even wait until his body is cold and they are already picking the bones like the vultures they are." Everyone stayed clear of the queen. They had never experienced the sharpness of her tongue before.

Belardos's death changed the overall religious atmosphere of the capital radically. The quiet calm that Belardos had engendered gave way to uneasiness. The priests, who should have been helping the people to achieve a sense of well being and continuity, merely upset them. The widespread differences in the approach to worshipping Bel and the other gods left the people feeling confused and leaderless.

Not only was there the struggle for power among their priests, but also between their gods. The people were never sure they were worshipping the right gods at the right times. Who do we listen to? Who do we believe? With Belardos there had been no doubt that his loyalty was to Bel Marduk. Some, however, felt Bel should be subordinated to Inanna, who was the chief ancient goddess, and Astarte was her second. The chaotic atmosphere reigned even in the funeral service as the body of the high priest was placed in the ground with the conflicting messages that were being given.

As if the unrest in Babylon wasn't enough, a messenger from General Nebuzaradan in Jerusalem warned Nebuchadnezzar of more discord in the Judean capitol. Jehoiakim, the King of Judah, was not pleased that the Babylonian presence in the country had not been lessened in the ensuing six years. He was acting offended, saying since the original take over from the Egyptians, he was not allowed to really rule his own country even though he had been left on the throne. It seemed Jehoiakim had forgotten to be grateful he was alive to be a small part of a much larger empire. Nebuzaradan was recalled to Babylon to help Nebuchadnezzar assess what needed to be done to take care of the growing rebellious attitude.

"I guess this is what being king is really all about," Nebuk commented to his wife. "I should have known things were going too good to last. Now we will be kept busy with both religious and military politics. There is so much that I'd rather do than dealing with all these little skirmishes. My hope was that political intrigue ended when my sister and her husband were banished."

"My dear husband, you certainly didn't become King of the Babylonian Empire by being so naive. Surely you realize your sister and her husband are only just a few of the people who would love to replace you on the throne. You know, any position of authority draws people who want to be in that position themselves or have someone whom they can control. It's part of the job." She laughed, "I think it was written into your coronation.

"Oh, really, I don't remember that part."

"I have an idea; if you don't like being king, we can always retire to the mountains of the north where my people came from. There you can just be plain ordinary Mr. Nezzar."

Nebuk joined her in laughter. "However, the idea of just being a plain citizen is completely out of the realm of possibility. I must see to this realm. It's my joy, my goal, my vision . . . my nightmare."

"Yes, my dear husband, all yours"

"I suppose you are right about people being what they are, Mara. I do realize there is more to ruling the greatest empire on the face of the earth than just building the great city of my dreams. In the meantime, Mrs. Nezzar, speaking of ordinary people, I forgot to tell you that I got a report on Belana and Youini."

"Oh, really, I was wondering about them just the other day."

"They have made it in the desert. They have established a small business on the caravan route to Tabo and apparently they are keeping soul and body together."

Mara mischievously grinned, "And probably charging a fortune for a drink of water."

"I never thought they would be able to survive. It must have been a real struggle having to forgive each other as well as learning to do hard work. I'm glad I didn't put them to death."

"I am, too, Nebuk. I believe they fell into the same trap that destroyed your father. If he hadn't been so consumed with his hatred of you, they might not have been so eager to poison him."

Nebuk sighed, "They were just part of that whole situation which I'm glad is over."

"So am I. Perhaps the hardship of the desert will give them a new appreciation for life—their own, if not ours."

"Yes, and I am sure Prince Ananni will be a better person without his parents' influence. Nabonidus told me recently, when I was in Ur, that he thinks there has been a change in Ananni's attitude. You know, Ananni, just like our Nabonidus, never really had politics in him. He and Nabonidus have been working rather closely together; in fact, they have become friends. Ananni and his wife have been to Nabonidus's house numerous times. Did you know, Prince Belo-phane has disappeared?"

Mara looked surprised. "No, I didn't".

"So has his sister Princess Oonda. We assume that they have gone to join their parents in the desert. We are watching to see if they show up out there."

"I thought that they were forbidden to be with their parents?"

"That's true, but I'm sure Belo-phane was so disappointed that he will never become king, he couldn't stand to stay here. Hopefully, he will be of much less trouble out in the desert than at Ur. I can still see him resting his hand on the throne at my father's funeral. He could hardly wait to sit on it."

"Well, at least those problems are over, and you, my dear husband, King Nebuchadnezzar, have much more to do than sit here chatting with your wife. She, of course, loves to have you do so, but I know you must get busy."

"All right, slave driver."

"By the way, you do know, don't you, that you will have to send troops back with Nebuzaradan to get those Judeans back in harness."

"I suppose you're right, Mara. You seem to have taken up where our dear friend, Belardos, left off. That's good; I shall welcome any spirit guiding you can give me."

"I shall do whatever I can. But do not make decisions entirely on what I say or think. Please rule as you see fit. I am your queen, but I am not the ruler of this empire. It's your job, sweet husband . . . all yours."

As soon as Nebuzaradan arrived from Jerusalem, it became obvious that Mara was right in her assessment of the situation; the king would have to gather a large army to march to Jerusalem and quash any rebellion. Nebuzaradan was sure his being recalled to Babylon was the pretext the King of Judah would use to consolidate his power with the people and be able to urge them to support him in his attempt to take Judah back from the Babylonians. There had also been some intercepted secret messages sent to Egypt to try to enlist help from them.

Nebuzaradan did not arrive in Babylon alone, but with his wife, a beautiful Judean princess and his son, Aaron. Nebuzaradan presented Ruth to Nebuk and Mara. She was rather dainty and fit perfectly with her husband's short stature. Her shiny, long brown hair, deep blue eyes and infectious smile, merited approving glances when she and Aaron made their court appearance. Aaron a typical, mischievous two-year-old made himself at home in the throne room. His curly blond hair and laughing blue eyes were an oddity in a nation of dark hair and eyes.

Nebuchadnezzar and Mara were delighted with his family, but were surprised he had not told them of the marriage. When questioned, Nebuzaradan answered hesitantly. "I was afraid I might not be allowed to stay as the military overseer if it were known I had married a woman of Judah. I felt it might have been considered a conflict of interest."

"Zaradan, I know of your loyalty to me and this empire. I know you would do nothing to compromise your position. You've probably been harder on the people and yourself than you would need to be. But I can understand your position."

"Your Majesty, you are very wise. That is one of the reasons I feel the rebellious attitude is festering. I probably have been too hard on them."

"It is doubtful, but go on."

"Perhaps another person could work better with Jehoiakim. If you wish to replace me, Ruth and I will remain here with Aaron and stay out of the picture."

"Nonsense. Since you have told me all this, you are the only one who I would send back. Send Ruth's family here as soon as you get back to Jerusalem. They will be honored citizens and we will find positions for them to enjoy while they 'vacation' in Babylon. However, we shall need many more laborers to complete our work here at Babylon, so you need to be bringing as many more slaves as you can when you come."

"Thank you, your Majesty. Both Ruth and I appreciate your kindness to us and to her family. There are a number of artisans in her family who I think could be useful in the work here. Under your touch, this city has become a marvel. The walls are magnificent. This city, my king, is a fitting monument to your greatness.

"Thank you. It is coming along very well."

"Perhaps more slaves could make the building speed up even more. I'll bring the best I can find."

"When the rebellion is over, I shall expect you to bring the upper-class people back with you. Bring all the royal families and especially King Jehoiakim's wife and children. We'll decide what to do with him when the time comes, depending upon how serious his rebellion really is."

"Now, I have one further question for you, Zaradan. Did you know what the sex of your baby was going to be before he was born or did you have to wait until he arrived?

Nebuzaradan laughed, remembering the conversation that he and the king had many years earlier before Prince Awil Merodach was born. "Your Majesty, a very strange thing happened. Ruth's great uncle is a prophet in the land of Judah. He was the one who encouraged the people to surrender to you when we first arrived there. Do you remember that?"

"Oh, yes. That was unusual. What did he tell you?"

"He told us we would have a son. He also told us the conflict between the pagan beliefs of Babylon and the True God of Israel would be reflected in the way our son would develop, but that he would be a good man of God eventually."

"These religious things make me nervous, Zaradan, and here you are adding to the mystery of spirituality by having a son as predicted by a Judean prophet. By the way what was the prophet's name? I may want to talk with him when I come to Jerusalem—after you get the mess straightened out."

"His name is Jeremiah."

"Oh, yes, I seem to remember that name. I certainly wish someone would tell me where the power comes from that these different religions claim to have. I see the advocates of Bel do wonderful things and then I hear that prophets of the Judean God also do wonders. Someday when I have the time, I will find out what religion is all about. Until then, I shall continue to use these superstitions of the people to make them obey and work for me."

CHAPTER 15

If only Belardos hadn't died, this whole religious mess would not be complicating our lives, Nebuchadnezzar' thought. He was upset and angered by all the confusion that the replacement of Belardos was causing. In addition, the three main contenders for the position of high priest were all men whom he felt were definitely lacking in insight and wisdom to handle the job. Because of the very close relationship he had with Belardos, he was aware that any replacement was apt to be inferior in his eyes.

All of these men were confident that they could win the king's endorsement and were constantly pestering the king to attend various functions. He was invited to dinners, meetings and teas. He was expected to demonstrate his concern over who might be chosen the next high priest. In reality Nebuk didn't care who he was, as long as he could control him. There could be no interference with the plans he and Belardos had already worked out. Nebuk let it be known that he would await the council's decision.

Finally a priest was chosen by the High and Exalted Council of Bel Marduk. He was a small, hawk-nosed, unpleasant man with bad breath. When Nebuchadnezzar had to spend time with priest Zroybel, he always wished he were somewhere else. He consistently violated the king's airspace by thrusting his face directly in front of the king, bad breath and all. Now this unpleasant one was the High Priest of Bel. He was as much disliked, by the king, as Belardos was loved.

Zroybel, like a small yappy dog, was always ordering subordinates around to demonstrate his power and ability. In spite of being most obnoxious, he had, by his manipulations, achieved the powerful position of High Priest of Bel. He had forced the king to reckon with him.

Zroybel's ascension soon created serious problems. The subordinate priests, who had served Belardos so well, were being pushed out of their positions of responsibility. Nebuchadnezzar was especially concerned this religious turmoil was happening just as the problems with Judah were surfacing.

Nebuchadnezzar, after sending Nebuzaradan back to Jerusalem with a large contingent of soldiers, called all the priests to a meeting with him in an attempt to stop the priestly squabbling. This meeting with the priests was held just before the dedication of the king's recently completed residence. Some of the newly empowered priests were complaining that the king's palace should have been built after the Temple of Bel. Nebuk's intention for the meeting was to bring calm to the religious struggle, but the entire meeting was dominated by the angry words rival factions were throwing at each other.

Finally, realizing that reason would never work with these people, Nebuchadnezzar tapped his scepter on the floor to get their attention. "As you all know, the temple I have planned for the glorification of Bel is an enormous and wonderful undertaking. You've all seen the plans. I've devoted much time and effort to the accomplishment of this great project. If this quarrelling is not stopped immediately, I shall order the work on the Temple of Bel to be stopped completely. Then I shall change the order to build the temples of Innana and Astarte before any work is done on the new Ziggurat."

There was a corporate gasp and the king continued, "I am demanding absolute quiet coming from the Bel Priesthood, or I shall change my promise to my dear departed friend, Belardos, and force the glorification of Bel to come to a stop. It is totally up to you. Do as you wish, but remember, I rule this realm you do not. I will do what I want to do. You may be sure that if my wishes are not heeded, Bel will be only a minor god on the roster of our gods. It makes no difference to me."

Nebuchadnezzar's words stopped the wrangling, which was quickly replaced by a smoldering anger and threats to make the king very sorry if he did that.

True to his words, the work on the Temple of Bel and the ziggurat was slowed and accelerated many times during the years that followed, reflecting the temperature of their relationship. The conflict between the king and the priesthood was never fully resolved during the years Zroybel served as High Priest.

Adding to this uncomfortable situation, Nebuchadnezzar began having many bad dreams. Some of the old dreams recurred and new, frightening ones were added that left him sleepless and distraught. The strain began to show in his face and Mara worried about his condition. Even the ministrations of Belakah failed to bring lasting relief.

The opening of the new palace brought a measure of triumph to the king. It was magnificent with high parapet towers, a fitting tribute to the king and his architectural vision. Beautiful mosaics, colorful brick walls and impressive bronze gates made the palace a wonder to behold. The tapestries and hangings of brilliant colors, the finest that could be found, festooned the halls and great rooms.

The palace was located on the northwest side of the magnificent Processional Way. It was like the emblem on the king's scepter, the focal point of power, imposing the might of Babylon on all who entered the city through the main Ishtar gates.

The royal family moved into their new home with great pomp and ceremony. The general public, as well as royal dignitaries from around the world, toured the great structure and visited the home of their monarch.

The very first night in the palace was not a peaceful experience for the king. Not only was he exhausted from greeting the thousands of people who had paraded through the gorgeous new throne room, he was fighting off a severe cold. And to top it off, Zroybel had not even bothered to attend.

After his massage, sleep still would not come for the king. He got up, surprising his guards by walking the halls of his new home.

Stepping out onto the portico of the family wing, the fresh air and warm spring breezes began to quiet his mind. He walked down the wide stone steps to the grassy compound, sprawled on the ground, removed his sandals, his bare feet touching the grass and digging his fingers into the ground. The feel of the earth further calmed his nerves and soon he was drowsy and able to return to his bed. Almost immediately Nebuchadnezzar was asleep, only to dream.

It was a dream that had no meaning to him but nevertheless caused him to be upset. In his dream he felt himself fighting with beasts and evil powers. It seemed as though they were trying to keep him from understanding what the dream was all about. Upon awaking, he had no recollection of the dream, only a gnawing sense of its importance. He had no facility to understand why the evil powers didn't want him to know the meaning.

Nebuk was so preoccupied, straining to remember the dream, he wasn't functioning well. "I can't seem to make a decision. I don't seem to be able to put words together and my thoughts are all jumbled and off the subject. All I can think about is that dream. What was it?"

Mara, always sensitive to when Nebuk was troubled, asked him and he told her what was happening. She suggested, "Why don't you call Zroybel's wisemen to tell you your dream and what it means. It will give them something to do that might be helpful instead of spending all their time criticizing everything you do." The bitter edge toward the priesthood was still there.

Quickly calling in a scribe, the king sent messages to the heads of all the wisemen, astrologers, soothsayers and seers to send representatives of their craft to gather in the palace the next morning. They were told only that the king needed their services, that it was urgent and to be there.

As Belakah was giving him his massage, the king told him of the dream. Belakah, using his typical blind faith in Bel, assured the king that the priests of Bel would be able to tell him what he wanted to know. They had in the past; they would again.

Belakah's confidence and the massage had a calming effect on the king and he slept better that night, grateful again for having met Belakah.

At the appointed hour about twenty-five of the wisemen/seers were gathered in the magnificent throne room. Hangings, stitched in the finest needlepoint, depicting Nebuchadnezzar's war victories adorned the walls. His family symbols were painted into the plastered walls. A royal purple Persian rug extended the full length of the room to the raised throne. Nebuk urged them to come closer.

The high priest didn't seem able to look the king in the face since his recent snub of the palace opening and was trying to hide in the back of the room. Nebuchadnezzar was not disturbed; that way he didn't have to have Zroybel in his face as usual.

"Gentlemen, I have had a very disturbing dream. I need your help with this dilemma. Please tell me what my dream was about."

"We shall be most happy, Your Majesty, to do all we can." The high priest was gracious in his answer to the king. He realized that the king was asking them for help, which gave them, however slight, a greater degree of influence over the king than they had recently had. "Please tell us the details of your dream and we shall quickly give you the interpretation."

"That is the problem. I do not know the details; I can't even remember the general idea of the dream."

"Well, Your Majesty," a priest standing near the front of the group volunteered, "perhaps it is nothing that should be allowed to bother you, for if it has escaped your royal mind, it is probably not worthy of Your Majesty's second thoughts." This comment from one of the most knowledgeable seers brought smiles to the faces of almost everyone in the room, especially Zroybel, who enjoyed anything that made the king look less than regal.

The high priest, relishing the king's seemingly awkward position, continued in a condescending tone. "Think, Your Majesty, perhaps the thoughts will come to you. We shall meditate while you think." At a hand signal from the priest, all the men knelt down and began to mutter their prayers.

Nebuchadnezzar was irate. What did this jackass think he'd been doing? He held his composure, however, and in a few minutes the high priest asked him if anything was coming to him. "Oh, yes! It's coming to me, that you are not the great spiritual people you parade yourselves to be." The fire was in his eyes and tongue. "You can make up some fancy interpretation to cover when you need to, but when it comes to really knowing the truth, you know nothing. I am sure the last great man of Bel was Belardos and the rest of you are just fakers."

"No, no, Your Majesty," one of the priests responded. "We just need to know some of the details of your dream so we can then follow the trail to the true dream and the meaning."

"I don't believe you can tell me what my dream was unless I tell it to you first. That sounds like you all are less than what you claim to be. Seers, astrologers, magicians and 'wisemen.' Phonies, all of you." The king's voice echoed down the halls of the palace. Many of the servants, aware of the repercussions when the king was on the rampage were ready to make themselves scarce. It was going to be a rough time to try to serve him.

Zroybel spoke up, "Your Majesty, there has never been a time when we were able to tell the dream without the events being given to us. Even our highly respected Belardos, your friend, told you what your dreams meant after you told them to him."

"That may be so, Zroybel, but there were many things that Belardos told me, things that were coming before they transpired. He knew things in advance." Then pointing directly at the high priest, who had worked his way forward during the exchange, "I expect you, as his successor, with all this high-powered help you have here, should be able to tell me a simple dream."

"But, Majesty, we can only do what we have been trained to do. No one is able to first tell you the dream and then tell you the meaning of it. Perhaps the comment was right. It is nothing you need to be concerned about."

Nebuchadnezzar exploded, "Listen to me, and listen well. I have lost sleep over this dream and I know within me, it is a very important thing. I certainly would not have called you to this emergency meeting if I did not feel very strongly about it." Pausing to let the importance of his words settle in, and also to control his emotions, he continued, "You have two days in which to discover my dream from whatever sources you can find and then to tell me the interpretation. If you do not, all the wisemen and magicians, astrologers and seers of every persuasion, will be put to death. If you cannot give a simple dream and its interpretation, it is obvious you and your religion are false. I don't care what you teach to others, but you must give me the truth and if you can't . . . you're dead. This audience is over."

They were totally undone, the most frightened group of seers in the history of Babylon. What the king had asked for had never been heard of before. They were panic stricken. The men rushed to their books, charms and incantations. Their families were devastated. None could sleep. But the king slept very peacefully the next two nights.

When the two days were completed, Nebuk called the group back before him. They came very soberly and fearfully into the throne room. The high priest had appointed a spokesman who haltingly addressed the king. "Your Majesty, please tell us that you have remembered the dream, and you are ready for us to interpret it."

"You scoundrels, if I knew the dream, I would not tell you just to expose you as fakes. Do any of you have anything to say to me?"

"Yes, Your Majesty. Please give us more time. We will find an answer. I am sure." the spokesman continued.

One of Zroybel's assistants, spoke up, "Your Majesty, perhaps your dream was of a beautiful young girl and she turned your thoughts away from the lovely and good Queen Mara, and you were so embarrassed that you could even think such a thing and consequently it has left your mind?"

"A very unworthy try. Any drunk on the street could have

come up with such a story. For your efforts, you shall be the first one beheaded." The king motioned to Arioch, the captain of the palace guard. "Take them all to prison and begin rounding up all the rest of the so-called seers and put them in the hold as well. We shall have a public exposure of these idiots."

Having given the orders, the king left the throne room and returned to his chambers, the anguished, objecting voices of the "wisemen" ringing in his ears. One of the voices could be heard berating Zroybel, for causing the problem by snubbing the palace dedication.

The roundup began immediately with great numbers of the wise men being put into prison without even knowing why. Belteshazzar, the eunuch of Jerusalem, was on his way home when he was stopped and heard the reason for the arrests. He asked the guard who had come for him and Shadrach, Meshach and Abed-Nego, to take him directly to the king. The guard, well aware of the respect the king had for the four men, brought him to Arioch who took Belteshazzar in to the king.

Nebuchadnezzar, already upset by the "wisemen" and the dream, was further annoyed that a slave was being brought in to him. What possible thing could a Judean slave have to tell him concerning the matter of his dream? "Well, Belteshazzar, do you have information to tell me concerning my dream?"

"Your Majesty, there is a God in heaven who knows all the events and thoughts of a man whether great or small. My cousins and I will pray and we shall bring you the information that you seek. For the Lord our God is able to give you the thoughts that have escaped your mind. He is a God of loving compassion and does not want you to be without the information you seek. Only give us one day to pray and ask of our God. Please do not kill the wisemen before we have brought you what you seek."

"What makes you think that you can succeed where all the others have failed? Is your God greater than Bel Marduk?"

"Yes, Sire."

The audacity with which Belteshazzar spoke startled the king.

"Very well, be back here tomorrow by this hour with the answer or you will join the others on their way to death."

Belteshazzar returned to the house he shared with his three cousins, telling them "I have promised the king that God is able to give us the dream and the interpretation. We must pray and ask God to reveal what we need to know. We will be killed as well if we don't come up with the answer. However, I know that God is well able, so let's not waste our time in doubt but get busy asking God to give us the secret."

The men prayed individually for a while, and then they met to pray together. Finally Belteshazzar said, "We need to get a good night's rest, for we need to be able to hear from our god. Perhaps he will speak to us in a dream, as I am sure he did to Nebuchadnezzar. I believe this is the very reason why we were brought to Babylon to demonstrate the greatness of our God over these idols made of wood and stone."

During the night, as expected, God revealed the dream to Belteshazzar. He awoke thanking God and praising him in the Hebrew tongue. After the morning light broke, Belteshazzar shared the vision God had given him with Shadrach, Meshach and Abed-Nego. They were overjoyed and spent the time in thanking and worshipping God.

Belteshazzar sent a message to Arioch, the captain of the Palace Guard informing him that he was ready to see the king and would wait for his summons. Within minutes, Arioch himself was at his door to escort him to the king. "Are you sure, Belteshazzar, that you have the answer the king is looking for?"

"Yes, Arioch, I am very sure my God has given me the dream and the interpretation and the king will be comforted with the message he receives."

"I certainly hope you are right. He has been most troubled and when he has one of his moods, the whole empire is in trouble with him. Can you imagine what would have happened if all the wisemen and seers had been put to death and Bel Marduk deposed as the god of Babylon? It would tear the empire apart. I know that you do not believe in Bel and neither do I, but the empire's belief system is built around what their gods have done for the people."

Belteshazzar was ushered into the king's finely appointed private office, its massive wooden furniture with hand-tooled leather trimming shouted power and authority. The king was already there, pacing the floor. "Belteshazzar, are you able to tell me the dream and the interpretation?"

"The secret you have wanted to know, which none of your astrologers, magicians and seers could tell you, is very easy for the Lord. Your Majesty, there is a God in heaven who is able to reveal secrets and He is now going to make known to you what your dream was. Your dream was about the latter days and the future of the Babylonian Empire and the rest of the world.

"When you were sleeping in your bed, you had thoughts come into your mind about what would come to pass after your empire was gone. This was presented to you in a secret. This secret was for you to know. It was a means for the God of heaven to reveal Himself to you. He wants you to know Him. This secret is not for me or anyone else's profit, but it was given to me for you.

"While you were watching the scene before you, a great image, huge and magnificent stood before you. It was amazing and slightly frightening to behold."

The king sat down on his chair, leaning forward, his chin in hand and his elbow propped on his knee, listening with growing anticipation.

"The head of the image was of pure gold, and its chest and arms were of silver. Its stomach, loins and thighs were of bronze. It had legs of iron, and its feet were both iron and clay together."

"Yes! Yes, that's what I was seeing. Continue."

"As you were watching, a strange thing happened to the image. A large stone that had never been worked, like one of your building stones, struck the image on its feet and the whole thing, head to toe, broke into pieces. The iron, clay, bronze, silver and even the gold were pulverized and just like chaff in a summer breeze, they were blown away. The image was completely gone and the large stone that struck it, grew into a great mountain and filled the whole earth."

"You are absolutely right, Belteshazzar. That is exactly what I saw," the king said in an awestruck tone. "But what does it all mean?"

"Well, Your Majesty, you are a very great king. In fact, you are a king of kings. God has given you this kingdom with all its power and strength and glory for His purposes. You affect all the people of the earth; you are the ruler whom He has given to rule over both man and beast. You are the Head of Gold."

Upon hearing this, Mara, who had come into the king's office and had overheard all that Belteshazzar had been saying to the king, came and rested her hand on his shoulder and smiled approvingly at her husband. The years had not dimmed her beauty and her gentle quiet presence bolstered her husband who smiled gratefully at her.

Belteshazzar acknowledged her presence by a stately bow and continued the interpretation. "After you and your kingdom, another empire will arise which will be inferior to yours. Afterward another, the third, a kingdom of bronze will follow. These kingdoms will rule the whole earth. A fourth kingdom of iron, however divided into two legs, will be strong and brutal and will crush all existing kingdoms.

"When you saw the toes of clay and iron, you saw the strength and weakness of this kingdom and it will be strong and fragile at the same time. Clay and iron do not mix and when you add in the elements of many men or kings, it will be exceptionally weak.

"When these kings are on their thrones, God will set up a kingdom of his own. This kingdom will never be destroyed. It will never be up for inheritance or transfer. This kingdom of God will smash into pieces all the kingdoms that preceded it or that exist at the time. This stone or kingdom will grow bigger and bigger and will fill all the earth and it will stand forever. God will make this kingdom by his power. It is not the work of man.

"You, Oh Majesty, are the king at the beginning and God has

chosen you to know what will happen in the future. This dream is of God. It is sure and the interpretation is also sure."

King Nebuchadnezzar arose from the chair and bowed himself to the floor in front of Belteshazzar. When he lifted himself up he was barely able to speak. "Oh, Belteshazzar, what you have just told me is exactly the dream that I saw. Your God, whom you serve, is the God of Gods and the Lord of Kings. He is able to reveal secrets, secrets the gods of the other wisemen were not able to reveal."

The king sent Arioch, captain of the palace guards, to the prison. He released all the wisemen and seers that had been taken captive and brought them to the throne room. When they were all there, the King spoke to them humbly and in an even tone. "I have been given the dream and its interpretation by Belteshazzar." He briefly explained the dream and its meaning to the still trembling wisemen.

"Bring the gifts that were prepared for the revealer of secrets and interpreter of dreams." A necklace of gold, silver and precious stones was placed around the neck of Belteshazzar. Incense was ordered to be burned for him.

When these had been presented, King Nebuchadnezzar spoke again. "It is my will, my order, my command that Belteshazzar is no longer a slave, but a citizen of Babylon. In addition, he is to be the ruler over the whole province of Babylon. And even more, he is to be the chief administrator over all the wisemen of Babylon, including all you priests of Bel and that does mean High Priest Zroybel, as well. You see, the God of the Hebrews has been proven superior to all the gods of ours. There is a God who can give, tell and interpret dreams."

"Belteshazzar, what would you like to say?"

"Your gracious Majesty, I am grateful for the honor that you have bestowed on me this day. I am aware that the God of heaven, Who revealed these secrets to me, planned for me to be here to minister to you and to your empire, even to save these lives. It is my pleasure to serve you and I shall do so to the best of my ability.

"However, I would like to mention that my cousins were also deeply involved in praying and asking God to give us the answers to your dream. I desire that they also share in the reward. I would like them to assist me in doing the job you have given me. Also, I want to assure the other wisemen I mean them no harm. Please remember I was the one who prevented many of you from being executed yesterday. I will do my best to work with you to accomplish the greater glory of the empire."

The king applauded, "Wise words! Since you are in charge of the province of Babylon, you may appoint, with my complete approval, these young men to help you administer the province. I especially like the idea; it will allow you time to sit in the gate and administer justice to the people. It's obvious you have good judgement." With that the king dismissed everyone except Belteshazzar.

"You have proven to be the very best servant a king could have. I have to say something to you. I am very sorry I took your manhood away when I had you made a eunuch. It has bothered me very greatly. Can you forgive me for that?"

"Your Majesty, it has long been forgiven. You have not taken away my manhood, only my capacity to reproduce. I told you years ago, a man is not judged by the externals of his body, whether he is tall or short, thin or fat. A man is a man by what he is on the inside."

"I remember your words to me, but I am sorry for you, sorry that you can have no family. What can I do to make up to you for the loss?"

"Your Majesty, some things you can't restore, but one thing you can. I wish I could be called publicly by the name that was given to me and not by a name associated with Bel. My Hebrew name is Daniel, which means "God is my Judge." I would like to bear that name in the Babylonian Empire and not Belteshazzar.

"I will so decree. It shall be restored. If the dream and the interpretation are an accurate picture of the future, then I too, must believe that God is also my Judge. Daniel, my personal thanks to you and I shall be honored to have you as my loyal administrator. Babylon shall always be grateful for your services."

The relief over Daniel's interpretation of the king's dream was short-lived. It was bad enough Daniel was now the chief administrator of the province, but to be overseer of the wisemen of Babylon? To many, that meant a "heathen" foreigner was over the nationals. Here he was, a Judean slave, a eunuch, and of another religion. It was almost more than some could bear. Of course, to his face they were very nice, calling him Daniel and genuinely appreciative that they were alive because of his God's ability to discern dreams. Behind his back, they called him names and plotted against him.

Daniel took his new job as the ruler of Babylon in his usual, serious, careful way. The people not caught up in religious ego trips began to respect his fairness to the poor and the rich. His place of judgement in the king's gate was widely sought out and he brought justice to the entire empire. People from all over the known world were coming to Babylon not only to see the magnificence of the city and to court the king's favor, but to learn the principles and practices that governed the realm under Daniel.

And then rebellion broke out in the province of Judah and the empire's attention was shifted once again to foreign affairs. It was a hard time for Daniel and his cousins in their administration of Babylon. A war was heating up in their homeland, and here they were governing the city waging the war. They were accused of being disloyal to the empire and therefore should be replaced. It was also hard to administer justice when it seemed everyone was looking for a scapegoat upon whom to vent their feelings. Slaves, especially Jewish slaves, had always been sought out for such dubious honor.

Daniel, Meshach, Abed-Nego and Shadrach maintained their dignity, and as the king's respect for them grew even more, he increased their responsibilities.

With the help of the young Judeans, Nebuchadnezzar was able to pursue other pressing activities. It should have been the war, but war was not uppermost in the mind of the king. War caused a manpower drain; a manpower drain could curtail construction. Since construction was his relief for depression, Nebuk's moodiness and anger began to surface with more regularity.

CHAPTER 16

Nebuchadnezzar was extremely depressed. The building of his dream city was bogging down. Judah was rebelling and sowing discontent in her neighboring countries. These Judeans were robbing him of his greatest pleasure and must be smashed. Rallying what resolve he could, Nebuchadnezzar took the necessary steps to ensure the suppression of the problems.

King Jehoiakim of Judah, to all outward appearances, had been in submission to Babylon. However, his private actions were to prepare for war, even going so far as to arrange for Egypt to come to their aid.

When the plans to bring in the Egyptians became known to Nebuzaradan, he quickly alerted Babylon. In response, a large army was dispatched to the land of Judah. The Egyptians should have arrived to defend Judah against their archrival, Babylon; but when they heard the size of the reinforcements coming, they decided this was not the time to engage the enemy.

Left to defend themselves, Jehoiakim's advisors decided the time to strike was right and they began fighting the occupying army before any more reinforcements could arrive. Being outnumbered, the Babylonians hurriedly retreated northward from the city to a safe distance until the rest of the military arrived.

Nebuzaradan, wily leader that he was, used the Babylonian forces to march on the countries surrounding Judah who had aided in the rebellion. He first subdued them and then forced them to take action against the troublemaker, Judah. This attack by Babylon and their former allies caused division among the Judeans and soon the city of Jerusalem was surrounded and under siege. King

Jehoiakim was killed in the early days of the siege, probably by some of his own people.

Jehoiakim's son was only eight years old when he became king. He reigned for three months during the siege of Jerusalem, finally surrendering to the Babylonians. He, his mother and his brother were taken to Babylon as captives; and he was, despite his age, held prisoner for continuing the rebellion of his father against Nebuchadnezzar.

Nebuchadnezzar turned to Zedekiah, the son of King Josiah. He was the half brother of Jehoiakim and twenty-one years old. He had been too young to be taken captive to Babylon when Nebuchadnezzar first conquered Judah. Nebuchadnezzar's message to the new king was firm yet hopeful that the young man could learn from his brother's mistakes. He had to learn to rule in obedience to the laws of the Babylonians. It was a fact of life.

Relative calm returned to the Kingdom of Judah and soon thousands of captives were walking to their new home in the Province of Babylon. The military men, the craftsmen, and all the finest of the families were sent to Babylon. Nebuzaradan took all of his wife's people with him. They were given special privilege in Babylon just as Nebuchadnezzar had promised. Indeed, most of the people taken captive by the king were treated with respect and many prospered, becoming rich and valued members of Babylonian society.

Along with the captives, Nebuzaradan took most of the vessels from the temple to Babylon with him. He installed his chief-of-staff as the military commandant over the Province of Judah with strict orders to police the new government and keep the king guessing what Babylon would do next. "Keep them on edge so that they have no time to plan rebellion."

When Nebuchadnezzar heard the report from Nebuzaradan, he was relieved the Judeans were back under control. After all the years of the Judean conquest, finally having Nebuzaradan back as part of the palace advisory staff was pleasing to Nebuchadnezzar. He had great confidence in his military chief and was glad to be able to transfer even more of his own responsibilities to such a trusted leader.

Nebuzaradan suggested that Nebuchadnezzar send several of his most faithful Judean conscripts back to Jerusalem and allow them to show the people of Judah what a great privilege it was to be part of the Babylonian Empire. "That is a great idea. What an excellent way to calm the fears of the people who are still left in Judah. They certainly will be able to tell their people what a truly great person I am. I shall have to send Daniel; he has become my most trusted advisor on domestic policy. He will go and head the delegation to Jerusalem."

Daniel was delighted, of course, to be able to see Jerusalem again and wanted to take Shadrach, Meshach and Abed-Nego as well, but the king wanted them to stay and help get the new captives settled and keep the building program under control. So Daniel chose six other of the trusted Judean princes to go back with him.

It was certainly fortunate the three cousins did not go with Daniel; they were sorely needed to deal with housing and supply shortages as well as some of the more rebellious captives.

In the middle of all these problems, the king slid into a severe depression. Again, bad dreams plagued him. None of Mara's, Belakah's or any of the other courtier's attempts raised his spirits. Nothing helped until he remembered the dream that Daniel had interpreted. He decided he would build the monument of his dreams for himself, since he himself was the head of gold.

Acting as if nothing in the world ever bothered him, Nebuchadnezzar called his chief designers and began immediately to plan the statue. It would be very large and must represent himself. He decided not to place the statue in Babylon. Instead, he would create a park where people could go and enjoy a time away from the city. There this monumental statue of himself would be the center of attention. The Plain of Dura was nearby but not close enough to be incorporated into the city as it expanded beyond the walls.

Nebuchadnezzar determined that the best way to get an appropriate structure was to hold a contest to select the best design for the monument. He had used this technique many times before to create his fantastic buildings . . . why not the statue? The winner of the design would oversee the construction, and work closely with the king to see to the completion.

As usual, the king wanted the work to be done in record time. Soon all attention was on preparation for construction in Dura. Slaves were diverted from other building projects to prepare the grounds. As soon as the design, which he deemed worthy, was selected, the actual construction would begin. The king was happy with his new toy and went about smiling when he thought of his project. He was happy with himself.

Not everyone else was. Mara was not as enthused as the king over the monument. She was happy Nebuk was out of his depression, for however long, but she quickly voiced her objections to the project. "Monuments should be built after one is dead and gone."

"But, my dear wife, no one can build things as well as I can. Besides, I want to see it."

"I appreciate that, but it just further delays the building of the hanging gardens you promised me." She had longed for gardens similar to the ones that had grown on the slopes of the mountains of her north country home. "Have you forgotten you promised the next big project would be my gardens. It seems what you want is always ahead of what I want."

"I am the king."

Nebuk was happy. Mara was becoming unhappy; Zroybel was outraged. The promised glorification of Bel was not a top priority with the king. The high priest's top priority, a great temple, was on the list to be done, but it followed behind the city, the statue, Mara's hanging gardens and whatever Nebuchadnezzar could find to put in front of it. His anger was barely concealed and often vented to the other priests who fed into his resentments.

The Dura Plain project of his was one of those rare times when

Nebuchadnezzar did not listen to Mara's complaints. He promised
the work on the gardens would be resumed as soon as the statue
was completed. "You know I have built everything in Babylon for
all the people. Since I am the greatest King to ever live, it is only
fair that I have the monument fitting my greatness. I will build
this one thing for me, and then the gardens will be built for you."

The work progressed at great speed. The people responded
eagerly to complete this work quickly for their king. Not only was
he the greatest in his own sight, the people felt the same way
about him. It seemed he could do no wrong. They overlooked his
fits of depression and his ranting and raving when things did not
go his way. They even overlooked his crying in public when
something touched him deeply.

When completed, the statue was nine feet wide and ninety
feet high. The intricately built stone structure went together like a
puzzle and was covered with gold. The face was that of
Nebuchadnezzar. The body was a visual panorama of all the
characteristics of the king. It implied great strength, wisdom,
devotion and authority. Symbols and artifacts of his reign were
replicated by the design. Nebuchadnezzar was genuinely pleased
with the statue. The people came by the thousands to see it, to
marvel at it.

High Priest Zroybel came to see the king and complimented
him on the fine statue. "Your Majesty, this is a fitting representation
of you. We are certainly graced to have you as our king."
Nebuchadnezzar couldn't help but wonder what he wanted this
time. "We, the priests of Bel, would like to suggest that you have a
great festival every month for the people to come before your statue
and give evidence of their submission and allegiance to you. It
should be with the accompaniment of music and festivities. We
think all the people should bow down and worship your statue.
You represent all that is good in the country and you represent our
great god Bel to all the people."

Nebuchadnezzar didn't respond immediately for he seemed
deep in thought at the high priest's words. He was thinking his

very earliest thoughts about religion. *Use it to gain control over the people.* "I think perhaps you are right, Zroybel. I shall give serious thought to what you have suggested. Would you and your other priests be willing to oversee the festivals? Perhaps in this way we can get back on track with the elevation of Bel to the place we had originally planned."

"Oh, your Majesty, we shall be most happy to do all we can to implement your orders. We are here to serve you to the best of our ability."

"Yes, yes, I know." But Nebuk was thinking of the power and control that such a move would give him over any reluctant slave/ captives. *If they did not worship me, they could be put to death. That would solve some of our social problems.*

Zroybel was about to leave when the king called out to him, "Zroybel, see how quickly we can implement these plans. I like the idea. Do it."

"Yes, Majesty, we shall begin planning immediately."

Suddenly, Zroybel was really happy and to think . . . the king was too. The priests had been trying unsuccessfully to find a way to get rid of the Daniel's Hebrew influence over the king. They couldn't have asked for a better way. Nebuchadnezzar never realized he was being used. His own plans and pride made him a partner in crime with Zroybel.

The high priest returned from the palace to the Temple of Bel and told the other priests; they celebrated with much wine. The next day the festival plans, which were already well advanced, were finalized. Waiting two days before going back to the king to keep him from suspecting their plot, they received his approval without change.

All the Babylonian people and any foreigners in the province were required by the king's decree to travel to Dura at least four times a year to worship and bow down before the statue of the king. If a person was unable to go for legitimate reasons, they were to face toward Dura and bow down when the festival music sounded and the trumpets announced the worship time. Death by burning was the pronounced penalty for not worshipping in accordance with the law.

"Now," rejoiced Zroybel, "when the worship times come monthly, we shall watch very carefully to see if the Judeans worship as they have been ordered. We shall especially be watching Shadrach, Meshach and Abed-Nego. Too bad Daniel is out of the country. Oh, well, we'll catch him when he gets back."

On the first great day for the festival, the whole country was given a holiday. All except essential services were canceled to allow the worshippers to take part in the festivities. The music sounded, the trumpets blared throughout the whole nation and the people bowed down before the statue of the king. Many who did not worship as directed had their lack of submission duly noted by the spies the priests of Bel had assigned to the task.

The law allowed the people three months in which to conform to the decree. They had to make a pilgrimage if they were able. If they were unable, they were to bow down where they were. It was hard for the priests, having to wait three months for the report on the three important Hebrews. Their spies told them exactly what they wanted to hear. None of the three made even the slightest move toward worshipping the golden statue. Zroybel's glee knew no limitations. Contrary to his nature, he went around smiling.

Several days after the third worship event Zroybel sent the king a message asking for an appointment. Nebuchadnezzar dreaded the meeting with the priest, but set the meeting for the next day. Zroybel could hardly contain himself as he asked, "Your Majesty, did you indeed issue a decree that all must worship within a three-month period?" "Of course, I did; you know very well that I did . . . You wrote it. Were there many people who did not worship in the allotted time period?"

"Yes, Your Majesty. We have a list of slaves and others who refused both in their words and actions to conform."

Nebuchadnezzar spoke angrily to his scribe, "Have them tried and if guilty, put them to death in the brick ovens. Prepare the orders and I shall sign them right now." Turning again to Zroybel he inquired, "Were there any prominent men, upper class people who refused to obey my orders?"

"Again, yes, we have watched carefully to see that all obeyed your orders. We have found that the Hebrew eunuchs who are over the Province of Babylon, Shadrach, Meshach and Abed-Nego, refused to make any move to worship according to your order."

"Guard, bring these men to me immediately. I shall not put up with such insubordination. I don't care who they are." His rage mounted and the color of his face deepened toward crimson. "Who do they think they are that they can refuse my order. We shall see who is the greatest in this empire. I shall not allow it. I won't have it."

The king's rage reverberated through the marble palace. The king could be a very good man when all went well, but when he was upset, even if by family or close associates, look out.

When the men were brought before the king, it was obvious they had been handled roughly by the authorities, who thought harsh treatment would earn greater favor with the king. The men were pale with fright. The king was livid with rage. "I understand you do not serve my gods, but is it true, you refused to worship my golden statue that I have set up?"

"The charges against us are true." Abed-Nego spoke softly.

The soft, direct answer seemed to take the king by surprise and mollified his anger somewhat. "How could you have done this to me? You have been loyal servants ever since I brought you to Babylon almost ten years ago."

Nebuk paused for a long period of time, seeking to maintain his composure. "I shall give you one more time to change this situation. When the music and trumpets sound, if you will worship the statue I have set up, you will be allowed to live. But if you don't worship as ordered, you will be cast into the brick ovens to meet your death. Even your God can't deliver you from that." He pointed his finger at the men, his anger mounting again.

Shadrach spoke for all the men. "Your Majesty, we are not going to try to save our lives by saying we will think about it or perhaps we could worship. Time will not change anything. We can assure you, we will not worship the idol that you have set up. We will only worship the Most High God, who is able to deliver us from death."

The statement was so unexpected that Nebuchadnezzar was speechless.

Meshach nodded his agreement and said, "We believe our God is able to deliver us. But if not, we still will not worship your gods nor bow down to the golden image you have set up."

By this time the rage in the king's heart was boiling and his face took on the most evil look anyone had ever seen before. "Heat the furnace twice as hot as usual . . . no, make it seven times hotter than normal. We shall see how these heathen pigs will like to be roasted. Bind these men and let me know when the furnace is ready. I shall be there to watch them burn. This will be a lesson to all the rest of the rebellious people."

The three men were taken from the throne room directly to the prison. The Priests of Bel and some of the nobles who had worked for the three, jeered as they were led away. They were called heathen dogs, traitors, and spit upon by the fickle crowds as they passed by.

When the fire was ready, the soldiers paraded Shadrach, Meshach and Abed-Nego to the location of the furnace. Slaves manning the bellows allowing the furnace to be hotter than usual were sweating, and couldn't work for more than a short time due to the extreme heat. Flames of fire were leaping out of the opening where normally the bricks were safely placed in the furnace by means of long handled paddles.

The searing heat forced the guards, trying to get the men into the furnace, to back off several times in their approach. Finally the king shouted at them, "Get them in there if it kills you." As the guards lunged forward, pushing the men into the opening, they fell down in front of the door. Other guards rushed forward, grabbing their fallen comrades, and attempted to drag them out, only to be overcome themselves. All four of the guards were dead.

The excitement over the death of the guards subsided somewhat and Nebuchadnezzar was more than a little distressed at the deaths and his own erratic behavior. *I hate how much I'm acting like my father*, he thought. Rather than continue thinking like that he turned his attention to the furnace. As the smoke cleared, from where he was sitting he could see into the furnace and his face turned ashen. "How many men fell into that furnace?"

"Three, of course, Your Majesty."

"Then why do I see four men loose and walking around in the furnace? Why are they alive? Who is the fourth man? He must be . . . be . . . their God." Nebuchadnezzar ran from his seat and got as close to the furnace as he could stand to go. Cupping his hands to his face he called to the men, "You servants of the Most High God, come out of the furnace. Come out here."

Shadrach, Meshach and Abed-Nego crawled out of the furnace, praising God for their deliverance. The assembled observers and guards were all talking at the same time as they looked at the three men. "They are not the slightest bit burned. There is no singeing of their hair. Their clothes aren't damaged in any way. They don't smell of smoke. They aren't even sweating."

It was hard to believe what they had just witnessed. "But we saw them go in with our own eyes. We all smell of smoke more than they do." Later these eyewitness accounts spread to all the empire and no one dared to question the truthfulness of their experience. Some of the earlier spitters, now bowed to the three men as living gods.

King Nebuchadnezzar spoke in a loud voice so all the governors, princes, priests and officers could hear. "Blessed be the God of Shadrach, Meshach and Abed-Nego, Who sent an angel to deliver his servants from the fire of the furnace. Blessed be these servants of their God who, by giving their bodies to be burned and refusing to worship any god except their own, have turned the heart of the king and changed his word. I hereby change the decree of worship of the image of gold."

"But Your Majesty, your law can't be changed," a few legal purists objected.

"I have the absolute power in this empire and I have just changed the law." Glaring at the courtiers, he asked, "Who is going to stop me?" Nodded agreement swept the crowd. "Besides, we can all testify that these men went to death and came back again. They have paid their debts, and now no one else will have to.

"I forbid any people, nation or tongue to speak anything amiss against their God. If such speech is heard they shall be cut in pieces and their houses destroyed. There is no other god who can deliver, as has the God of Shadrach, Meshach, and Abed-Nego. These faithful men shall not only continue in the government of Babylon, they shall be promoted."

The three men bowed themselves to the ground, thanking God for his goodness and ability to deliver them. They stood to their feet and saluted the king and thanked him for his kindness in restoring them to their positions of leadership.

"Please come to the palace; there is more that I wish to speak to you about." When they were alone, the king questioned the men, "Who was the fourth person I saw with you in the furnace?"

"We are not sure, but the Most High God has promised that he would send a deliverer, a Messiah, who would deliver us from our sins. Whoever he was, he certainly did deliver us."

"Were you afraid when you were being forced into the furnace?"

"Afraid? No! Terrified? Yes!" laughed Meshach. "It's much better to look back on a miracle than forward hoping for one. Miracles are seldom announced in advance, Your Majesty."

"At least you have the hope of one. I am not too sure what would have happened to me, for I have no god able to deliver as yours."

"Your Majesty, as Daniel told you, you were set upon your throne to be God's instrument in this world, for this time. You can indeed trust the God of Heaven who made you king and who has spared your life, if you will allow yourself to do so." Shadrach looked hopefully at the king as he spoke.

"It is not always that simple, for I am a king, a great king by the words of your God through Daniel. But for me to leave the religion the entire empire is built upon and bring a whole empire to trust in your God is, for me, too great an impossibility. I may be the great king your God is using for his purposes. However, I do not feel very worthwhile, especially today. I realize this image and fiery furnace thing, was a trick by the leaders of my religion, to get rid of you. It also bothers me I could be so out of control and angry that I would lose the ability to think rationally and even worse, act like my father. For this, I owe you an apology."

"Don't let that bother you, great king, for we knew in advance what the plan was and as you can see, it is very hard to get rid of followers of the God of heaven."

"For that I am very grateful. Can you ever forgive me for the terrible injustices I have forced upon you from the very beginning?"

"Your Majesty," Abed-Nego spoke up. "Our God has made provision for the forgiveness of sins. Every year, when at home, on the Day of Atonement, we sacrifice a lamb as payment for our sins. Since Almighty God can forgive the sins of a man, we as mere men can forgive the things done to us by another man even if he is a great king."

To those words Shadrach and Meshach agreed and the king was so moved that he was unable to speak, the emotion of being forgiven so strong. When he had recovered enough to speak, Nebuchadnezzar said, "Had I been taught as a child what you have, perhaps this world would be vastly different. Perhaps there would be greater peace in the world and perhaps men would not do to each other what they do. Perhaps families would be able to love each other and grow up happily. Perhaps . . . Well, thank you gentlemen for being good to your king. This terrible thing will never happen again."

The next day all that King Nebuchadnezzar had promised the three men was issued in decrees. The mandatory worship was stopped; the exaltation of Bel was slowed to a snail's pace, and the men were promoted to greater authority in Babylon.

True to his word, Nebuchadnezzar was careful not to allow the traps of politics to interfere with what he thought to be the best policy for the most good for most of the people. The captives of Judah were given especially gracious treatment. They were allowed to worship the Lord God as they saw fit. They were able to keep their feasts and to start the synagogue system of worship, which lasted through many centuries.

When Daniel returned from Jerusalem three months later there was great rejoicing between the cousins. Daniel had been able to bring a measure of peace to the court in Jerusalem and Shadrach, Meshach and Abed-Nego were able to bring peace to the court in Babylon. "It is amazing how God works to take care of things."

CHAPTER 17

Crisis begat crisis! No sooner had Nebuchadnezzar made things right with Shadrach, Meshach and Abed-Nego than trouble erupted with Zroybel and the rest of the priests of Bel. They were petrified with fear that the king was on the verge of becoming a Hebrew convert. This, of course, was not the case, but their paranoia resulting from trying to have the three Judean princes put to death fed their irrational thinking. The priest's plans to eliminate the Hebrew influence backfired because of the Most High God's miraculous delivery.

Now the princes were further exalted and the Zroybel priesthood's bankruptcy exposed. The people were unanimous in their support of the king and his changing the decree. The miraculous deliverance brought great respect for the three men, but also a spiritual crisis. Many people began to have grave doubts as to what they believed. They were fearful and unsure of anything the priests of Bel pronounced, viewing them with suspicion. But as with all crises of thought, it was easier to live with the familiar than to make major changes. Soon they were following Bel Marduk as before.

After waiting a respectable period of time, Zroybel requested an audience with the king regarding the resumption of building on the new Temple of Bel.

The large Ziggurat had been completed, but Nebuchadnezzar had no intention of allowing any construction on the temple to interfere with plans for Mara's promised hanging gardens. When Zroybel came into the throne room, Nebuchadnezzar did not speak to him, only nodded his head in acknowledgement. Angry thoughts dominated the king. This man caused me to make serious errors in judgement and now here he is begging for favors. If only I could send him to the furnace. I'm sure there'd be no angel to rescue him.

Finally he spoke, "Zroybel, I have had about all I can stand of you. I am the king and you are the High Priest of Bel. You were never my choice for the job and I would really like to replace you with someone more of my choosing. However, the council elected you, and I will abide by their choice. But you will not be able to have things your way." Zroybel stroked his sparse beard, his anger mounting as he listened to the King. The color of his face betrayed his rising temperature.

Nebuk continued. "Stay out of my way. Your religion is as corrupt as you are. Leave me now. If I need you, I shall send for you."

Zroybel half bowed to the king, signifying his outward compliance, but his brain was shouting defiance. After leaving the room, he muttered to his aides. "He will be sorry. I shall show the power that is in our hands." Zroybel's eyes snapped with excitement as he became a man on a mission. "We may have failed to eliminate the Hebrew menace, but we won't fail again."

Daniel brought the king news of the government of Judah. He had spent a lot of time with King Zedekiah, his cousin, trying to convey to him that Nebuchadnezzar had been ordained of God for the purpose of bringing discipline to the land of Judah. Daniel tried to stress to Zedekiah that conformity to the way that Babylon ruled the world would produce benefits for the country. Zedekiah, however, seemed mainly impressed by Daniel being so high up in the Babylonian government. He assumed this would be helpful in their future relationship and could be exploited.

Daniel reported many positive things, but also shared the concerns that he had about Zedekiah's being a real hothead when he didn't get his own way. Although they were related they really didn't know each other very well, since Zedekiah was seven years younger and they were miles apart on spiritual matters. This made Daniel suspicious of where Zedekiah was headed, because the way he acted, he was not really interested in following in the "ways of the Lord."

Daniel made other comments about the advisors of the king. They seemed to be men of reason, and Daniel felt a steady course would be followed, at least in the short run. He advised close watch on any building that could be for military purposes.

"Thank you, Daniel, for the report and your good work in Jerusalem. I am certainly glad you weren't here when the episode of the statue took place. I am sure you, too, would have been in the furnace with your cousins." Daniel grinned and nodded in agreement with the king's assessment.

The king continued, "Daniel, I have never felt so foolish and so used as in this episode of the brick furnace. I have prided myself on the way in which I have conducted this government and myself. And to think I could have so mistreated Shadrach, Meshach and Abed Nego because of my ego—it's very shattering."

Daniel answered in his typical fashion, "God's miraculous deliverance of my cousins from the furnace has served to make them much stronger in their faith. Sometimes I have felt they depended too much on me. Now, they have a confidence that God is able to do through them what He pleases and that He can be trusted to take care of His own, any time and any place."

Nebuchadnezzar thought to himself, *I really don't like these sly 'innocent' little sermons these men always give me, but I am really impressed with them. They are some of the most trustworthy men in my entire kingdom. It must be their faith in their God that makes them better than the rest of the people.*

Nebuchadnezzar was genuine in his praise of the men as he spoke to Daniel. "I am certainly glad that you men are on my side. Your God seems to have favored me in my choosing the four of you from the princes of Judah. I am personally glad you are back and that you will again take up your duties here in Babylon. We've got a backlog of legal work that needs to be done. Would you please see if you can get the gate judgements back on schedule?"

"Yes, Your Majesty. I am glad to be back in Babylon for I

know this is the place God has ordained for me to be. It was good to see Jerusalem again, but it is good to be back home. I shall get to work and see what needs to be done. Again, thank you for the privilege of traveling to Jerusalem. Your trust in me will not be for naught."

"I should perhaps warn you that you will probably have more trouble with the priesthood of Bel. I have put them on notice that their building projects are very low priority since their plotting to kill you all through the statue worship. I don't think they will be very cooperative."

Daniel answered, "Nothing will deter the carrying out of God's plan for the government of Babylon, so we'll just take it day by day."

After Daniel left his office, Nebuchadnezzar smiled to think how providential had been his fortune in meeting Daniel and his cousins. *I doubt the realm would function nearly as well without them. Certainly the building of the city of Babylon would not have progressed as smoothly if I had to administer the provincial things that these men do.*

Nebuk's good mood carried over to home and telling Mara of the report of Daniel and how happy he was to have such good and trusted servants. Mara, who had been worried about the changes in his moods, was happy for his lightheartedness. Hoping to capitalize on his improved mood, she suggested that it would be a good time for them to get away from the palace and travel to the north country to visit her home. "Perhaps you could get more ideas for the development of the garden plans you've started."

With Nebuk's peaceful frame of mind, Mara knew he would want some project to occupy him. Since the ideas for the gardens had come originally from her home country, she hoped the trip to the north would preserve his happiness for as long as possible. Getting his mind back on building was always good for him. Now that Daniel was back, the administrative burden was lighter. It was decided that they would leave for the north in two days.

That night as Belakah was giving Nebuk his massage, he

commented, "You seem very relaxed tonight, Nebuk. I am glad that you are feeling well." Quietly working, Belakah tried to ease into further conversation about the upcoming trip. "However, I haven't been feeling too well myself just recently. I've been very tired. Perhaps it would be best to have someone else care for your bath and massage when you go on your trip."

"Belakah, you know I couldn't possibly have anybody else. No one is as good as you. You've always been there when I needed you and I am confident you will be ok. Just get me finished and I will get the rest of my bedtime things done myself. You get some rest."

"Yes, sir, I shall." With that Nebuk turned over and Belakah began to finish his massage. As Belakah bent over, he collapsed on top of the king.

Nebuk grabbed him and asked, "Are you all right?" There was no answer. He appeared to be dead.

Nebuk was frantic. "Mara! Help."

Mara came running with a palace guard. "What is the matter, Nebuk? Are you all right?" When she saw what had happened, she sent the guard for the physicians and helped Nebuk lay Belakah gently on the floor.

"He's dead," Nebuk cried. The pain was deep and sharp, like a sword wound piercing him. He dearly loved the eunuch servant who had become such a close friend and adviser. "Every man that I love dies. And just like Jeleu, he died in my arms. I can't stand it," he sobbed, deep, wrenching, uncontrollable sobs.

The king gathered his composure long enough to get through the funeral and burial. As soon as these responsibilities were over, he slipped into a deep depression. Nothing, neither the building plans nor the travel plans to gather ideas for the gardens, could shake him out of his black mood. "Mara, you'd be better off without me. I'll just leave and you can run the country." She became very apprehensive that he might take his own life.

And then the dreams returned. It was as if Belakah had held the dreams away. Every major dream he had ever had was replayed, from the one Daniel interpreted to the horrible ones which were associated with his father. Constantly replayed was the one of being made a eunuch.

He awoke screaming several nights in a row and there was no Belakah to comfort him and reassure him that everything would be fine. Mara did everything she could to console him, but he would not be comforted. He even dreamed of how Belakah had sent the bad dreams away and how embarrassed he had been by the servant's methods. He refused to eat. He could not sleep and he felt isolated from all of his family. Only Daniel was able to reach him.

As suddenly as the depression came, it lifted for a few days. Then it descended again, this time with even more intensity. Whenever he had anything to do with Zroybel and the priests of Bel, he would surely feel depressed. This periodic depression and relief occurred for the better part of a year. When he felt good, the world was a wonderful place. When he felt bad, the whole world trembled.

In one of the bad times, reports began to come to the palace from Judah. King Zedekiah seemed to have done a complete turnabout and was now rebuilding and stocking the fortified cities. He was visiting all of his neighbors, returning with gifts that signified treaties of friendship and possibly mutual defense. Finally, the most crucial factor, he refused to pay the tribute that had been levied against him. This was war.

Nebuchadnezzar was pulled out of his depression by sheer virtue of the demand placed upon him. He summoned Daniel to come to help him begin his strategy. The only alternative left to him was to further intervene in the Judean country and this time it would not be an easy way of dealing with the land. He began to prepare his nation for what he hoped would be a quick, massive intervention in the Kingdom of Judah. A large army was conscripted and huge supplies of equipment and food were gathered for the upcoming battle.

"Your Majesty," Daniel advised him, "don't place any more vassal kings on the throne. I think you should replace the monarchy with a governor who will not be able to promote the kingdom as a life station, but serve at the your discretion only."

Nebuchadnezzar was again surprised at the ability of the Judean prince to be willing to bring the monarchy, his own family, to a halt for the good of the Babylonian Empire. "Daniel, it constantly amazes me that you can devote yourself so fully to my empire even at the expense of your own kingdom."

"Your Majesty, you have been more than gracious in your dealing with my homeland. I am personally grateful you have dealt so kindly with my kinsmen. I know you have done much as a favor to me. Also, Your Majesty, I have told you many times, the things that you are doing are not just your ideas. The Most High God has given you this empire and I believe you are the one who is to bring the needed discipline to the Judean people for their sins in turning away from their God."

"Daniel, I wish with all my heart that you were able to embrace the god Bel Marduk. Then I could replace that rascal Zroybel with the only truly spiritual man in my entire empire. You would make a great High Priest."

"You flatter me, Your Majesty, but that will never be possible because the Most High God is greater than any other god either real or imagined. I serve him and him only, remember?"

"Yes, yes, I know and I had better not allow these sermons of yours to continue, or you might convince me to become a follower of your God. He certainly has proven Himself to be more capable than Bel . . . I had better not talk this way. Either you will convert me, or my critics, who seem to find out everything I say, will think I am a traitor to Bel Marduk."

"As you know, Your Majesty, I wish above all things that you would know and love the God of heaven and you would, indeed, lead this great nation in honoring him. As for being a traitor, you would have to take lessons to learn how to do so."

"Thank you, Daniel. You are indeed a gift to me from . . . whatever god."

The excitement that war preparations bring energized the

capitol for the next few weeks. The people, filled with mixed emotions of victory and loss, were worried. Young soldiers, ready to prove their capability, flaunted their muscles at every opportunity, especially to the young women who watched shyly from the sidelines.

Nebuchadnezzar again commissioned Nebuzaradan to head the army, while he himself would travel to Riblah, north of Judah, nearer to the time that the war was finished. He planned to confer with other heads of state to keep them from getting any ideas from Zedekiah's rebellion.

Plans for his personal involvement in the war brought to Nebuchadnezzar a sense of control that he frequently felt lacking. The vastness of the Babylonian Empire often left Nebuk feeling isolated and asking himself, "how is it that I can control the whole world, but I can't conquer me?"

Nebuchadnezzar gave his final orders to Nebuzaradan. "When I get to Riblah, bring Zedekiah to me, preferably alive. Bring his whole family. Do whatever you need to do to bring the entire Judean question to resolution. Destroy any and all fortified cities. Take whatever prisoners necessary. Bring the majority of the able-bodied people to Babylon as slaves. We can use them to finish the rest of the construction. What you can't take with you, burn or destroy so that there will be no further opportunity for insurrection. I will not tolerate any more of this nonsense."

Nebuzaradan took the word of the king literally. He laid siege to all of the fortified cities surrounding Jerusalem. Ramat Rahel, Beth-zur, Beth-shemesh, Arad and Engedi were all destroyed. The last two cities to fall were Lachish and Azekah. Finally, Jerusalem itself was under siege. Even rumors of the approaching Egyptians did not stop the final breach of the walls and capture of the city, which was looted and finally burned. The temple was destroyed after the rest of the vessels of worship were removed to be taken back to Babylon.

Nebuzaradan, when he entered Jerusalem, expected to find the king and capture him, but he had escaped. Informers told him that King Zedekiah had fled to Jericho. When the Chaldean forces found him, he surrendered, realizing that the fight was over. He was sure his surrender would result in mercy from Nebuchadnezzar.

The destruction of the Judean kingdom had taken longer than had been expected. King Nebuchadnezzar became very impatient with the progress of the war and as the reports of the siege wearied him, he went back to his first love . . . he continued his building. When the war was finally winding down and Jerusalem was reported taken, the king and his courtiers traveled to Riblah for the meeting with all the heads of state in the empire. It was in front of all of them that Nebuchadnezzar was planning to stage the judgement of Zedekiah.

The captured Judean king was to become the example to the rest of what happens when you don't play by the Babylonian rules. Instead of the mercy he was hoping for, Zedekiah was taken to Riblah. Here he was tried before the Babylonian heads of state and was forced to watch all the rebellious Judean nobles and his own young sons put to death in front of him. Then his eyes were blinded so that the last visions he had would be of his children's deaths. He was then taken to prison in Babylon.

King Nebuchadnezzar addressed the heads of state he had gathered together for this conference and to witness the trial of Zedekiah. "You have this day seen the high cost of rebellion to the Chaldean/Babylonian Empire. Some of you were brought into the empire under my father's leadership; most of you under mine. As you know, we have been most patient and considerate in our treatment of the nations who have come under our protection. However, you can see, after severe provocation, we can be very harsh. It is not my will this type of treatment be given to any of you. It, of course, is up to you as to how you wish to be treated."

The threats were so graphic; the effect, unmistakable by any of the kings and governors who still ruled their countries. They were very attentive to all the king had to say. His final assurances to them were taken as not only a threat, but as a promise of good, depending on their behavior. Some of them realized the king had been far-more fair in his treatment of them than his father had been. On balance, Nebuchadnezzar was not an unkind ruler.

The cost of rebellion against Babylon and the Chaldean army was very high indeed for the entire country of Judah. The royal family was almost completely destroyed except for the ones in captivity in Babylon. All the best families, with the exception of those who had followed the advice of Jeremiah and defected to Nebuchadnezzar in the first battle, were even now marching the many miles to the land of Babylon to serve their appointed time of captivity. The walls of the city were destroyed. The temple was completely destroyed and all the remaining vessels of the temple taken captive.

Thousands of people were forced to march to the province of Babylon. Here they began their slavery and continued building Nebuchadnezzar's great city, already one of the most amazing in the world. The people who remained behind were largely the people who, believing the prophet Jeremiah, had defected early to the Babylonian rule or were the very poor and disabled. The chances of either of these groups of people fomenting rebellion were rather slim.

Nebuzaradan returned to Jerusalem after delivering Zedekiah to Nebuchadnezzar in Riblah. He had two jobs yet to perform for the king. First was to install a new governor over the province of Judah (it was no longer to be considered a kingdom). The king's choice was a Babylonian loyalist by the name of Gedaliah, who befriended Nebuzaradan and introduced him to the family of his future wife.

Nebuzaradan's second mission was to find the prophet Jeremiah, if at all possible, and reward him for his faithfulness in trying to save his country from this final destruction that he had predicted. He was found in a prison at Ramah. When he was released, he was given the choice of going with them to Babylon, being cared for by the Nebuzaradan's forces; or staying behind and helping the governor administer the country.

Jeremiah hesitated to answer and Nebuzaradan said to this

faithful man, his wife's great uncle, "Why don't you remain here where you can do the most good for the people. I will give you your choice of any land you would desire. We shall provide food and support to take care of you for the rest of your life."

Jeremiah's, "I shall stay," made Nebuzaradan very happy. He had come to love the land of Judah, the people and especially this old man. He felt very badly about the destruction and the deportation, but he was very aware that the people who remained needed the spiritual help of someone like Jeremiah.

Nebuzaradan was sure he had done his duty to both the king and to the land of Judah. He was pleased the way things had worked out. He could now return to Babylon, to Ruth, his Judean wife, and feel what he had done was for the best.

When the new slaves arrived in Babylon, the city was engulfed with the overwhelming task of settling the large number of people. Fortunately, many of the slaves had relatives in the city and the surrounding countryside. The order went out that all Judean people should open their homes to the newcomers until quarters could be made available. Just outside the walls of Babylon large suburban housing areas were being developed. The largest Judean settlement was along the Chebar River. It was not really a river, but one of the many canals which had been developed for irrigating the very fertile farmlands.

The King wisely ordered construction of housing for the new captives. This slowed down the other major project, the hanging gardens for Mara. Now the slaves were happy, but the queen wasn't. She was angry. "Nebuk, I am sick of all the war, killing and more and more slaves getting top priority in my life. I am tired of being patient; I want my gardens finished."

"They will be; they will be!" Since Mara was Nebuk's mainstay, he had to do whatever he could to please her even if that meant not pleasing the rest of the people. It became a very delicate balancing act to try to please both parties. It was a very stressing situation for him.

He had to live with Mara, but had to hear all day long the

complaints coming to him through all the governmental channels. The resources of the province of Babylon were strained to the limit. The king became more and more agitated and finally depressed. The only solace he found was in walking out in the countryside where the breeze whispered peace to his mind and the grass and trees helped him feel alive.

On one such walk, he made the decision to pursue the gardens; for that not only would please Mara, but would also help him. He knew he was headed for trouble if he didn't get control of himself.

The gardens he had envisioned were difficult to design. The flatness of the land in the Shinar Plain where Babylon is located did not lend itself to hillside gardens. Specially designed features were needed to create the atmosphere of the hillsides with their sunny and shady areas. In his mind he saw the gardens hanging overhead with vines and flowers cascading down, giving shade to the visitors below.

Walking and thinking about the garden's development brought the inspiration he needed. Just as he had cut out stone channels to carry water to various parts of the city, he could cut out larger channels and plant the flowers and vines in them. They could be suspended on pillars, which would allow for people to be under the gardens, and still allow the gardens to receive sunlight and rain. In dry weather the gardens were to be watered using unique lift pumps he had already designed. They could easily be built in many places along the inside wall of the city, but especially where the interior portions of the walls had not been completed would be excellent.

He was as excited as a little boy with his idea and set to work immediately. He called for his architectural engineers to help him with the technical details and they, too, became excited about the uniqueness of the garden's construction. They also noticed that since the double walls had been made wide for chariots to travel easily on top of them, people would be able to enjoy the gardens from the top as well as from the bottom.

When Nebuk returned to the palace, he tried hard to hide his excitement from Mara as she asked sharply, "Have you made any progress on the garden plans today?"

"What do you expect me to do? Stop everything and just spend time on the gardens? Well, that's just what I did do today, and wait until you hear what I've come up with." Mara became just as excited as her husband. She was doubly pleased, for not only were the plans progressing, but also her husband was out of his depression and alive again. When told it would take some time for the pillars and channels to be cut out and readied, Mara suggested the laborers get back to building houses for the slaves as quickly as possible so when needed they would be ready to work on the gardens. Nebuk breathed a sigh of relief; Mara's sunny disposition was back.

For several weeks things were on the upswing until one night Nebuchadnezzar was awakened with a fearsome dream. "I must get someone to help me," he thought. "I will send for the wisemen first thing in the morning."

CHAPTER 18

The dreams had been coming to the king with greater intensity and frequency. He usually awakened in the middle of the night with at least two dreams fresh in his mind. Often he had difficulty remembering which parts of the dreams were related to each other. Some of the dreams were just repeats of previous ones, which had been interpreted earlier.

The recurring dreams were not usually a problem unless they involved his father accusing him of being unfit to rule. The dream of the large statue with him being the head of gold was always a pleasant dream even if he didn't understand about the large stone smashing the statue. It calmed him when it replayed in his mind. *At least the God of the Judeans thinks well of me, even if my father didn't. Why is my father's opinion of such great importance? But why can't I shake the feeling of being unworthy? Why is there no relief to the doubt of my worth? Here I am the greatest king of the greatest empire the world has ever known, and I still feel unworthy.*

With the death of Belakah, a great source of Nebuk's comfort was gone. Realizing how much he had depended on the eunuch caused him to miss him even more. Thinking of Belakah only served to intensify the dreams. In order to improve relations with the priests of Bel, Nebuchadnezzar would call them in to interpret his dreams. They were delighted to do so and often gave very lengthy interpretations, which served primarily to make them feel like they were regaining the upper hand that they once had with the king. Frequently they gave very comforting views of the dreams and sometimes their ideas were absurd.

Nebuk would never have called the wisemen of Bel to interpret the dreams if he had known of a conversation months earlier between

Zroybel and his top advisors. "I am having trouble with my dream potions not working as well on the king as they should. My spirits tell me that there is opposition to what we are trying to do to the king. I think that it is Belakah who has done something to block the dreams from working."

"Perhaps we should get rid of him so that the channel to the king is open and we can do what we wish with his mind."

"An excellent suggestion. Please take care of that for me." In the usual fashion of the spirit world, spells were cast which resulted in death. Belakah and the king were totally unsuspecting of this vicious warfare in the spirit realm. Since the powers of Bel could not work against Belakah's powers which came from Bel, and definitely not against the power of the Most High God, the interference had to be removed. The priests failed to understand that Belakah was one of the few positive aspects of Bel worship for the king. Removing Belakah removed the king further from Bel devotion.

Each time the king called for his wisemen they were uneasy until he told them his dream. They remembered only too well that they could have been put to death over not being able to tell him his dream and the interpretation.

It was not easy being one of Nebuchadnezzar's seers. It was almost impossible for them to admit the Hebrew prince from Judah had saved their necks, let alone acknowledge he was in complete charge over them and almost everything else in the Babylonian kingdom.

This time when they responded to the call from the king, he was visibly upset by the dream he'd had. "Gentlemen, the dream I have seen has come to me in what seems to be the most urgent of terms. I feel as though it's some kind of a warning, a premonition. I want you to tell me the meaning of the dream."

"We shall do our best, Your Majesty. Please tell us the dream as you remember it."

As Nebuchadnezzar began the telling of the dream, the wisemen corporately relaxed. "I had just come back from inspecting the building sites of the gardens. I was very pleased with the great design I had created and I was happy. I lay down expecting to sleep very peacefully. I was not upset in the slightest. When the dream began I became very agitated and finally fearful. By the time it was finished I was extremely troubled.

"There was a great tree. It kept growing and growing until it became very large and strong. It reached to the very heavens and people could see it from all over the earth. The leaves were full and the branches loaded with fruit so that everybody could eat from it. Animals found shelter and shade under its branches. It was good for everyone.

"Then I saw a holy being come down from the heavens and shout to ones below to chop down the tree, strip off the leaves, throw the fruit away and chase the animals out from under it. The birds of the branches were chased away as the branches were cut off. This holy being told them to leave the stump and the root in the earth in the tender grass of the field and bind it with a band of iron and bronze. He said that it should be wet with the dew of heaven. Let him graze with the beasts on the grass of the earth. He said to let his heart be changed from being a man to being an animal and let seven years pass over him.

"Then I knew that the decision for this to be done was by the decree of holy watchers and the sentence was given by these holy ones. They said this was being done so the living may know the Most High rules in the kingdom of men and gives it to whoever he will and he gives it to the lowest of men.

"That's my dream, gentlemen. I will give you some time to deliberate and return to me with your interpretation."

"Is there anything else you can tell us about the dream or any thoughts that came to you after you dreamed it?"

"No, that was it. When I awoke I was filled with dread and panic. I could hardly breathe and I knew it was something very important to me, and that I needed to have the interpretation. I did not sleep the rest of the night, and I have pondered what the meaning might be. I know nothing more than what I have told you. Please hurry with your interpretation. I feel it is urgent; I need to know what it is all about. Please return by tomorrow at this time or before if you have found the answer. Thank you."

The wisemen hurried to their books and studies, agreeing to meet in four hours to determine what they had found and pool their ideas. "After all, we have to do a good job for the king. You never know when it will mean our lives. Even more, we don't want another victory for Daniel, do we?"

Zroybel was smug in his feeling they would soon be able to depose Daniel from his favored spot. He was convinced the spirits that he had commissioned to trouble the king were indeed working for him. "Since this dream is from Bel, then we, as priests of Bel, should surely be able to give the interpretation."

At the appointed hour the wisemen assembled in the high priest's temple offices. They came dragging in with few if any hopeful looks on their faces. They compared and none of them had come up with much by way of interpretation. The biggest problem was the change from the tree, an inanimate object to a human being. Another major trouble spot for them existed in the dream where the term The Most High was used. Bel Marduk had never been called in those terms before. They had some rather ragged thoughts, but nothing that fit together with each other's ideas. Zroybel was nervous and scolded them, "Think, you dunces, think. Don't you realize what is at stake here?"

Of course they did, and their nervousness grew as the apprehension mounted in the room, accentuated by Zroybel's incessant pacing back and forth. His hawk nose seemed to be peering over each shoulder in the room. Finally he suggested, "Let's take each phrase of the king's dream and analyze it together. Perhaps we can get the interpretation through group inspiration." That also ended in failure. They decided to stop and pray and offer sacrifice to Bel Marduk, Innana, Astarte and other of their assorted deities.

It was a very tired and ragged-looking bunch of not-so-wise men who had to confront the king the next morning. Zroybel, as usual when things were not going well, carefully positioned himself far in the rear of the pack. The appointed spokesman for the group spoke up. "Your Majesty, we have toiled all night long seeking the answer to your dream. We kindly request that you give us a little more time in which to work. We are just now coming to the place of finding the key to the unfolding of your dream," he lied.

King Nebuchadnezzar listened patiently to the prepared excuses. "Had you men been as clever in giving me some kind of interpretation as you've been in giving excuses, I would have at least something to think about. However, I am not surprised you do not have any answers for me." His voice and anger were rising. "You can only answer little things that don't amount to anything important. You can bluff your way just so long and at the moment of truth, you are lost.

"Please leave. I am sending for Daniel. But have no fear for your lives; for he would only plead that your lives be spared, so I will save him the trouble. If you were as willing for him to live, as he is for you, perhaps you might have more spiritual power." With that the wisemen slipped sheepishly out of the palace, following their leader.

When Daniel arrived, the king quickly rehearsed the dream and asked him if he could give the interpretation. "My so-called wisemen are not able to do so. I know that the Spirit of the Holy God is in you and I believe you are able."

Daniel walked around the king's office, praying quietly. The more he walked and prayed the more distressed he became. Finally, the king said, "Daniel, don't let the dream or what you are getting of its meaning bother you. Just tell me the truth."

"I can do no other. I wish most sincerely that the dream and the interpretation were on your enemies that hate you and not on you. You are the great tree you saw, that grew and became strong and reached the heavens that could be seen by the whole earth. Your leaves and fruit were abundant and fed many. You gave shelter to the animals and the birds perched in your branches. You are that great tree and your influence has reached the whole world."

"You saw the holy one coming from heaven, telling men to chop down the tree and destroy it but to save the stump. Leave it in the earth and band it with iron and bronze in the grass of the field. You are to be wet with dew and you are to graze with the beasts of the fields for seven years. This is the decree of the Most High God which will be coming upon you."

"You will be driven from men and you will make your dwelling with the beasts of the field. You will eat grass like an ox. You will be wet with dew from heaven for seven years. This is to teach you that the Most High God rules in the kingdom of men and gives it to whosoever He chooses. Since He commanded the stump and roots to remain, your kingdom will be restored to you, when you learn the lesson that heaven rules."

When finished speaking, Daniel was in tears and the king was speechless at what he had just been told. In his heart he knew what was being said was the truth, and whether he liked it or not, it was fact.

Daniel spoke again to the king, "O Great King, let me give you my advice in light of this dream and interpretation. I hope you can accept what I am saying to you. Break with the sins of the past by getting God's righteousness. Cancel out your iniquities by showing mercy to the poor. Perhaps there can be a way around this and you will continue to prosper."

Nebuchadnezzar was pensive but anger began to come to the fore. "I am the head of gold and now I am the great tree. What possible sins could I have that I would need to break, and what iniquities would be canceled by my being more kind to the poor than I have already been? The dream itself tells how I have fed and sheltered all that are under my shade. I am greater than others who may need to repent and deal with such things. Besides, your interpretation sounds like this dream is a sure thing and therefore nothing I can do will change it."

Daniel listened to the king and realized he was right. There were not going to be any changes. The king would have to go through what was forecast for him. He spoke quietly to the king.

WAYI

"Your Majesty, there was no intent of condemnation for you in my words. As you will recall when I began the interpretation, I wished the dream and its meaning were for your enemies. That is still my wish, for you have been to me the kindest and greatest king the earth has produced. I shall serve you in the future as in the past. I meant no offense."

Again, Daniel's soft answer took the edge off the king's anger and he spoke quietly. "Daniel, I know there was nothing in your mind of evil intent. I only wish my mind were as pure in thought as yours." He paused, troubled by the interpretation. "I do not know what the dream will mean, but I wish to have things assured in the event they transpire just as you have said. I wish you to become Prime Minister of the Babylonian Empire. In the event that I am not able to serve this nation for seven years, I wish the fate of the world to rest in your hands and not in the hands of others, including the hands of my sons."

Nebuchadnezzar called for his secretary and proceeded to draft a decree stating that Daniel was to be vested with all the power of the monarchy in the event the king was indisposed for any reason short of death during the next two decades.

Daniel was amazed at the confidence the king was placing in him and the power he was so ready to allow him to wield. Even more, Daniel marveled at the gracious fulfillment of God's plan for his life. Here he was a slave, allowed to interject the faith of God into the lives of the people of a pagan realm even as it was being used as God's judgement on the nation of Judah.

Both Nebuchadnezzar and Daniel were poised and ready for the dream to be fulfilled but nothing happened. Daniel occasionally struggled with doubts over the words he had been given. Yet, deep within, he continued to feel they were real. Nebuchadnezzar, after a few weeks had passed, pushed the dream and its interpretation into the far recesses of his mind. He busied himself in finishing the hanging gardens, the great walls and several smaller projects that had been neglected. He felt contented with the building he had done since he first came to Babylon seventeen years earlier.

One particularly lovely evening he and Mara were riding in their coach through the city and then up on the walls. They drove around the completed city center. Construction was still continuing outside the walls, but inside was his beautiful, carefully laid out city. It was very much like the one he had seen in his dream in which he saw his as-yet-to-be-born son sitting on his throne. Mara's gardens with their cascading vines and flowers were breathtakingly beautiful in the late afternoon light. The sky was brilliant with shades of red and gray as the day drew rapidly to a close.

Returning home, Nebuchadnezzar looked over the city from his palace balcony and said to himself, "This is the fulfillment of all my dreams. I have made this city beautiful. I have made it great. The empire is greater than ever. All my father did was only a prelude to the greatness that I have brought to this land. I am indeed the greatest king that has ever come on the scene. I have done a great thing. I shall be remembered for all time. People will speak of me down through the ages with awe for all that I have accomplished. Of course, I could not have done it alone, but they would not have done it without me. It is my vision. I did it."

While Nebuchadnezzar was speaking these things to himself, a voice came speaking clearly to him. "King Nebuchadnezzar, a full year has passed this very day since you were spoken to in the dream. The kingdom is departed from you. You shall be driven from men and will live like an animal. All that was spoken to you by Daniel will be fulfilled."

Before Nebuchadnezzar could ask a question he was taken with a fit of coughing. Then he grabbed his head and cried out in great pain. Mara heard his cry. Just as she came to the balcony, he started to fall; Mara caught him and eased him to the floor, screaming for help. The servants quickly got the doctors to come to attend the king. Fear gripped all in the palace as the word spread concerning the king's attack.

Mara tried to get him to respond to her, but at first he was not able to move. The doctors feared a blood seizure in the brain, but it did not seem to be what they usually treated. After what seemed like forever to Mara, he began moving about and tried to open his eyes. She tried again to get him to respond to her, "Speak to me, Nebuk. Tell me what is happening to you." He tried to speak and at first no sound would come out. Finally he said "Arma."

"What did you say, dear?"

"Arma. Wash a massher wibb em." The rest of his words were totally unintelligible. He tried over and over to make them understand without any success and he began to cry. Mara was also in tears. She was panic-stricken and called for Daniel to come and help her.

When Daniel arrived he took charge, relieving Mara having to deal with the government as well as the pain of dealing with Nebuk's illness.

The entire efforts of the palace were mobilized to help the king—to no avail. The only thing they found that calmed his agitation was for him to be taken out and allowed to walk in the fields. Physically he was well, but his mind would not correspond. He drooled and fumbled with his food. His brain seemed severely damaged.

Often time brings healing; as time went by the king looked less and less like he would recover. Daniel assumed full responsibility for the government as the king's decree had ordered. Mara reinforced Nebuchadnezzar's decree concerning Daniel's role, stating that it was the king's wish recorded over a year earlier. It was an especially hard time for Nabonidus, Aia and Awil Merodach. They were upset about their father and didn't understand why Daniel was given the control of the government and not one of them.

Explaining the dream, the interpretation and the events as they affected the king was nearly impossible. Daniel believed the king would be restored at the end of the seven years. Mara hoped that it would be so. The children refused to believe at all. The priests of Bel, especially Zroybel, believed against it with all their strength.

The king's condition rapidly became so difficult that he was spending most of his time outside being watched over by servants who were loyal guardians. The outdoors was the only relief that was found for his distress. The more he was allowed to roam free in the fields, the more struggle it took to get him back into the palace for the evening and bed.

The final break came when he attacked and killed one of the nurses trying to feed him his evening meal. The palace staff was irate that this maniac, once-loved king or not, was allowed to roam the palace grounds without any thought given to their protection. The people were upset. The palace was upset. The royal family was upset and desperate to do the best for the king. The priests of Bel continued working to eliminate the king from their future. Finally a coalition of various factions came to the queen and demanded the king be removed from the palace so life could get back to normal.

Daniel had already prepared the queen for the events that were coming. She realized she would have to relinquish control over her husband's life and trust the God of heaven to care for him during the remainder of the seven years. But in her heart she couldn't let go. She cried and pleaded with Daniel to find another way. She plotted to take him away and live in hiding with him alone somewhere, until one day when he turned on her and struck her.

Mara tearfully called for Daniel. "I can't take this any more. I'm at my wit's end. You've got to help me—what shall I do?"

"Mara, you must give up to the demands of the people. You know the prophetic word that the king would be driven away by the people into the wilds."

Daniel arranged for a series of Judean slaves who had been sheepherders in their homeland to become the ones to give general oversight to the king's welfare. They were to graze their sheep and cattle in an open area several miles from the capital where the king was being placed. They were to watch for any problems he might have. They were not to try to deal with him directly, only watch for his safety. Guards were stationed surrounding the large area set aside for the king, in which he could move about freely.

A shelter with food, clothing, bedding and necessities was

provided in a section of the field protected from the worst of the elements. There were trees giving shelter from the burning sun and providing fruit for him to eat. The best possible arrangements were made for the king to live in the wild and yet not be completely on his own. And so the great Nebuchadnezzar became a man of the wild. He left the greatest empire known to man to become the least of men, living among the animals.

As soon as Nebuchadnezzar realized he was free to do whatever he wanted, he set off on a run and refused to have anything to do with any of the people who had come out with him, including his wife and family. He was now a free man and the very brain damaged toward society was now leading him to make the choices he needed. Just as instinct guides an animal, so instinct began to guide the King of the Babylonian Empire. He became an animal.

He avoided the shelter unless severe storms were coming and he would go into the shelter only until they passed. He ate grass. He foraged for his food. His hair grew long and covered his body like feathers of a bird. His fingernails were like claws and he used these claws to dig and open nuts and plants for the food locked within them. He slept in the open, refusing the shelter bed. He awoke day after day with the dew of the morning on him, washing his body for the next day's survival.

During the early days of the seven-year exile, Mara would travel to the wilderness area to get reports from the watchers. Occasionally she would see him. As he became more and more animal-like in his looks, she found it harder and harder to see him and to believe that he would ever be restored. She continued to send the things necessary for his survival, but was dismayed the clothing and food was not touched. When she finally saw him without clothes, wandering among the rocks looking for food and saw him eating grass, she quit coming at all. "I just can't stand to see him like this. I can't stand it."

Mara found solace in these dark days in spending much of her time in her hanging gardens. It was there she still felt Nebuk's closeness.

Through frequent consultations with Daniel, Mara gave him her perspective on Nebuk's thinking, which helped the Prime Minister in his direction of the government. Little by little Daniel gently told her of the God of heaven; how he is the one true God and how He, and He only, is worthy to be worshipped. Mara had many questions; through her friendship with Belardos, she had become a very devout follower of Bel Marduk. Zroybel's treatment of the king, the other Judean princes and of Daniel himself caused her to become disillusioned with the priesthood. She had seen the dreams and their fulfillment in her husband's life and now here she was hoping and waiting for this dream to be completed with her husband's restoration.

"Daniel, is it really possible my husband will be restored? Can I really believe that? Is there really hope for a future for him? Tell me all you can about the dream and its meaning."

Daniel carefully traced the happenings leading up to the king's breakdown. He rehearsed the dream, the failure of the priests of Bel to interpret, and Nebuchadnezzar's expectation that they would not be able to find the interpretation. He told how agitated he had become when he was called in and had to tell the king what was given him by the Lord. When he explained the meaning, how Nebuk accepted it as true and yet refused to do anything that might have helped him escape the consequences of the dream.

As Daniel was describing the series of events that took place, Mara commented on the day. "I remember how calmly he told me about the interpretation of the dream that you had given him. He took it all very matter-of-factly, but it really frightened me."

"Do you remember, Your Majesty, it was exactly one year to the day after the dream, His Majesty was boasting of his accomplishments when the attack came upon him."

"Yes, I have thought about that many times. Since that happened exactly one year later, do you suppose it will be also on the same day that Nebuk will be restored to me?"

"I wouldn't be at all surprised if it were to happen just as you have said. I think it would be well, for you to think in terms of planning a welcome home celebration very shortly after that day."

"Daniel, if my husband comes home on the day of the seventh anniversary, I too, will become a follower of the God of heaven."

"Your Majesty, I wish that you would not have to wait so long to know the peace and the joy that comes from following the one true God. However, I shall pray and ask the Lord to grant you your wish so you may know that the God of heaven rules in the events of man."

The next three years passed with steady monotony. Daniel's rule of the empire was just as if the king was still there. He made decisions based on what he knew the king would want. He used every opportunity to tell the people the king was coming back and would be resuming his reign. Many of the people laughed at him out loud. One said, "only another lunatic would believe that the lunatic king would be back and on the throne."

It was very disheartening to hear such words, but Daniel did not let their skepticism deter him from being the best regent an empire could have. He refused to sit on the king's throne, but sat in a chair beside the empty throne in an act of public submission. Even his enemies were at peace with him because of his integrity.

Daniel was especially grateful the Lord had given him favor not only in Babylon itself, but also in all the various monarchies Nebuchadnezzar had taken into the empire. Almost no rebellious activity was reported back to him at all. When events requiring a firm hand came forth, the local military emplacements were able to handle them without major problems. The Chaldean/Babylonian Empire was running smoothly.

The one unresolved area of strife was with Nebuchadnezzar's children. They could not accept their father placing a foreigner in charge instead of them. Mara was left standing between them and Daniel. She tried her best to bring them together into some form of understanding but with little success. Gradually they even began to separate themselves from her.

With agonizing slowness the seventh anniversary crept closer and tension in the palace increased. Would the king really come back? Again the staff was afraid to hope for such a miracle. Whenever a report came from his watchers, the question uppermost in everyone's mind was, "Does the king seem any better?" Most were afraid that the queen's heart would be broken.

The night before the anniversary, the queen could not sleep. She paced the floor, kept most of her servants up as well and cried. She found herself praying. "God of heaven, if you are real and who Daniel says you are—I want you to prove it to me tomorrow."

Daniel and his cousins were also praying, but with much greater faith. They were asking God to vindicate his name and reputation in this land of unbelievers.

Zroybel and the priests of Bel were also praying, praying the king would never recover and Bel would not allow the intrusion of the foreign God to gain a greater following in the land committed to the worship of Bel. "Let it be known who is the greater god."

CHAPTER 19

The sun had just begun to streak the eastern sky. The cattle, making up his herd, began to stir. Gentle sounds welcoming the new day indicated that life continued in the waking world. Nebuk stood up slowly into his normal slouched posture. Then within him came the urge to stand straight. He stretched himself into the more comfortable, albeit unfamiliar position. Raising his head, facing the brightening sky and looking up into the heavens filled him with a sense of being. A peace filled his ravaged mind and he raised his arms in salute to the new day. As he did so, understanding returned to him.

He found his voice. The first words out of his mouth echoed over the gentle plain. "I bless the Most High God." It felt good to speak. "I praise and honor Him who lives forever and ever." The sound of Nebuk's voice scared the cattle who ran away from this strange animal, who could now talk. It felt even better to be thanking God. "His power and dominion are everlasting. His kingdom is forever from each generation to the next. All the inhabitants of the earth are as nothing. He does according to His own will in heaven and on earth and no one can change His course or has the right to say 'what are you doing?'" The words poured forth from deep within.

At first, Nebuchadnezzar exulted in praise and then he bowed himself to the God of Heaven, acknowledging his sins of pride, arrogance, and self-sufficiency. "Oh, Most High God, please forgive me. I am sorry. Transform me into the man I should be. I have been vain and self-centered, filled with pride. Forgive me, Oh, Lord God."

Just as his understanding returned, so did his memory. He

remembered the many days, nights and all the years that he had spent in the wild. He remembered the foraging for food and the struggles to stay alive in that hostile world. Now he remembered with pain having killed an attendant, remembered striking Mara and being away from his wife, family and his throne. Intense pain and remorse followed these thoughts.

He looked closely at himself, seeing now for the first time the desperate condition not only of his heart, but his body as well. Naked, dirty, with hair streaming almost to the ground and a waist length beard, his fingernails were long, hooked growths that he could hardly stand to look at. Then he remembered the shelter and headed for it.

There he found water and soap with which to wash. He found the clothing Mara had left for him. It was alarming for him to look into the shiny metal plate that served as a mirror. He had tried to run the comb through his hair. It was so matted and snarled that he could only gather it together and knot it to stay out of his face. When he emerged from the shelter, he looked almost like a human being again.

In spite of knowing how he looked, gratitude filled his heart and mind and he continued to thank and praise God for his restoration. Just as he was beginning to wonder how to get back to Babylon, he spotted two of the watchers. He had often seen them, but they had been nothing to him until now. He approached them and they seemed apprehensive and afraid, seeing him clothed. "My good friends, don't be afraid of me, for I am no longer demented as I was. The God of Heaven has given me back my reason and I praise Him for doing so."

The mention of the God of Heaven caused the Judean sheepherder-watchers to rejoice and they came running to meet the king with tears in their eyes. "The dream, the prophecy, the interpretation was truly all from God and now the king is restored. Blessed be the Name of the Lord who has performed this miracle. How may we help you, Your Majesty?"

"Please help me get back to Babylon. I must get back as quickly as possible. I must get back to my family. I want all the world to know that the God of Heaven is indeed the true and only God, and He has fulfilled His promise to me."

Great happiness filled the three men, and their rejoicing bonded them together, the king with the Judean slave shepherds. There was no sense of separation between them. They were overjoyed; the king of Babylon had been restored and his restoration was going to be used by God to bring glory to Himself. The world would surely know now that He is the Great God of Creation and no other gods should be honored before Him.

"Do you have a knife with you? Could you cut these awful fingernails?"

"Oh, Yes, Sire."

"I needed them to survive, but now I can't function with them. I can hardly stand to see them." He held out his hands and the shepherds carefully pared off the grotesque hooks. "Thank you. Let's get going."

They had only walked a short way when they saw a chariot coming in the distance. As it drew near the men could see Daniel and his guards. Even before the chariot had fully stopped, Daniel swung down from his seat and saluted the king. The joy in his heart was evident. There were tears in his eyes and a catch in his voice as he spoke, "Your Majesty, welcome back. We have missed you sorely."

"Blessed be the God of Daniel, who has become my salvation. Blessed be the One true God, King of the Universe. I honor and bless the Name of the Lord. Blessed be God, Who has done great things for me." The two men embraced and laughed and cried for the goodness of the Lord.

When Daniel made a move to help the king into the chariot, Nebuk leaped in and with one arm reached down and lifted Daniel into the chariot with him. It was obvious the king was strong and in good health.

The king and Daniel both thanked the shepherds who wished the king God's speed and waved as they drove off. They would have much to tell their families of their being there when the king was restored. Daniel directed his driver to head straight for the palace as fast as he could go. Daniel and the king talked all the way back.

When the walls of the city came into sight, the king began to weep. Tears of gladness, surely, but also tears of sorrow that the city had literally become his god and that he had been so blind to the realities of life.

Then the parapets of the palace were spotted and Nebuchadnezzar became very excited. There on the wall was his beloved Mara and his eldest son and daughter, their spouses and his youngest son, all waiting and hoping for his return.

When they spotted someone beside the guards in the chariot with Daniel, they became excited and when he waved to them, they began screaming for joy. The word spread rapidly throughout the entire city. "The king is back and in his right mind."

The king kissed each of his family on their tear-stained cheeks, recognizing gratefully their love and affection for him. "I am too filthy to hold you as I want to, but that will change when I am cleaned up."

Mara spoke up, "I have arranged for bath, hair cut and the manicure. The servants are all standing ready to assist you. Only do not take too long. We are ready to make up for seven years of your absence. We've all got a lot to tell you and lots to ask you. The physicians will also want to certify that you are all right."

Nebuchadnezzar looked at his family and said, "First, there is one thing I must say to you. The God of Heaven has fulfilled His word to me and I want us to honor and glorify Him."

"My dear husband, if I had not come to believe in the fulfillment of the word of the Lord, you would not have all these people waiting for your arrival. I know the God of Heaven is the true God. Now hurry back to us. Then we can talk."

The clean up process took far too long to please either the king or his family. When the king emerged, once again clean-shaven and dressed in his royal robes, they were amazed that the seven years in the wild had not aged him. In fact, he looked younger, stronger and healthier than he had when he went away. He asked the barber to leave his hair a little longer than he used to wear it as a reminder of where he had been. His whole body was tanned but not weather beaten. His skin was smooth and moist from the dew that had covered him when he slept for the seven years out in the open.

Nebuk carefully held Mara in his arms. He kissed her gently but passionately. "We have a lot of catching up to do," Mara whispered to him and he smiled gratefully.

He proceeded to embrace Nabonidus, and Niyan and their four children, the youngest, a six-year-old, whom he had never seen.

He laughed when his grandson asked his dad, "what happened to the ugly man that first came to see us?"

Speaking to Nabonidus again, "Daniel has told me of your support to your mother during these trying times. Thank you, my son."

He greeted his daughter and son-in-law and the new baby which had been born only three weeks earlier. When he embraced Awil Merodach he asked him, "where is your wife?"

"Father, I have chosen a woman to be my wife, but she refused to be here since this was to be a family reunion. I shall bring her to meet you shortly."

"You had better!" he chuckled and he gave his son an affectionate squeeze.

When the time of family reunion was concluded, Daniel led the king to the throne room to meet the hastily assembled court. The room was crowded with officials who stood to their feet and broke forth into thunderous applause as the king entered.

Nebuchadnezzar was moved to tears as he stood in front of all the officials of the empire. He was unashamed. Daniel escorted the emotional king to his throne, presented to him the royal scepter and bowed himself before the king. One by one the officials paraded before him, pledging their loyalty and support to the returned monarch; he in turn extended the scepter to them. When Shadrach, Meshach and Abed-Nego passed by, the king embraced them, calling them his first teachers in faith.

When the reception line was finished the king stood to his feet. "I have some things to say to you. First, it was the God of Heaven who brought me low and then brought me this restoration. I praise and honor him. Second, I want to honor Daniel who refused to take advantage of my absence from the throne to advance his own or the cause of his people. I have been told that he did not rule from my throne, but only sat nearby as he held the empire together. He is the banding of iron and bronze, which enabled the empire to continue in my absence. I wish to thank Daniel for his faithfulness to the God of Heaven and to me his king. If I had been half the man that he is, I should never have spent seven years in the wild learning to be a true servant of the Most High God."

The entire audience stood to their feet and honored Daniel who in turn gave the praise to the God of his fathers, the God of Heaven.

Finally when he and Daniel were alone together, Nebuchadnezzar hugged the man with such force that it nearly took Daniel's breath away. "Daniel, how can I ever thank you for all you have done for me and for this empire? Your example of true servant-hood must be made known to the entire realm. I want you sitting with me in all public appearances and in all judgements that I make from the throne. You shall be seated on my right hand. I cannot rule without the direction of the God of Heaven and I cannot rule without your aid. Will you do me the honor of serving with me?"

"Your Majesty, I shall be delighted to assist you in whatever ways I possibly can. I have tried my best to preserve the empire during the time you were away, and I do need to spend time with you so you will know what has been done. But, Your Majesty, please do not forsake training your sons to succeed you when the time comes. They need you to show them how to be godly men as well as a king."

"I'm grateful for your concern, and welcome your advice. I shall need even more than that. I need you to instruct me in the way of the Most-High God. I am but a child in spiritual matters. Please be my father in the ways of the Lord and I shall try to be so to my children."

Daniel raised his hands toward heaven and gave praise and thanks to God for all He had done in bringing him to Babylon, in bringing the king to the Lord Himself and in bringing the king back to the throne. The king joined him in praise.

It took the king a period of time to learn all that had transpired, in the seven years he was gone. He realized the value and importance of all Daniel had done during those years. He was very happy that he had not invested the power in his sons, for they didn't have the stability needed to hold the empire together as Daniel had exhibited through his trust in God.

As Nebuchadnezzar began to incorporate his sons into the ruling process, it was very clear Nabonidus did not want to be a king any more now than when his father first assumed the throne. "Father, I am not in the least bit interested in being the king. I want to continue my research of our history and ancient peoples. I like being a professor and teaching others our great heritage."

Nebuchadnezzar shared with Daniel what Belardos had told him about Awil Merodach being the one who was to be his successor. Daniel said, "Do not be afraid to train him to be king, for God is not opposed to that step. However, he will not be king very long."

Daniel's remark excited Nebuchadnezzar, "That agrees with what Belardos said and that Nabonidus would eventually be king after his younger brother. "It is very interesting to know things in advance like this."

"It really is not so important to know the future. It is far more important to know the God who directs the future. I feel those future things will take care of themselves as we trust The Lord God to guide us in our preparation."

Nebuchadnezzar told Nabonidus, "I know you do not want to be king. I feel that Awil Merodach should be the one to succeed me. I have only one condition that I will impose on you. If in the event that your brother should die or be unable to rule, you must be willing to step in and do so." Nabonidus agreed readily, for he was almost nineteen years older and sure his brother would outlive him.

When Nebuchadnezzar told Awil Merodach of his decision and of the Belardos prophecy, his son was ecstatic. "Father, I have long felt my destiny rested in being your successor and now you have given me the right to expect to be king and not be jealous of my brother. I always thought he should be the rightful one."

"Your brother has never wanted to be king. Our struggles with your grandfather and all the palace intrigue was more than he could take. He is delighted that the responsibility will rest on your shoulders and not his."

So the specific training for Awil Merodach to become the next king of the Chaldean/Babylonian Empire began in earnest. There were many functions to ruling the kingdom that Nebuchadnezzar could turn over to his son, allowing him to gain the experience necessary for a ruler. The king tried to incorporate all the experiences he wished his father had given him. It was pleasing to Nebuchadnezzar to have his son so closely involved with him.

Awil soon learned the ropes and found most of the duties of king very much to his liking. He liked the feeling of power that accompanied the monarchy. However, he didn't like the changes that were coming into the empire, now that his father was a believer in the God of Heaven.

Both Nebuk and Mara were very interested in the things that Daniel taught them concerning the Lord. They had grown up in the openly permissive and overly indulgent realm of the Chaldeans in which there were many gods who fought with each other for supremacy. Bel Marduk had been the generally accepted super god in Babylon, but the many others all had adherents who were willing to fight for their god's reputation. It was hard for Nebuk and Mara to realize that there was not only a superior God, but that he was indeed the only God.

Through studying the scriptures Daniel had given him, Nebuchadnezzar began learning the ways of the God of Heaven. Slowly the distressing realization that faith based on the teachings of Bel, and the other gods, which most of his people and his own family endorsed, simply was unbridled self-indulgence. He remembered that as a young man, he had speculated about controlling the people by the means of sexual behavior. He remembered thinking that religion was not really a belief system, but a gratification of a lower nature.

In trying to bring a higher morality into the realm, Nebuk tried to explain the difference in the two belief systems to his sons. He found them very resistant, especially Awil Merodach. Awil, being such a young man opposed any limitations to his erotic impulses. Even though he was soon to be married, he had an appetite for all the lovely young women who were more than willing to be that close to the power of the monarchy. Nebuk could hardly say anything considering his own earlier history.

The sexual excesses of the Chaldean Empire had always troubled Mara from the days when she was one of her husband's dancing girls on his fifteenth birthday. She tried with little success to share her feelings with her son. He made it clear; he did not want to hear it.

"Look, Mother, you can say all you want, but this austere sexual ideal that you and father seem to have adopted since your conversion to the Judean faith is fine for people your age, but for the young, really alive people of this city, it will not do. If I am to become the next king of the empire, I certainly do not want to revamp everyone's belief system and impose a new one on them. I believe in a free, do-as-you-please life style, as long as it doesn't interfere with the rest of society. The next thing you will be telling me is that relations with the male temple prostitutes is wrong, too."

"Son, that is one more of the many things I am trying to tell you that is wrong in this society. All this sexual expression was never the intention of God, and his plan certainly did not include men with men and women with women practices. These things are forbidden in the law of God."

"Don't misunderstand me, I am very grateful that father is back as king and on the throne. But what I was afraid of has happened. You have accepted this foreign God and his law as being for us. We are not Judean. We have our own gods. I personally like what we have here in Babylon. My very first sexual experiences were with the male prostitutes in the temple and there is nothing wrong with that."

"If it offends God, it is wrong. And if it offends Him, He is ultimately the One to whom we will have to give answer. It is for our own good that we do that which pleases Him."

"Mother, you can have your religion, but just don't try to force it on me. I intend to be my own person and do what I, as the future king of the empire, feel is right for me."

"But my son, is that what's best for all the people?"

"I believe what is best for me will be good for them also. If not, I'll still be the king."

It was useless to try to argue the point. Only God could change the mind of King Nebuchadnezzar, so that would probably be the case with the future king as well. Mara was pained, as she thought of the things her son might have to go through to gain the wisdom his father had learned by his experiences.

The truths of their new faith had revolutionized their thinking. It affected the way they treated their family, the way they treated the people and especially the way they treated the many slaves they had brought into the country. Their attitudes toward the slaves had always been evenhanded. They never allowed any dissension or rebellion to go unpunished. Now, they saw the slaves as people who had feelings and who deserved humane treatment in every area of their lives.

No longer was castration considered the prime means of keeping their male slaves docile. Adequate housing was provided for the slaves. They were allowed to live with their wives and children without fear of being separated. Eventually, slaves were allowed to own land and create wealth for themselves, and children born in the land were not considered in servitude.

Agriculture was absolutely essential to the large thriving metropolitan area of Babylon. Many thousands of people lived outside the walled city and needed to be fed. With the favorable climate in the Tigris and Euphrates valley and Nebuchadnezzar's very effective irrigation system, food was plentiful.

As the years went by the renown of the Babylonian Empire spread beyond the borders of the known world. People came wanting to see for themselves the glory of the City of Babylon, its famous hanging gardens and the marvels of irrigation, and to confirm the reports of the greatness of King Nebuchadnezzar. For the rest of his days, the king was always showing with pride the greatness of the city and telling people of the greatness of the God of Heaven.

Construction, which had been done in the city of Babylon, began to be imitated in many other cities in the empire. Ur once again developed into a very prosperous city. The advances in building techniques, which Nebuchadnezzar had developed, helped Ur overcome the loss of the governmental offices. It now became the center of asphalt production because of the underground petroleum, which bobbed to the surface of the rivers and many oil ponds dotting the area. Asphalt came into major use in construction as one of the main binders, which helped hold the brick and stone construction together. Only later did it become used in paving roads.

Those who had known the king earlier in his life were amazed at the change in his personality and demeanor. No longer did the bad dreams send him into severe depression. In fact, the mood swings and depression were things of the past.

Nebuchadnezzar enjoyed life. He spent time with his family. He tried his best to reassure his sons and his daughter that they were very important to him, remembering how his own uncertainty had warped him.

His great joy was in spending time with his grandchildren.

Through them he came to understand how his father had truly enjoyed his grandson before the family had drifted so far apart. He was able to forgive his father for being so distant with him. He not only forgave his father for his rejection, he also forgave himself for judging and condemning his own father. He rejoiced that his family was close to him.

Nabonidus' son, Belshazzar, was a great source of joy to him. The young boy liked to be with his grandfather and in the throne room whenever he could arrange it. He liked all the pomp and pageantry the monarchy represented. He loved sitting on his grandfather's throne and pretending that he was the king. Nebuchadnezzar often thought his oldest grandson should really be the rightful heir to the throne, but this was not his father's wish and so the future must rest with God.

Nebuchadnezzar had been back ruling the empire for a number of years and his sons had taken greater interest in the kingdom when Daniel came before the King and to ask a favor. "Your Majesty, your sons have taken increased responsibility in your rule. I want them to have your full confidence, and I don't want to stand between you and them. Therefore, I would like to be relieved of my major duties to spend time in seclusion and service to our God. I would like to become semi-retired."

"Of course, Daniel, what is it you would like to do?"

"I have always liked the country around the Shushan palace in the many times that I have traveled there with you and on state business. I would like to have a place in the area where I might read, write and entertain any people who might come to see me."

"You shall have the Palace at Shushan. I shall arrange for it to be at your pleasure."

"Your Majesty is too kind. I do not wish that big a household. I merely need a small place that would accommodate myself and two or three servants who need an easy life."

"You may have anything that is part of the palace holdings in the area, and please feel free to make the palace your home, if you

so desire. Only be careful of the Medes and the Persians who are
lurking not too far away," he laughed.

Daniel thanked him and began to turn over much of his
responsibilities in the government to Awil Merodach and
Nabonidus. He let them know he would be available whenever
they needed him. Awil was more than thrilled to have the
opportunity to wield more power and he liked being in control.
The young prince thanked Daniel and was very happy to learn
that Daniel planned to spend only part of the year in Babylon and
the rest in Shushan; that way he would be of lesser influence.

Just before Daniel was to leave for Shushan, Nebuchadnezzar
had another of his dreams. This one was similar to the first one
Daniel had interpreted, except that he could see the head of gold
only down to the lower part of the chin. He could not see the neck
and the chin seemed to recede and hide from view. People were
watching the head of gold and it disappeared and nothing was
left. The dream disturbed the king, because before and in all other
repeats of the dream, he had been able to see the whole statue.

When Daniel heard the details of the dream, he told the king,
"You will not see the end of the Babylonian Empire, but people
alive at the present time will see the end of the first great empire
that the dream statue represented. You are still the head of gold
and you will not reign for too many years longer. Prepare your son
to do the best job he can, but realize the empire will come to an
end fairly soon after your death.

"I am an old man, Daniel, and I have ruled this empire with
your help for nearly forty years. That's a long time for any king to
survive in this turbulent world. Without the God of Heaven being
my strength, even before I knew who He was, I never could have
accomplished all that has been done. I am awed at the escalation
of the greatness of the empire. It has exceeded anything that I
could have ever believed possible. I am a blessed man, to have been
restored and to see this great increase. I knew that the empire
would come to an end sometime, but I had hoped that would be
thousands of years later."

"Remember, in the original dream, one day the God of Heaven will smash all the man-made kingdoms and establish one that will live on forever. I believe we shall be a part of that final, glorious Kingdom of God."

"So be it," the king whispered softly. He embraced Daniel and sent him to Shushan.

The next months were emotionally wearing on Awil Merodach. He became restless to gain the throne. His jealousy over the greatness of his father's reputation and his anger with his father's faith in the foreign God caused him great unrest. "When is he going to die and let me rule?"

Nebuchadnezzar was not unaware of his son's impatience. He remembered his own feelings many years earlier when he could have cheerfully deposed his own father, who stood in his way. He smiled as he worked with Awil and saw his frustration. Speaking to his son, he said, "Son, I know you desire to be the ruler of this vast empire. I have done my best to train you to be a worthy sovereign. There are a few areas in which you still need training. The first of these is patience. Greatness comes wrapped in patience. I remember the seven years I spent in the wild learning the hard way what greatness really is. Second, you need a source of strength outside of yourself. You need to know the God of Heaven as your own friend."

"That is all well and good for you and mother, but I've heard all I want to hear about your God of Heaven." That not only closed the conversation with Nebuchadnezzar, but Awil's eyes as well.

It was just two years later that Mara discovered that King Nebuchadnezzar II had died peacefully in his sleep. His aged and wrinkled face accented the contented smile on his eighty-one year old countenance. His death was not unexpected as age took its toll on his body. The physicians told Mara what to expect. "He will just not wake up sometime." The state funeral attended by dignitaries and representatives from all over the world gave Mara the opportunity to deliver the king's last message to his people. Her voice was strong in spite of her personal loss as she read.

"My dear people of the Babylonian Empire, my family and

friends. For much of my life I sought to be the greatest monarch ever to live, to be the "Pride of Babylon." My goal was to outdo my father, Nabopolassar, and my namesake, Nebuchadnezzar I. Prophetic dreams seemed to point to my importance. I believed I was truly the great one. Seven years of demented wilderness experience taught me that the way of greatness is the way of humility. Now I know that only the God of Heaven is truly THE GREAT PRIDE OF BABYLON. Sincerely, Your humble servant, Nebuchadnezzar II."

EPILOGUE

After the death of Nebuchadnezzar, his son Awil Merodach, spelled by historians as Evil (and he probably was), became the king of the greatest kingdom devised by man. Nabonidus and his family returned to Ur; a lot of conflict had developed between the brothers. It soon created great difficulty for their mother.

Mara returned to the area where she had been raised. She had always loved the mountains of the north. Even the fabulous hanging gardens that Nebuchadnezzar had built for her to enjoy had never erased the longing for the hill country. She lived there peacefully until her grandson, Belshazzar, ascended the throne; at his request, she returned to be in Babylon. She died of a heart attack shortly after the invasion of Babylon by the Persians.

Awil Merodach reigned two years after his father's death until his brother-in-law assassinated him. Nergalsherezer had finagled his way into power through his sister, the queen, and then killed the king so that he could take over the throne. Nabonidus was much too afraid of the political situation to attempt to regain the throne for his family.

Nergalsherezer ruled the empire for four years, during which time the political struggles became very intense. His son, Labashi-Marduk, succeeded his father for a very short period of time. He was killed by a group of nobles loyal to the Nebuchadnezzar household, who brought Nabonidus to the throne, thus fulfilling his promise to his father.

Nabonidus succeeded in bringing a measure of stability to the empire simply by virtue of being the great king's son. As quickly as possible, he established his son Belshazzar on the throne as co-regent. Nabonidus went into the Arabian Peninsula to study the native culture and look for the remnants of his Aunt Belana's family.

During this time the famous "handwriting on the wall" episode happened in Babylon. Belshazzar was on the throne when the Persians laid siege to the city. The Babylonians were confident the city was impregnable and they refused to worry about the impending invasion. "It couldn't be done" was the watchword. As if thumbing his nose at the invaders, Belshazzar called all his nobles to a feast and used the sacred vessels from the Jerusalem Temple that his grandfather, Nebuchadnezzar, had taken. In the midst of the revelry the mysterious handwriting appeared on the wall. None of the astrologers and magicians could interpret it, and Belshazzar was so panic stricken that he called Mara, his grandmother, to the banquet hall to tell him what to do.

Mara advised him to call for Daniel who was also in the city at the time. He came and interpreted the handwriting predicting the end of the Babylonian Empire. That night, just as Daniel had told them, the Persians diverted the river through newly constructed canals and came into the city through the dried up riverbed. The empire was easily taken. The silver chest had arrived; the head of gold was completely gone.

Printed in the United Kingdom
by Lightning Source UK Ltd.
9656000001B/13